FREDDY'S BOOK

ILLUSTRATED BY DANIEL BIAMONTE

FREDDY'S BOOK

BY

JOHN GARDNER

ALFRED A. KNOPF NEW YORK 1980

THIS IS A BORZOI BOOK
PUBLISHED BY ALFRED A. KNOPF, INC.
Copyright © 1980 by John Gardner
All rights reserved under International and
Pan-American Copyright Conventions.
Published in the United States
by Alfred A. Knopf, Inc., New York,
and simultaneously in Canada
by Random House of Canada Limited, Toronto.
Distributed by Random House, Inc., New York
LIBRARY OF CONGRESS CATALOGING IN PUBLICATION DATA
Gardner, John Champlin, [date]
Freddy's book.
I. Title
PZ4.Q23117Fr [PS3557.A712]   813'.5'4   79-16681
ISBN 0-394-50920-X
Manufactured in the United States of America
Published March 19, 1980
Second Printing, March 1980

NOTE: A key event in *Freddy's Book* (*King Gustav
& the Devil*) is drawn from a tale in Mark Helprin's
collection, *A Dove of the East and Other Stories*.
Numerous passages here are drawn, slightly
altered, from other sources.

FOR MARCUS

I · FREDDY

I was in Madison, Wisconsin, on a lecture tour, when I first met Professor Agaard and his son. I was there to read a paper, brand new at the time (since then, as you may know, widely anthologized), "The Psycho-politics of the Late Welsh Fairytale: Fee, Fie, Foe—Revolution!" The lecture was behind me, a thoroughly pleasant event, as usual, at least for me—a responsive audience that had laughed at the right places, perhaps here and there shed a tear or two, asked the kinds of questions that let a speaker show his wide-ranging knowledge and wit, and applauded with generous gusto when it was over. Now I was deep into one of those long, intense celebrations that put the cap on such affairs, making the guest feel gloriously welcome and the audience (those who

make the party) seem a host of old friends. The whole first
floor of the house was crowded; a few may have drifted to the
second floor as well; and from the sound of things, there was
another party roaring in the basement. I think I never knew
whose house it was; probably the elderly professor of antiqui-
ties who'd met me at the door, one of those bright-faced,
bearded fellows with a great, hearty handshake, a thundering
laugh, and a pretty, younger wife. I don't mean I was indifferent to who my host was; not at all. I have been, from childhood upward, a gregarious, infinitely curious being, quick to
strike up friendships wherever I travel, always more than
willing to hear the other person's side. It was no doubt those
qualities that led me to my profession, history—or more precisely, psycho-history. In any event, as I was saying, the night
was hectic, as these things always are, and the party was
already under way when, trailing associate professors and
graduate students—my face bright red, I imagine, from my
long climb up the icy flagstone steps (I'm a heavy person, I
ought to mention, both tall and generous of girth)—I arrived, divested myself of hat and coat, and began my usual
fumbling with my pipe. Crowded as the house was, I couldn't
catch more than a smattering of the hurried introductions.

Whomever it belonged to, I remember thinking it a splendid house, elegant and fashionable: vaguely Tudor but ex-
ceptionally airy and, with its wide arches, its crystal chan-
deliers—a thousand reflections in the walnut panelling—a
place wonderfully aglitter with cheerful light. Except for the
kitchen and numerous brick islands of thriving plants, the
whole first floor was carpeted in oystery light gray. Talk
rumbled, oceanic; silverware clinked around the white buffet
tables. I'd moved to my usual theater of action, backed
against the drainboard in the large, bright kitchen, where I
could be close to the ice in its plastic bag and, thanks to my
height, could command every corner of the room. On every

side of me, guests with their glasses were packed in so tightly that only by daring and ingenuity could one raise one's own and drink. There were the usual smiling students, heads tilted with interest, eyes slightly glazed, possibly from drink but more likely from mid-term pressure and lack of sleep. Heaven knows it's not easy for our graduate students—the competition, the scarcity of jobs; one's heart goes out to them!

So I was holding forth, enjoying myself. It may be true, as occasionally someone will point out to me, treating the thing as an established fact, that for the most part the students and professors pressed around me are interested only as one is in, say, lions at the zoo; but I would stubbornly insist that there are always exceptions, even the possibility of some signal exception: some young Gibbon or Macaulay not yet conscious of how good he is, who hangs on every word of the sparkling-eyed, silver-haired visitor from Olympus (the lower slopes), hunting with ferocious concentration for what, in time, he'll find he has inside him. One is always a little checked by that not-too-remote possibility—one tries not to speak too rashly, give bad advice—but I, at least, am never utterly checked. One plays the game, follows wherever drink and inspiration lead; what harm? I was the guest celebrity, every word worth gold; but I was only one in, excuse the expression, a galaxy of stars. Everything I said was sure to be contradicted next week when some other famous scholar zoomed in; and everything I said—no question about it—I emphatically believed for that moment. "You have such confidence, Mr. Winesap!" people tell me. Shamelessly I reveal to them my secret. On paper I say anything that enters my head, then revise till I believe it; but in conversation I count on others for revision. I rather enjoy being proved—conclusively and cleanly—to be mistaken. It's Nature's way, I like to think: the Devonian fish corrected little by little through the ages into the milkcow, the gazelle, the princess with golden tresses who refills my glass. Young professors poke my chest with their index fingers, their faces pocked and sweating, their bright eyes bulging. "Nonsense!" I sing out, or "Interesting! Good point!" Behind them, men my own age, with trim gray moustaches, smile knowingly at the floor. I can guess what they're thinking. They'd like to know how I, a mere poet of a historian, have become what I've become, while they, so responsible and reasonable, so well-armed with evidence and fit to be trusted to the last jot, tittle, iota, and scintilla, are only what they are. I could tell them the answer: "You inspire no confidence, my learned friends! You don't eat enough! You're skinny!" No doubt in their heart of hearts they know it. "Never mind," I could tell them in a gentler mood, "in a thousand years we'll all be suppressed events in a Chinese history book."

We were discussing monsters. I'd written a trifling, amusing little piece on the roots and rise of the American big-foot legend, and the people around me were asking me now, though it had nothing much to do with the article I'd written, to explain my ideas on the popular appeal of monstrosity ("from *monstrum*: a showing forth," as a wiry little graduate student pointed out—a young man worth watching, as I mentioned at the time). I was carrying on in the highest spirits—needless to say, I'd had a good deal to drink—and just as I was making a particularly interesting point (I felt), a bespectacled, doll-like professor at my left broke in loudly, peering with fierce attention at the sherry in his glass, the corners of his mouth twitching nervously outward, "I have a son who's a monster."

I smiled, quite thrown, glancing at the faces around me to see what response I ought to make. The man was either mad or in deadly earnest, and in his presence my casual

spinning of theories seemed indelicate to say the least. No doubt those around me felt the same embarrassment, but from their looks one would have thought they hadn't heard him. I stroked my moustache and looked back at the professor just in time to see him roll up his large, glinting eyes at me—fierce blue pupils trapped in red and white webbing— then look back as if in terror at his sherry. He raised his hand, not looking up, timidly inviting a handshake. "We haven't met," he said. He had, like so many university people, the queer habit of making his words just a touch ironic, and sometimes, as now, he would close off his phrase with a curious little *baa* of a laugh, a sort of vocal tic. "I'm Professor Agaard," he said. *"Baa."*

It was an odd introduction. Among other things, one rarely hears anyone at these gatherings call himself "Professor." I studied the top of his head with admiration: a large, pale, liverspotted dome; frail wisps of hair. He was older than most of us, surely past retirement; probably professor emeritus, I thought.

"How do you do?" I said, grasping his small, rigid hand. Awkwardly, hardly knowing what else to do—smiling and bending my head to show interest—I said, "Your son, did you say—?"

He glanced at me in horror, as if only now did he realize that he'd spoken it aloud. The others were all studiously gazing at their drinks.

I smiled harder, throwing him help. "I imagine all our sons can seem monstrous at times." I laughed heartily and gave his small fingers another earnest squeeze.

"Oh no," he said, looking at me sternly, almost indignantly, focusing hard through his thick, tinted glasses, "I mean it literally." Then he glanced at those around us— blank faces, frozen winces. It was clear that even he, for all his singularity, was aware that he'd broken the polite conventions, darkened the tone of things. No wonder if he was flustered; he must have been as painfully aware as I was that his colleagues did not like him. Perhaps he scorned his students and graded too fiercely, with the result that his classes were smaller than other people's, stirring his colleagues' resentment. Perhaps he was believed to give out a crushing excess of information—he looked like that type—or shirked committee work, or consistently took the wrong side in things. Whatever the reason, he was clearly unpopular, and now, as often happens to people in that plight, having made a small mistake—perhaps not even knowing what mistake it was he'd made—he was evidently thrown into a panic. Unable to think of a way to back down, and having missed my invitation to make light of it, he looked to left and right, his expression grim, then back at me, his eyebrows lifted, eyes wild, and made his radical decision. "Ah!" he said, and then, loudly: "Excuse me!" Without another word, he snatched back his hand, ducking and turning at the same time, found a small opening in the crowd, and fled. I stared after him, no doubt with my mouth open.

"You must've got to him," a fat, bearded red-head beside me said. He was laughing, his two plump, small-fingered hands closed fondly around what looked like a glass of straight bourbon. His hair was parted in the middle and curled up sharply on each side; if we hadn't been so crowded, I'd have glanced down to see if he had satyr's hooves. He let go of his glass with one dainty hand and gave me a pat on the shoulder. "Never mind old Agaard," he said, laughing again. If I'd been startled by Agaard's look of woe, I was even more startled by the red-head's look of merriment.

Before my friend the red-head could carry the matter further, one of the people I'd been talking with earlier broke in again, poking between us with his nose like a chicken, and, like it or not, I was caught up once more in the scholiast's game, paring popular notions of the "queer" and "unearthly" from notions of the "monstrous." Time slipped out from under me; I forgot all about Professor Agaard and his son, and at last, when there were only a few of us left, the clean-shaven, neatly combed graduate student who'd been assigned to my service made signs that, really, we ought to be on our way, if I was willing. I hated to leave such a sociable haven, even now that most of the others had gone home; but reluctantly I finished off my drink, found my hat and coat, and followed him down the steps and the icy, buckling sidewalk to where his car sat, alone under a streetlight at the corner. It was a foreign car, trim and new, the kind that makes a person of my size hug his knees. But I was in a mood to hug myself. Wonderful creatures, all of them! A splendid occasion!

It was just as we were pulling in at my motel—one dim light in the office, the sign turned off—that I remembered the brief, peculiar conversation with the doll-like old man and asked, "What is this business about Professor Agaard's son?"

"Agaard?" the young man echoed, ducking his head, peering past the steeringwheel, making sure he was approaching the motel in exactly the right way—that is, approaching where the sign said ENTER, not EXIT, and driving very slowly to outwit the malevolent ice.

"I believe he said his son is a 'monster,'" I said.

The young man glanced at me as he'd have done if he believed my revealing the truth about the Agaards would bring ruin on the Department—throw him, with his degree now made worthless, to the wolves. It was nothing of the kind, I knew; nothing but the alarm of a young man uncom-

fortable where the rules turn vague, drawn against his will
toward the fogbound marchland where honest concern and
the gossip's ingress merge. Surely the personal affairs of his
professors were not his business, his eyes said, though his lips
remained thoughtfully pursed. I knew him then; should have
known him all along by the stiffness of his elbows as he
drove: he was one of those good second brothers in the fairytales, the one you could almost but in the end not quite put
your money on. Out of virtue, he believed, come success and
security; turn aside for an instant, and the abyss will leap
around you with a shout. Poor devil, I thought, trying to put
on charity—"third and mightiest of the three magic rings,"
as I like to say at meetings. (No one is amused.) Nevertheless, his look somewhat chilled me. I remembered the look of
distaste all around me, those cobra glances, when the old
man had spoken about his son. I half wished now that I'd
made Professor Agaard stay longer and tell me what he
meant. The young man stopped the car; we'd arrived at the
door. "I don't think I know a Professor Agaard," he said,
and gave me a cool little smile. "I'm in American." With two
fingers he adjusted his glasses.

"I see," I said. It was an interesting solution. My young
friend would go far in this icy-hearted, ethical age. But then,
of course, the poor fellow wanted to get home to his wife, be
able to get up for his classes in the morning. It's easy to be
harsh; take the bolder way! I nodded, smiled again. Over-
head, the stars shone like tiny bits of frost. I was depressed a
little by that sudden reminder of the immensity of things,
universe on universe, if the Hindus are right—giant after
sprawling giant, each pore on each body a universe like ours.
I opened the door. "I'm sorry to have kept you so late," I
said.

Gratefully, mindful of his manners, he stuck out his
hand. I shook it. "Good-night, Jack," he said.

"Good-night," I said, and, after an instant, "Good luck to you, my boy!" I got out and carefully shut the door. He waved as he pulled away; I waved back. I went up to my dim, comfortable room, staggering just a little—increasing instability of the planet, no doubt; also too much gin—drew the covers back, undressed, went to bed and, at once, slept like a bear.

T HE FOLLOWING MORNING, rising late, I found a letter awaiting me at the desk. I opened it on my way to breakfast in the sun-filled café-restaurant, puzzled for a moment over the wobbly, old-man handwriting, awkward and full of starts as a minnow's trail, dropped down to the signature, and felt a shock of something like morning-after guilt. The letter was from Professor Sven Agaard. With the full name before me, I realized at once that the queer old man I'd met last night was the well-known Scandinavianist, easily one of the most re-spectable historians of our time, though only for one fat book, published some thirty-five years ago. In fact, I'd as-sumed he was dead.

It was a long letter, and at first I could do nothing but stare at it in distress, though technically, of course, I'd done nothing wrong. Try as I might, I could make no sense of this guilt I was feeling, but there was no mistaking that it was guilt. It did not seem to me, though perhaps I was mistaken, that it was anything so simple as my not having recognized his name.

At last, seated with my tea, awaiting my toast and scram-bled eggs—small groups of chattering diners all around me, having mid-morning coffee or perhaps early lunch—I flat-tened out the somewhat wrinkled letter on my placemat, glanced around me once, then hastily read through it. The first two pages were a long, serpentine, and, it seemed to me, quite mad apology for the way Professor Agaard had intruded with his personal affairs. He was a silly old fool, he assured me. (I mused over that one. False modesty? Some old-world politeness I was not understanding? Something about it made my skin crawl, to tell the truth; I set it down, tentatively, to my sense that I'd wronged him. I read on.) He would not blame it on the wine he'd drunk, though the wine had no doubt had its part in the business. Nevertheless, having intruded so far, he could see that it was only right that he invite me to his house, if I was interested, since it was wrong to introduce some teasing suggestion and then refuse to say more. He was not, like me, a traveller, he said, a man who could be comfortable in any world he entered. (That too seemed over-modest. I knew for a fact that he'd been born in Sweden and had at one time travelled widely; but this too I let pass.) If he'd erred in life, he continued—winding cautiously in toward his point—it was probably in giving in too easily to this weakness, keeping himself too aloof from things. Indeed, it was entirely possible that, concerning certain matters, he'd made grave mistakes; perhaps I could advise him. Needless to say, he said again, he was profoundly sorry for having troubled me, and if he was wrong to write this letter, as some would undoubtedly say he was—"rude heads that stare asquint at the sun," as Sir Thomas Browne so aptly put it . . .

My breakfast arrived. I ate without noticing, reading through the whole thing again more slowly, and then yet again, wondering what under the sun I'd stumbled into. It was a pitiful letter, there was no mistaking that, but there was also something else that I couldn't quite put my finger on, an elusive hint of anger, at very least an edge of nastiness.

The letter had a repeatedly-copied-over look. Considering its length, the professor must have worked at it half the night. On the final page there was a telephone number and the word *unlisted*, underlined twice, then directions to his house, somewhere on the outskirts of the city.

I had at first no intention of accepting the invitation. I was scheduled to fly down to Chicago that afternoon—I had a lecture in two days, and a number of old friends I was hoping to visit, former colleagues at Northwestern—and even if I were free, it was clear that the invitation had caused Sven Agaard such distress, such a torture of close reasoning on morality and social responsibility, that to accept might well be the act of (there it was again, that ridiculous, empty word) a monster. On the other hand, I thought—frowning and pressing my fingertips together—the letter had something like an anguished plea in it. Perhaps, for all his apology and hesitation, and in spite of the hint of lidded wrath that escaped him, the old man was urgently hoping I'd visit. He was not an immediately likeable person, but distress is distress.

These last few words I spoke aloud, a thing I sometimes do when I'm reasoning with myself, and, realizing that I'd done so, I glanced around at my fellow diners. Only a head or two had turned; otherwise, no one had heard or cared, all happily occupied with their own affairs. I stoked up and lit my pipe to ponder the matter further, think it out properly, fair-mindedly. After all, my lecture had in some way touched the old man, I thought, or he'd never have written such a letter. For my conscience' sake, if nothing else, I must decide this matter on some basis more solid than whim.

I sat for several minutes, smoking and drinking tea, weighing the matter on this side and that. If Professor Agaard really was in need of advice, as he'd suggested—if he really had made, as he'd said, "grave mistakes"—it seemed unlikely that he'd get help from the colleagues who'd responded to him with such indifference, if not hostility, at the party. Considering all the trouble I'd put him through—his embarrassment last night, his labor over the letter—perhaps refusing him would be the worst thing I could do. I could hardly deny that I was curious, in a way; not wildly curious, but curious enough to take some risks, no question about it.

Then another thought struck me: Had the old man approached me and spoken to me, and then afterward written, because in fact—or partly—he disliked me? despised, as some people do, my rather hopeful view of things? Was he one of those too numerous so-called "hard" historians who seethe at the very mention of psycho-history? In my irrational bones I had a feeling it was so. The idea, naturally, made me cross for an instant. I have always tried to be, so far as I know how, a just man, not needlessly unkind. Life itself may be unfair—I've never denied it—but how odd that I, a stranger just passing through, as the folksongs say, should be held responsible! Very well, I thought, no reason to go see him. Sorry, Iago, I'm dining with my wife!

On the other hand, of course, he was, or had been once, a superb historian in the high, thin-aired field I myself did my earliest work in, thirty-some years ago—a man I'd have been honored to serve, if I could. . . . Abruptly, rising to pay my check, I decided to postpone my trip to Chicago and go see him, possibly meet his son.

I made some phonecalls—one to my wife, one to Jack Jr. (who teaches English at Whittier), one to the airport, several to friends, and one, finally, to Agaard, to say that I was happy to accept. He suggested—a certain odd distance in his voice, a sound like sea-roar or wind behind him—that I come at about three.

Around noon, a heavy snowfall began, so heavy that by eight that evening, though of course I didn't know it at the time, the whole country would be transformed, the Madison airport socked in. At 2:15 I checked out of my room and, carrying the only bag I had with me—a small, old-fashioned one, the kind one associates with the visits of country doctors —hailed a cab. All through the city and out into the suburbs the driver grumbled about the weather, the inefficiency of the snow-removal people, the self-interest and stupidity of politicians. "One of these days," he said again and again, hunched like a wrestler over the steeringwheel, speaking so grimly you'd have thought he was referring to some definite group and plan; then he'd clamp his mouth shut, letting the matter drop. The motor pinged and clattered, the fenders rattled, the broken shock-absorbers banged with every bump as we flew up toward Agaard's. I sat forward, smiling and nodding with interest, elbows on my knees, straining to hear above the noise of the cab as if the driver's anger might give me some clue to what awaited me at the professor's. Absurd, of course. The driver was a thoroughly socialized, perfectly normal human being. Every word he spoke he'd said hundreds of times before to his hard-up, slow-witted family and friends, who agreed with him completely.

We came to a sparsely wooded area, a section with which the driver was unfamiliar. Every few blocks—or rather, every few crossroads—he would pull off the road, roll down his window, and lean out, squinting, trying to see what the sign said. It was clear that he resented being out here in the country. Every vehicle we passed was a Jeep or a pickup truck, and in every driveway, or so it seemed, some dog raged, mad-eyed and snarling, feinting at our tires. At last he found the roadsign he was after and, since he'd slightly passed it, angrily hit the steeringwheel, then backed up, spinning as if punishing the car for its stupidity, and we made our turn. We ascended a knoll—the woods were thicker here; dark, still pines, all strangely tall—and made out, on our right, a few lighted windows pale as fog, and a huge, vague outline like the prow of a ship—Professor Agaard's house.

The driver stopped the cab. "What is it," he said, "insane asylum?"

"It belongs to a university professor," I told him.

The driver scowled up at it, taking a cigarette from the pack on the dashboard. "I thought so," he said. He glanced at me, appraising, then back at the house. "Damn if I'm going up the driveway. *No* way."

"Why not?" I asked a little sharply.

"Ice. Never make it."

I studied him, perhaps making sure he wasn't hiding some darker reason, and just that instant his match flared, lighting up the stripped-down, shabby interior of the cab. He leaned close, cocking the cigarette toward the flame with his stubbly lips and squinting like a man with one eye. "Eight dollars," he said.

It was an outrage, heaven knew; but the driver so obviously knew it himself, even giving me a squint-eyed, stubtoothed smile, that I accepted my luck as if Providence had sent it—I was on expenses anyway—paid him, got out (there were no dogs in sight, though those we'd passed on the road were still barking), and, carrying my bag, made my way through the needle-fine, blowing snow up the hill. Behind and below me, I heard the cab pull away, heading back down toward the lights of the city, leaving me in heavier darkness.

It was a gloomy old place, chilling as a barrow—not at all my kind of thing—and the closer I got to it, the gloomier it became, also the quieter. I arrived at a kind of graveyard gate, writing over the top, formed of rusty iron letters, too many of them missing for the name of the place to be readable. I thought, inevitably, of creaky old allegories, demented gothic tales—a thought that began in amused detachment but ended somewhere else, so that a shiver went up my spine. The place really did give off the smell, or rather the *idea*, of death. Who would have chosen such a house, coming to Madison as a young professor, except for the reason that once it had been a splendid residence—wide porches, sunken gardens—and even now might be brought back, as he must have thought, might be made a grand place in which to raise a large family, give parties? It hardly took second sight to make out that the young woman who'd dreamed of playing hostess here was no longer among the living, or that the young professor who had proudly, somewhat fearfully taken the deed and mortgage had been changed, by various accidents, to another man entirely.

The gate stood partway open, just a narrow gap. I held my bag in front of me and, pushing against wind, went through. I was in among the pines now. It was as if I'd all at once lost my hearing.

Before I had my glove off to grope for and ring the bell, Professor Agaard was at the door. "Come in!" he shouted. His voice cracked out like a trumpet, belligerent and fearful. The door he held open, just a foot or so, was huge; he clutched the edge with both hands. It had heavy locks on it. He was smiling as if in panic, dressed as he'd been last night, rumpled suit, dark, frayed silk tie. "Terrible out," he said loudly, somewhat accusingly, "I'm surprised you bothered."

"It's not as bad, down in the city," I said.

"No, I don't suppose so. It never is."

After I'd stepped in, slipping my hat off and stamping to knock off snow, he pushed the door shut, leaning against it with his back like a child—and no wonder: the man was even smaller, more doll-like, than I'd remembered; the top of his head came no higher than the middle of my chest. He drew off his spectacles to wipe away steam and grinned, looking at me up-from-under like a ram, his pupils almost hidden by his eyebrows. His dentures were overlarge and gray. "Come in and have a nice cup of tea," he said. He half turned, then turned back for a moment and shot me a look, his eyes frankly boring into me like a child's, then put the glasses back on; also the grin. "I see you came by taxi." He seemed to disapprove, maybe thinking it would be hard to get rid of me.

I shrugged, apologetic. It wasn't easy to tell what emotion I ought to feel. The old man was at once deferential and, it seemed to me, crabby; perhaps he himself wasn't certain what he felt. He was avoiding my eyes now, that much was clear; but whether from shyness or from a wish to hide his dislike for me I couldn't make out.

"I hope you weren't too badly cheated," he said. His expression suddenly became prissy, struggling to be a smile. It was a look I'd see on him again and again, as if, though he tried to see the humor in things, all this world were distasteful to him, sadly disappointing to a spirit of his antique refinement and sensibility. He shot me another little look, eyebrows sharply drawn inward, at once stern and baffled. What I'd wrung my fingers over now seemed obvious: he'd been hoping I'd turn him down.

Since I'd come, however, he decided to make the best of it. He seized my elbow and began to steer me through the gloom of the hallway toward the tall, closed door at the farther end. The hallway was like an ice-box, the air as cold in here as outside and not much less drafty, stirred as if by cavewinds. When he opened the inner door, heat poured over us as from a furnace. "These old houses!" he said, with a bark-like laugh, waving me through the door, wincing as if the house were a punishment he'd been sent—unjustly, for the crimes of someone else.

We were in a cavernous livingroom with a threadbare Persian rug, an unlighted chandelier, here and there a lamp among the frail, spindly pieces of furniture. Most of the light in the room was thrown by a great, rolling fire in the fireplace. It glowed dully on the wainscoting, the backs of books. (Surely he'd made the fire for my visit, I thought, and for the same reason moved the two chairs up close to it, between them a low antique table with brass-ball clawfeet and a black-glass top. Perhaps the old man was even now of two minds.) His books were everywhere, shelved, crammed, stacked on all sides of us, some in English, others in foreign languages, mainly German and Scandinavian. Here and there one could make out dark paintings, framed documents. I'd been looking around for several seconds, giving up my hat, coat, scarf, and gloves, and nodding absently to his stream of complaints—irritable little shouts—when I noticed, with a start, an enormous black cat sitting prim and motionless near the fireplace, watching me with round yellow eyes. I must have jumped.

"Oh," said the professor, his face falling as if the day were now spoiled, "that's Posey."

I bowed to the cat, then after an instant's hesitation—still carrying my bag, which the professor had neglected to take from me—moved nearer, rather formally, as if to show them both that I'm a lover of cats, as usually I am. (My wife keeps four of them.) The cat remained motionless; not a whisker stirred. The odd thought struck me—strictly a passing fancy, but for a split-second one that made my neck hairs tingle— that perhaps *this* was the professor's son. The ridiculous thought came and went almost too fast to register. One knew by her name and could see by the grace of her neck and shoulders that the cat was female; and anyway, of course . . . I glanced at the professor. He stood bent forward, as still as the cat, his fingertips together, just touching his chin, his loose, webbed eyes looking up at me through slightly fogged lenses.

"What a beautiful cat!" I said. She was, in fact, with firelight edging her like a halo.

He seemed to consider it, his white lips stretched toward a tentative smile, as if he'd like to think it true; then he jerked his head, clenching his jaw so that his dentures clicked. "Eats us out of house and home," he said, and, turning to the cat, pretending to speak fondly but in fact showing something more like hatred, I thought, or anyway fiercely controlled impatience—"Isn't that true now, Posey?"

The cat looked coolly from the professor to me, then stirred, stretching, and moved away, over toward the side of the fireplace.

While the old man polished and inspected his glasses, stiffly holding them up and looking through them at the fire, then giving them another clumsy wipe with his hankie, I listened to the creaks and groans of the house, the crackling of firelogs and ticking of distant clocks, wondering where— above me or in some grim chamber farther in—Professor Agaard kept his son.

"Well, well," the professor said when his ritual was over, the glasses back in place, "let's see about that tea!" He bowed from the waist, turning as he did so, then scooted toward another door, perhaps one that led into the kitchen. His head, I noticed for the first time now, had at some time been mashed deep into his shoulders, possibly by arthritis, so that it would no longer turn from side to side. When he paused at the door, it was his whole upper body that cocked around to say, "Make yourself at home, Winesap! Posey, won't you show our nice visitor a chair?" He made his *baa*-ing noise, laughing at the joke, then left.

I looked at the cat as if inviting conversation—she seemed at least as ordinarily human as the professor—but the cat had lain down on her side, half closing her eyes, dismissing me. I set down my bag and rubbed my hands together, as if for warmth. "What a wonderful house!" I called, loudly enough to be heard in the kitchen.

The cat shrank as if she thought I meant to harm her, then relaxed, not quite forgiving. From the kitchen came no answer; silence like a judgment of Brahma. I sighed, picked up my bag, and drifted to the nearest of the bookshelves to look at the titles.

So I occupied myself for a good ten minutes. It was pleasant enough business, since I'd written my dissertation on medieval Scandinavia—a subject I've rarely thought about since—virtually the only subject in Agaard's library. He had all the books I knew, which was hardly surprising, and a great many more I'd never heard of. Other than those he had only a few old novels, Tolstoy and the like, and an occasional book of verse. Outside the tall, round-topped windows I could see nothing but blowing snow and darkness, though it was still mid-afternoon. There were vertical shadows, puzzling for a moment, until at last I realized they were bars to keep out burglars—or to hold something in. Finally the old man returned, pushing an elegant teacart, dark walnut—perhaps I was seeing here the hand of the long-vanished mistress of the house. On top of the teacart he had a tarnished silver tray. The cat raised her head, alert.

"Ah!" I said, "wonderful!"

"The tea's old and stale, I'm afraid," he said loudly. "I'm sure you're used to better."

I recognized or imagined something snide in his tone, but

having no idea what it meant or what to do with it, I said with a broad wave, "I'm not fussy. I wouldn't know stale from fresh."

Though his mouth smiled, I saw when he rolled up his eyes that I'd said the wrong thing. It was the duty of a man of my good fortune to know the difference, he seemed to say. He, if he'd been blessed with opportunities like mine . . . I was beginning to see my situation here with Agaard as hopeless.

As the old man poured the tea his thin hands shook and he muttered to himself, a habit I was glad to see in him, since I share it. Yet if he hadn't been muttering—cursing, perhaps, or expressing astonishment at some remembered or legendary outrage—I would of course have mentioned my admiration for his work. I couldn't help but wonder if he blocked me on purpose, not that the performance wasn't convincing. When he'd filled my cup, over on the cart, he started toward me, walking carefully, looking hard at the cup and saucer, still muttering, now and then crunching his dentures. A few feet from me he stopped, turned at the waist to look around to his left, then looked back at me over his spectacles, raising his eyebrows.

"Didn't you want to sit down?" he asked.

"Thank you," I said, blushing no doubt, and stepped over, still carrying my bag, to the chair nearest the fire. He followed with the tea, muttering again, and when I'd put my bag down and carefully lowered my bulk onto the seat, mindful of the bowed-out, fragile legs, the plush-covered arms held upright by a charm—the chair so narrow that the arms lightly brushed my body on each side—he placed the cup and saucer not on the table between the two chairs but in my hands, as carefully as he'd have done for a child, steadying them a moment, making sure I had them balanced, then

raising his hands from them slowly. Though there was sugar
on the teacart, he did not think to offer it or place the dim
cutglass sugar bowl on the table. I decided to do without. He
returned to the cart and poured a saucer of milk; stiffly,
carefully carried it around behind the farther chair over
toward the fireplace to set it on the scuffed black tiles for the
cat, who came over to it at once; then finally poured tea for
himself. When he too was seated with his cup, the three of us
forming a little circle in the light—high, flitting shadows on
the bindings of books and the lumpy, dark wallpaper—Professor Agaard said, "Well now."

I waited. He said nothing more, only stared into his lap.
Perhaps half a minute passed. I sipped my tea.

At last I said, "I must say, Professor Agaard, you're a
great hero of mine. One of the most important books I—"

"That was a long time ago," he said. He spoke with
finality, like a man clapping a box shut.

"All the same," I began.

"It's a painful subject," he said.

"I'm sorry."

"Thank you."

We drank our tea in silence. He sat with his toes pointed
inward, his face turned away from me.

An agonizing two or three minutes passed. The cat
watched us with the innocent malevolence of her carnivore
nature; indistinct shadows craftily began inching across the
ceiling and floor. The silence stretched on, acutely embarrassing for both of us, surely; I must think of a way to break
it, I kept thinking. I cleared my throat, a time or two, little
half-involuntary growls like a sleeping dog's, but nothing
came. I hadn't felt so self-conscious and uncomfortable since
the days old Slash Potter, my thesis director, would require
me to sit waiting in his high marble office while he thumbed

through my latest revisions. Not that it was all Agaard's fault, it struck me. It was I who, hoping to flatter him, had demoted myself. As I suspect may be clear already, I did not actually like old Agaard's book, though I'd been vastly impressed when I was younger. I still respected it, of course. It was, and is, the work of a mind I do not hesitate to call far superior to my own. His gift for languages, his absolute originality, his uncanny intuition, all these were awesome; indeed, I wouldn't be disposed to quarrel with the widespread though hardly universal opinion that the fellow is without parallel. Nevertheless, I don't care much for the book.

Be all that as it may, the fact was, I could see now, that I had lied to him, in effect. Perhaps it was from the falsehood itself that he cringed, verbally slapping my hand away, refusing a charity that had in it no true *caritas*. Time grew heavier second by second. Then by lucky chance I thought of Jack Jr.—how we, two intellectuals (perhaps not in the sense that Sven Agaard was, but by no means fools), could sit smiling with affection, serenely silent in one another's company for hours at a time. At once, as if the thought of my son had released me, I found myself saying—leaning forward, trying to sound at once concerned and hearty—"It must be difficult, living here alone, having to take care of your son. He does live here with you, I presume?"

"Oh yes, he lives with me," the professor snapped, raising his head, then lowering it, pointing his nose at his knees again. Though I watched him closely, his eyes gave me not the slightest clue to where the son was kept.

After another little pause I remarked, smiling, tilting my head to show interest (any slightest movement, I was finding, made the chair creak), "I imagine it must all be rather painful."

He nodded, smiling grimly, raising his cup to drink.

"Yes, it would be natural to imagine that." Above the rim of the teacup he gave me a look of what might have been fury.

I looked down, once again shrinking a little, struggling to sort out my confusion. Was it possible, I wondered, that it had been someone else, some malicious prankster, who'd written that letter inviting me up? But I'd mentioned the letter on the phone; it was Agaard who'd written it, all right. Had he changed his mind, then? gotten cold feet? Perhaps one couldn't blame him; I'd have to know more about his son to judge. Certainly if he wanted me to leave, I'd leave at once. I should let him know that. I glanced at my watch, then at Agaard. "Good heavens, it's after four," I said. "I have a plane to catch at eight." Only as I said it did I hear how ridiculous it sounded. Trying to save myself, I said, "Does it take long to get to the airport?"

"Twenty minutes," I thought he'd say with a murderous sneer and a *baa*; but again he surprised me completely. He leaped up and went to the window, then blanched. With a voice and expression that might have been extreme alarm, he said, "Look! It's snowing! You have a plane out tonight?"

"It's at eight," I repeated uncertainly, guardedly.

Professor Agaard stood perfectly still for an instant, hands clasped tightly, torso cocked forward, staring as if in growing surprise at the storm. At last he shook his head and turned back to me, eyes narrowed, stepping grimly toward his chair. "It will never take off," he said. "Right to the last minute they'll say the planes are flying, and then, with apologies, they'll post a one-hour delay, and then another, and then another; what do they care?" He gave a laugh, waving one arm. "The airport can be packed like a can of sardines, people can be sleeping all over the floors, little children can be bawling, they'll go right on lying— company policy, not to mention human nature! *Baa!* Take my word for it, Winesap." He closed his right hand on the back of his chair. "They'll never take off. I know these storms out of Canada. I've lived here for fifteen years." He seemed to consider sitting down, eyebrows driven inward toward the bridge of his nose, eyeballs slightly bulging, then decided to remain standing.

Again I was baffled. It sounded for all the world as if, despite the sneer, the misanthropic snarl, he was asking me— almost begging—that I stay over, keep him company. The thought, I must confess, made me shudder. "Well—" I began. I sat motionless in my spindly little chair, or rather hovered just above it, my elbows rigid, weightless on the arms.

"No, no," he said emphatically, clicking his dentures and bending stiffly toward the teapot, "it will never take off. I doubt that you could even get a taxi in weather like this." He shot an angry or maybe terrified look at the window.

I too looked. It was like night out; a gloomy, shifting marchland beyond which lay heaven knew what.

"Of course we have beds here—no shortage of beds, such as they are!" He gave his sharp little *baa*, his expression triumphant. "Here, have more tea," he said, and hurriedly came at me with the pot.

H<small>E WAS A</small> difficult man—never in my life had I met a man more difficult, now snivelling, now snarling, now cackling with glee, always with his mind somewhere else, I had a feeling, turning over and over that secret or guilty confession he couldn't quite find it in his heart to let loose of, much as he might wish to—stroking it with his fingers, clutching it greedily to his bosom, watching me, his chosen antagonist, with unrelenting vigilance in his dim, crafty little eyes. It was not just his son, I was by now persuaded; he'd made graver mistakes than by chance giving life to a "monster," as he'd called him. I gave the old man time, sitting there opposite him, our shoes almost touching. It was surely true that no planes would be flying from Madison that night. If Agaard was a mystery, both generally speaking and from moment to moment, I needn't be in any great hurry to get to the bottom of it. I'd figure him out. And of course the old man was hoping I'd catch him; or a part of him was. I had nothing to lose, nothing except the chance, back in the city, of finding more congenial company—if nothing else, the tinny cheer of some motel TV. I began to enjoy myself. *En garde*, Agaard! It was you who threw the glove!

At the moment Professor Agaard was busy bringing it to my attention that, like most members of the human race, I am a scoundrel. "'Pseudo-history,'" he said, with a scornful little headshake. I blinked, not sure whether it was a joke or a slip of the tongue, and tentatively corrected him, my tone ironic: "Psycho-history." He nodded, accepting the revision without interest, giving the air a little bat with the back of his hand. He made a face as if, either way, the term repelled him, as no doubt it did. I couldn't really blame him. I'd felt that way myself when it first became popular, mostly in con-nection with fanciful, unfriendly biographies. We'd shifted to wine now, the old man trying to trick himself, perhaps. He was drinking rather quickly, as if his throat were parched and the wine had no more taste than water. In point of fact, I might mention, the wine was excellent. It surprised me a little that, disliking me as he did, the professor hadn't brought out Gallo. The fire beside us had burned down to a few glowing embers. The cat was asleep. Old Agaard had resisted my every effort to turn the conversation to his son, ducking in distress from every faintest hint, willing to chatter like a magpie on any and every subject but the one that, we both knew, had brought me to his house. "What a curious thing for an intelligent man to spend his life on!" he said. " 'Pseudo-history'! I take it you call yourself a 'pseudo-historian'? *Baa!*" His face had grown whiter as the room grew more murky; it was as if he had on powder.

I thought of correcting him again. Was he deaf? or was it simply that once Agaard got an idea in his head it was there, firm as bedrock, to the end? I decided to let it pass. I smiled, in fact. Pseudo-history. Why not? It had a ring to it. Anyway, our point of disagreement was substantive—never mind the name!

"Oh, I don't know," I said. "I think one could spend one's life in worse ways." The backs of my legs ached from the strain of keeping part of my weight off the chair. My gestures were constricted—a thing I never like—by my wish to do no harm to his miserable antique. "It's true," I said, "that psycho-history is not always a terribly serious pursuit. It's sometimes trivial, nothing more than a pleasant enter-tainment—not that that's all bad." I flashed him a smile. "I mean of course studies of the 'deeper implications' of Lyn-don Johnson's bathroom jokes, or the social attitudes se-creted away in castration imagery in the tales of Paul Bunyan. Yet we learn things, here and there. Any way of looking at the past is still looking at the past." I glanced at him, carefully waving my wineglass. Again his eyebrows were rammed inward against his nose. "We're after the same things you are, you know. The twists of human pride, hu-manity's age-old survival tricks."

"Pah!" he said, then laughed. *"Baa!"*

It annoyed me, of course. No one likes his life's work dismissed quite so lightly, not even a man who, like myself, holds all effort to be at least partly vanity, a heroic, death-defying labor of bees making honey that will rot in a season. To cover my annoyance—and perhaps nervousness (he did, of course, make one conscious of limitations)—I put my wineglass on the floor beside my foot, got my pipe and to-bacco out, and began to load the bowl. I prudently stopped myself from asking if he'd mind if I smoked. "As I'm sure you know," I said, soberly catching and holding his eye, "our work is no more fanciful than the next man's, in the end. All history at least from the days of Thucydides is in a way 'pseudo-history,' as you call it—the tale of human struggle as it's told by the side that won."

"I know all that," he snapped. (I had it coming, I'll admit. I'd gone just a little sentimental there; downright self-righteous.) He got up to put another log on the fire. The cat came awake and shrank back, then fled at his approach. "All history as fiction," he said, "psychological projection, 'a distant mirror'—et cetera, et cetera." As he was about to bend toward the log he paused and turned his whole torso to look at me, rolling his eyes to the corners like a horse. "It's ex-tremely useful stuff, you'll tell me." He waved toward the ceiling, bitterly ironic, and put on, again, his prissy look. "What's heaven itself but pseudo-history? Yet we all die the happier for it, eh?"

"Some do," I said cautiously, lighting my pipe.

He barked—literally barked like a dog—then bent down, picked up a log, carried it to the fire, and dumped it in. Sparks flew wildly. One fell on his trousers. He slapped at it. "I'm not against religion," he said angrily, as if at the spark. "I'm not against fairytales either, for what they are. What I mind is historians that say anything they please. That's what your discipline encourages, Winesap! Why do people choose it? Why is it the rage in every supposedly re-spectable university from Harvard to Berkeley? *Baa*. Because it's easy, that's why! No grubbing around in Latin or Old Slavonic, no sorting through dirty old books in the basements of libraries! Just hunt down sexual metaphors and allusions to 'dusk' in the papers of Thomas Jefferson! (You've read Garry Wills' piece demolishing that, I hope.) So these eager intellectuals of the Now Generation come flooding to your courses—their courses, I mean; I don't mean you personally, necessarily; you've done serious work from time to time. I mean those others, my busy little colleagues, the ones who were 'Marxist revisionists' five, ten years ago, and before that cracker-barrel Toynbees." He stopped, panting a little; he'd lost his thread. Then abruptly, remembering, he raised his arm like a general, plunging on: "They flood into your courses, which helps the F.T.E., brings in money to the department; and they pour out their fairytale histories of 'Blacks' and 'Chicanos'—*baa*—the history of people who have no history, which brings them federal grants, 'research' assistants, free trips to the Bahamas to lie in the sun and write Freudian reconstructions of the Great White Sugardance!" He stood trembling, whistling like a bat.

My hand slightly shaking, I reached for the wine bottle and held it toward him. "Have more wine," I said, and smiled. Angry as he made me, I had to give the old man an A for rhetoric.

He laughed, a kind of snort, eyes widening behind the thick, tinted lenses. "I admit it, Winesap, I'm not very civilized. I'm rigid and inflexible, and I've never learned to put the truth nicely." He came a step nearer and held his glass out. I poured. When he'd swallowed a little, standing there in front of my chair like a student, his head only inches above the level of mine, he held out the glass again, this time pointing at my chin with it. "I'll tell you the trouble with trying to learn history from fairytales," he said, strong emotion in his voice. He came toward me a step, crowding me, still pointing. "They're mindless—even the best of them!—all bullying, no intelligence, no moral profluence, ergo no real history! Static! They're exactly true to life, those dreary flats between historical upheavals. The handsome prince comes; he finds his beloved and they live happily ever after; and no one any longer speaks or sends cards to the stepsisters." He leered.

I nodded, reserving judgment, half inviting him to continue. Though he clung to his image, his argument had made a sudden, uncharacteristic skip of theme and logic—had leaped, arms and legs flailing, toward chaos. Perhaps we were about to get somewhere.

His voice became still more emotional, barely in control. "People like you, Professor Winesap," he said, "may *pity* the stepsisters, the wicked old stepmother. You may try to understand them by some theory of dream-analysis. You may even work it out that the cruel old witch who's behind it all is of use in the world, provoking those she injures toward greater benevolence." He turned around jerkily, preparing to step to his chair again, but remained where he stood, bent forward, pointing back at me with his glass. "It never occurs to you that the beautiful princess and the wicked old witch believe exactly the same thing: Anything at all, including cunning and lies, will work for the beautiful; nothing helps the ugly."

"That's true," I said lightly, "that never occurs to me."

He *baa'd*, then went to his chair and abruptly sat down. "Well, it's a fact, Winesap. Take my word for it!"

I nodded, pushing my tongue into my cheek. I could see why they felt as they did about him, those people at the party—why Agaard, in his troubles, could turn only to a stranger.

He was saying, almost a shout, "I've had experience with

the happy, blessed people of the palace, if you follow my metaphor."

"The lucky ones."

"Exactly." He looked at me fiercely, as if I were the cruellest, most unfeeling of the lucky, then glanced away. Yellow flames leaped up around the log he'd put on, though I'd have sworn, a moment earlier, that the fire was dead.

He swallowed a little wine, then said, feeling he'd gone too far, no doubt, relaxing a little by an act of will, bringing his foot out from under his chair, "Well, you can't teach an old dog new tricks. I prefer the old-fashioned ideal of history. Hard-won facts, incontrovertible proofs."

I nodded. The trouble with incontrovertible proofs, I might have told him, is that they shut down conversation, inspire not mutual exploration through debate but scorn and attack. You prove that your man in his castle of logic and hard-won facts got some trivial detail wrong (I might mention the term psycho-history), and as his knights come fleeing in dismay to your side—blushing, stammering, hitting themselves for shame—you blast his elegant fortress to Kingdom Come.

"If history were done properly," he said, "it would make us better *men*."

I avoided his eyes.

"Men and women," he said, clumsily correcting himself.

"We're not in disagreement about that," I said. I decided to let it rest there, a truce agreed upon by mutual misinterpretation.

If he was trying to think of some new way to attack me, nothing came to him. It wouldn't have mattered anyway, I thought. I no longer cared; his opinion was no longer of interest. Let him tyrannize his students, his son. It wasn't my sport.

He stared for a long time, unmoving, into the fire, his eyebrows jammed inward, eyes darting here and there. He too could see that we'd come to an impasse, a classic stalemate; let him break it if he could. Then it seemed to me that I heard something move, somewhere above us. When I glanced at him I saw that Agaard had heard it too, though he was careful not to turn or look up. I continued to listen and heard it again, perhaps the sound of a chair being dragged across a floor upstairs. In embarrassment I drew back my foot, noticing that I'd been tromping rhythmically not on the claw of the tableleg but Agaard's shoe. He cleared his throat and glanced at me—we both looked down—then turned his toe inward, out of my way.

Now we both sat motionless, the whole house utterly still, like the hush between heartbeats. The sound came again.

All at once Agaard said, "You haven't asked about Freddy."

"I thought I had," I said. Our glances met and dropped again, two rams backing off. Quickly, I said, "I meant to. I'd be interested to hear."

He put on a pained smile for a moment, then let it twist to unabashed woe and turned his face away to stare at the high, dark windows, no neighbor's light anywhere, so far as I could see; then he whispered something and, snatching off his glasses, covered his eyes with one hand. I sat more erect, startled by his sudden emotion; I was half out of my chair. He sat rigid, regaining self-control, then lowered his hand and said sternly to the table between us—his hands relaxed, as if his body weren't involved, his eyes squinting for sharper concentration—"He's a sensitive boy. He writes poetry, in fact." His laugh barked out; then instantly his face was serious again. "I don't know if it's poetry. Long things in prose, vaguely historical. He used to let me read it. Lately . . . I suppose I must have said the wrong things."

"This writing he does," I began, groping.

He shied away. "We used to send him to school, or have tutors in. He's extremely bright. You might not think it, to look at him. Most people, one glance . . . Freddy's problem, when it's endocrinological, goes along with slow-wittedness. You see a boy like Freddy, you naturally assume . . . But in Freddy's case it's genetic. He's smart as a whip and painfully sensitive. That's why we keep him home." He shook his head crossly, and his voice, when he spoke, was close to breaking. "You've no idea what it's like out there, for a boy like mine —the nastiness, the torment, not to mention the danger. Not that it's so wonderful in here, you understand." He shot me a look. "I don't fool myself. I was fifty when he was born. His mother was younger, of course. She was killed when he was nine—a highway accident." He raised his hand abruptly, as if saluting the Führer. What the gesture meant I have no idea.

When he drew back his hand I leaned forward slightly, forehead lowered. "I don't think you mentioned what's wrong with him," I said.

"No." His pale lips jerked back. "No, not yet. I'm sure you're curious!" He pressed his hands to his knees and leaned forward, about to stand up.

I looked down, puzzled at his suddenly turning on me again. "Remember, I came because you asked me, Professor." Now both of us were rising—stiffly, formally.

"Yes I know. Also for other reasons."

I kept silent a moment. "The world's not perfect," I said at last.

"Yes. Not perfect," he said. He pushed up his glasses and touched his eyelids with the index finger and thumb of one hand. He whispered something, wincing, arguing with his demons, then moved ahead of me, turning back to see that I followed, toward the door he'd gone through for the tea and then later the wine. It did lead, as I'd supposed, to the kitchen, a large, gray-walled room like the kitchen in a home for the aged or some hospital in the slums. The appliances—refrigerator, stove, washer-dryer—were thirty years old if a day. The pots on the stove were large, the kind used by restaurants.

He took me through another door that led to a pantry, scented with rat-poison and general decay, white discoloration like lichen on the walls, then down a high, narrow hallway leading to what had once been, apparently, the servants' quarters, a section of small rooms that he now kept locked off—a nightlatch on the door, which he opened with a key from his small, cluttered ring. The ceilings were lower here, the rooms sparsely furnished, the wallpaper less gloomy—cheap and plain—a sitting room, bedrooms, a bathroom, a doorway that led, as I was soon to learn, to the narrow back stairs. At the first of the servants' rooms I stopped in my tracks. Pieces of wallpaper hung down like stalactites, the windows were partly boarded up with plywood, and in the walls there were holes, as if someone had stood in the center of the room firing cannonballs. Bits of lath showed like dry, broken ribs; in one place even the flooring had been broken. I went to the window—a few of the windowpanes were intact, barred but not boarded—and I stood for a moment fingering my cooling pipe and looking out. Snow and desolation, dark trees, then nothing, a shifting wall of gray.

Professor Agaard stood with his head thrown forward, lips clamped together, his small hands clasped behind him. "Freddy was ten," he said. "He'd been naughty, and to punish him we locked him in his room." He gestured. "This room. He has another room now, upstairs. They'd told us at school he had terrible tantrums, but of course we had no idea; this was the first we ever saw of it. Not that we hadn't seen signs, of course. . . . It was a hard time for him. Needless to say, they tried to force me to institutionalize him. He was at that time still a child. Not a 'small child'—*baa*. But the teachers he'd have had there, and the creatures he'd have been locked up with, day after day! Idiots, crazy people . . ." He closed his eyes. "But the teachers above all. Those fools you talked with at the party last night, they're risen saints by comparison!"

"Surely you're just a little hard on them," I said. I reached out, without thinking, and touched his arm. He stiffened as if in fear of me. "You should try to get to know them," I said, drawing my hand back, "talk with them a little."

"Talk with them!" he exploded. "Look there, Mr. Winesap!" He pointed to the window where I'd just stood looking out, and after a moment I realized that he meant me to notice the bars. I suppose, having noticed them earlier, I was not as impressed as he'd hoped I'd be. He turned toward the door to the back stairs and pointed. "And look there!" On the door there were three heavy locks. I remembered the big iron locks I'd seen on the front door and nodded, suspending judgment. "Talk with them, you say?" he yelped. "Shall I leave that poor odd child in the care of the cleaning girl— supposing I could *get* a cleaning girl? Is that what you suggest? You look at me harshly!" His scornful smile twitched briefly, then failed, sagged toward panic. "You've misunderstood. It was *Freddy* who put those bars on the windows and locks on the doors, not I!" He jerked his head back and woefully laughed.

I squinted, fingering my pipe, trying to understand. "Are they frequent, these tantrums?"

He looked puzzled, then annoyed, as he would at a dull, persistent student. "He hasn't had a tantrum in years." He peered into my face as if wondering at the depth of my stupidity. "Come," he said at last, "come up and meet him."

To my surprise, the latches on the door to the stairway were not locked. As Agaard started up the steep, narrow steps ahead of me, I asked, "Are you saying he locks people *out?* that is, locks himself *in?*"

"That's what he does all right!"

I hesitated, feeling duped, trifled with. But I said, still moving cautiously, "I can see that would be worrisome. Do you know what sets him off?"

He glanced back guiltily. "Anything! Everything! A knock at the door, a truck in the driveway—my telling him to turn off his light—"

"You mean if no one bothers him—"

"Exactly!" he exclaimed. He'd reached the top of the stairs now. He stood catching his breath, his fist clenching the railing. "Leave him to his miserable little paradise of books, his cave of old maps and print"—he gestured with his left hand, strangely childlike, exactly as if the spirit of a child had taken possession of him—"leave him alone and he's happy as a clam! But rouse him out of it—even let him imagine you're *about* to rouse him out of it—he begins to lock things. Seals himself off. Not in bad humor! all very quiet and methodical. And he'll open them again if you insist—though Lord knows he doesn't like it! You'll say I've spoiled him, but believe me, it's more complex than that. I don't mean I'm not to blame—how could any child grow up normal, living with an odd duck like me? In any case—" He put his hand on the top of his head, apparently hunting for the thread he'd lost. He said, "You see, Professor Winesap, he's made a world for himself—and why not? The outside world frightens him—not that he shows it much: simply gets his locks out, maybe prays a little, or buries himself in his books."

"Prays?" I said.

Agaard sighed, looking down at the old worn carpet between us. "When he was small we had a woman who took care of him, a Mrs. Knudsen, one of those hellfire fundamentalists. I'm afraid she put the fear of the Lord into him. The hellfire part's behind him now—we're Presbyterians. But he still gets down on his knees sometimes and . . ." He gestured vaguely. "He was very fond of her—for good reason. She was as kind as she knew how to be, a far cry better than the people who got him later—the school he went to, the hospitals—"

"Surely the university hospital—" I suggested.

"Worse than the snakepits!" He laughed angrily and began again to make his way down the hallway. It was long and windowless, lit by three bare bulbs. He touched the wall with the fingertips of his right hand as he walked. "He was happy there at first, but then he began to break things. They took a dislike to him—understandably, I suppose. He was difficult at the time, didn't speak much English. . . ."

"You've tried private psychiatrists?"

"Psychiatrists," he hissed, half turning. "You use the plural, Mr. Winesap. I see you know about psychiatrists."

"Just the same—" I began. With a part of my mind I was musing on his various uses of my name: "Winesap," as to a student; "Mr. Winesap," as to an underling; "Professor," never without a sneer.

"It's gotten out of hand," he was saying when I returned my attention to him. "Utterly out of hand."

"I can see that," I said—not so much a lie as a stalling action.

He raised his left arm, a gesture again oddly childlike, or

puppet-like, pointing nowhere. He spoke more softly now, hurriedly; we were apparently close to Freddy's room. "As I've said, I think, he reads day and night. There are very few books in this house he hasn't read, and of course I bring him whatever he wants from the library. I act as his teacher—it's been a great pleasure, in many ways. I don't mean to sound like a boastful father, but . . ." He scowled, then changed direction. "As I mentioned, I think, for some time now— more than a year, close to two years—he's been working on a book of his own."

"Interesting," I said, glancing down the hallway in the direction we'd been heading. "A book about—"

"As I told you, I haven't seen it."

I nodded, apologetic and baffled. Something rubbed against my leg and I looked down. The cat, Posey, had found the open stairway door and come up. I looked again at Agaard. "He's told you nothing about it?" I asked. "That is, he sees no one in the world but you, and for two years he's been working on a book, and in all that time—"

"Not a word," the professor said. He crinkled up his lips, his eyebrows jammed together again.

"When you take him his supper," I said, "or sit in the same room reading, does he—"

"Never," he snapped. "Not a word, not a hint!"

I nodded, then started down the hall again as if I knew where I was going—perhaps I did, in fact, following the cat —but again the professor caught my arm.

"One other thing," he said, "he's read your books." He tipped his head up, as well as he could, given the stiffness. "He's a kind of 'fan.' "

I took my pipe from my pocket, tamped the tobacco, and lit it. When I'd taken a few puffs, I stepped forward abruptly, reached down, and picked up Posey. I held her against my chest with one hand. Professor Agaard looked at me; then we continued along the hall. At the end he bent forward to knock on a door, waited a moment, then called, "Freddy? Unlock your door, Freddy!"

The boy pretended not to hear, though we knew he had to.

"Freddy?" Agaard called. "We've got company, son!"

My heart jerked, hearing him say "son." I'd never used that word on Jack Jr.; it hadn't been the way we, as they say, "reached out." The way Agaard used it, it was like a blind man casting a net over the side of what might or might not be a ship. The boy, I was sure, couldn't help but hear it as I did. How could he not answer?

There was a sound then; some heavy movement. The cat craned her neck. A lock on the door clicked, a dead-bolt slid open, a chain-latch scraped, and at last a startling voice said, "Wait a minute, Dad. I'm not dressed." The voice was sweet, like a young singer's. Agaard saw my surprise but made no comment.

We stood listening and heard him move away across the room; then, softly, the professor pushed open the door, stepped in, and gestured for me to follow. I obeyed, stroking the cat as I did so, the pipe clenched hard between my teeth.

"Freddy?" the professor called again.

The cat tried to jump. I held onto her. It was a large room, plain and clean-swept as a forest floor, bookshelves in rigorous order on every side; against one wall, half blocking the window, an oversized, specially made desk, very plain, with two neat locks on it, and a great sturdy chair to match. Around the chairlegs there were smooth iron bands. The giant furniture threw everything else in the room awry, what little there was—a few pictures on the white walls, framed pen and ink drawings of viking ships, carefully and elegantly done in a slightly old-mannish hand, rendered as if for an expensive picture book. They were signed "F.A." It came to me only somewhat later—perhaps because they seemed professional and seemed to have been professionally framed— that the pictures were by Agaard's son. On the prow of one of the viking ships a king in a horn-helmet stood looking thoughtfully at a hawk on his wrist. Agaard, when he saw me looking at it, looked away.

The room was so spare one could see everything at a glance: a closet door with a lock on it, a long table with five perfect constructions—three ships, two dragons—nothing else on the table but a neat stack of stainless-steel razor-blades. What defined all the rest, of course, was that immense desk and chair. They made it seem that the room itself was from a picture book, or better yet, a stage-set, for across one end hung a dark green curtain. Beyond that, presumably, the professor's son crouched, hiding. My gaze stopped and froze on an enormous bare foot that protruded, unbeknownst to its owner, no doubt, from behind the curtain. It was the largest human foot I'd ever seen or imagined; if the rest of the body was proportionate, the creature must stand eight feet tall or more. But it wasn't just the size of the foot that made my heart race. The thing was visibly unhealthy, bluish gray with red blush-spots; bad circulation, lack of exercise. How the poor creature had gotten to this state God only knew, or God and Agaard. "Out of hand," the old man had said. I accidentally mumbled the words aloud, causing the professor to glance at me, then look away.

"Freddy," he called, "remember I told you Mr. Winesap might visit us? Well, he's here. I've brought him to see you." There was a pause. "Freddy?" Agaard glanced at me, then moved over to the curtain to poke his head in and talk with his son. Though he talked as loudly as ever, the heavy curtain muffled the sound; I caught only one phrase from Agaard: "I *want* you to." Freddy answered with only a polite syllable or two, his voice low, so that I couldn't catch the words. I continued to look around. There was a typewriter on the desk, spotlessly clean, a very old electric with a thick gray cord, a cord heavy enough, one would have thought, for a welding machine. Beside the desk stood a large wooden box, no doubt a wastepaper basket, with a wooden cover, locked.

The professor drew his head back outside the curtain now and, whether or not with his son's permission, reached up and snatched the curtain open. The look on the professor's face was like mingled anger, fear, and triumph. There before us, half-turned away, sat a monstrous fat blushing baby of a youth, his monkish robe unbuttoned, his lower parts carefully covered with a blanket. All around him, neatly stacked, lay papers and innumerable books, some closed, some open, arranged about him in a perfect fan. The skin of his face and arms and chest was pink-splotched, shiny. He was as big as some farmer's prize bull at the fair, big as a rhinoceros, a small elephant. I exaggerate grossly, but such was my impression that first instant. The brute effect of encountering him there—suddenly shown forth as the curtain gasped on its old metal rings—was, if anything, greater than my images suggest. His eyes, when he turned to glance at me, just perceptibly nodding, were red-rimmed, huge behind the gold-rimmed glasses; his childish pink lips were drawn back from his teeth in what I recognized only after an instant as a sheepish smile. His expression was pitifully eager, yet at the same time distrustful, alarmed, not unlike his father's when he'd met me at the door. One side of the giant's upper lip was slightly lifted, delicately trembling with what might have been disgust—perhaps disgust aimed at himself. He pretty well knew, no doubt, what a strange sight he was, there in his cell. His pallet was a king-sized mattress with a steel-gray blanket over it, behind it a stern brass lamp on a low wooden table buried in carefully stacked books. From a string tacked to the ceiling above his head hung a red paper-and-balsawood dragon with extended wings and a queer thick belly.

"Freddy doesn't make paper dragons anymore," Agaard said proudly, as if Freddy weren't there.

The giant's blue eyes stared straight at me for a moment, the lashes blond, like his frail beginning of a moustache; then he began to move—all of him at once, it seemed—his arms rising as if lifted by some external force, the fat, dainty hands clenching a book as if to hurl the thing in rage. But he didn't hurl it—had never intended to, I saw—only drew the heavy white arms and the book up nearer, as if to dismiss us, free us to go back to our presumably more interesting adult pursuits, and bent closer to the page. The cat, clamped against my chest, struggled.

"I've brought you a friend," Professor Agaard said, moving closer to the boy, pretending he thought Freddy hadn't heard. "Mr. Winesap, this is Freddy."

With a jerk of my free hand I snatched my pipe from my mouth. "How do you do?"

Freddy sat motionless, not breathing, it seemed, his face and neck red, his eyes still eager, the rest of his face guarded. Fat bulged everywhere, blue-shadowed. The whole rounded body was as sickly as the foot, surely too heavy and weak to stand up, I thought; he couldn't have stood anyway in this low-ceilinged room. I felt a flash of anger at the professor beside me—the idea that a father could allow this to happen to his son!—but I struggled to quell it. I knew, I told myself, nothing whatever of how it had happened, for all the father's talk.

I remembered the cat I'd been clutching all this time, and carefully lifted her from my bosom and set her down on the mattress like an offering. She ran around beside him and stood there, back humped, just out of Freddy's reach.

"Aren't you going to say hello to Mr. Winesap, Freddy?" Agaard asked.

"Good afternoon," Freddy brought out, looking down, almost a bow.

"I'm glad to meet you," I said heartily, and thought of reaching out for his hand, but then—from cowardice or fear of embarrassing him further—did nothing.

"Well, so how are things, son?" Agaard said.

The giant boy glanced at his book as if eager to get back to it, then shrugged, slightly smiling.

"Did you notice it's snowing out?" Agaard said.

I stood puffing at my pipe, studying the bulging red dragon above Freddy's head until he glanced up at me; then I pointed with my pipestem. "Interesting dragon!" I said. "Is it Chinese?"

He half nodded. "French." He briefly grinned.

Agaard laughed, a loud bark that nearly blew his nose. "It *looks* French!" he said. "It looks like it *ate* too much!"

The giant half grinned again, uncertain whether to be insulted. He looked at the back of his left hand, discovering and inspecting a scab. "That's the way the pictures were," he said.

For a moment after that it seemed that none of us could think of anything to say. Then, bending forward—I think I saw it coming an instant before it came—Professor Agaard said sociably, his voice too loud, "I've told Professor Winesap about your writing, Freddy." He turned his head to me, a queerly mechanical movement, and urgently smiled.

I stared, nonplussed. Freddy briefly raised his eyes to mine, more alarmed than before.

Any fool could see that he'd heard and understood, that he was going through twenty emotions at once—trying to hide his confusion by turning his head and shoulders slowly and reaching out to touch the cat between the ears with two fingers, the faintest suggestion of a petting motion—but Agaard said, "Did you hear what I said, Freddy? I told him about your book!"

He gave me no choice. I took a deep breath. "Yes," I said, "yes, your father tells me you've been writing for some time now, Freddy!" I clenched my pipe in my right fist and poked at the dottle busily with various fingers, first one then another, of my left hand. "It's interesting—very interesting—that you're writing a book, Freddy! Fascinating!" He sat with his head bowed, looking intently at the scab on his hand. It unnerved me not to be able to see his expression. I was tempted to squat, get down level with his eyes, but I stayed as I was and continued heartily, trying to make it all sound friendly and normal, though my voice in my own ears rang false, theatrical, someone else's voice entirely: "It's not easy writing books! You know, that's the one place where all human beings are equal, I've often thought. It's an amazing thing when you think about it, Freddy! Whatever we may seem to be—humpbacked, tall or short, pale or ruddy, never mind"—I briefly interrupted myself, puffing at my pipe, lighting it—"whatever we may be in other ways, when we pick up that pencil we're all in the same boat." I looked for a place to throw the extinguished match, then put it in my pocket. "If there's one human nature, that's where we find it and take part in it," I said, "in carefully written books. Not just any books, mind you. Careful books! Books we've taken time on! You've been working on yours for quite a while, I understand." I glanced at his father, who was nodding, encouraging me, profoundly agreeing. Freddy said nothing. "You must excuse me if I sound as if I'm lecturing you,

Freddy. I don't mean to, not at all!" I laughed, turning away a little, looking again at his pictures. "You must think of it from my side, Freddy—think of my astonishment, meeting your father here and hearing what you've done. It's a very interesting solution, that's what I mean. Here you are, locked off from the world, in a way. . . ." I glanced at him; he was still looking down. "I mean, well, the message-in-the-bottle kind of thing, some such business—but the finest kind of message a mortal man can send. A man may say anything when he's just talking, you know, but when he's writing he has time to think it over and re-do it until it's right, send a message worth hearing! In a thousand years . . ." I moved to the pictures on the farther wall, hoping to seem to him less threatening. "When your father mentioned that you were writing a book, I was interested—fascinated—as a fellow writer. It's a lonely occupation, as everyone knows—which may be why we writers have such a feeling of, you know, *community*. I'm sure you understand! What I mean, mm, Freddy—" I turned to look at him, as self-conscious by now as he was. "Freddy, if you should ever want to show me what you've written, don't hesitate!" I said. "You can be sure I'll be interested! We'll all be!" I searched my wits for something more to say. I felt vile, weak in the knees, though every word I'd said was, in intent at least, true. I puffed at my pipe, clinging to it with both hands.

Freddy went on looking at the scab. Mentally, he'd backed away from us, securely locked some door.

"You hear that, Freddy?" Professor Agaard piped. "Jack Winesap would like to read your book!" When the boy said nothing, Agaard said, "Wouldn't you like that? Wouldn't that be nice?"

After a moment Freddy said, almost too quietly for us to hear, "You don't know I've got a book."

Agaard said nothing—stiffened a little, possibly; slightly paled.

I looked from one of them to the other. "Come, come, Freddy," I cajoled, "your father's proud of you! I know how he feels; I've got a son myself."

Freddy did not look up. He said very softly, "He doesn't know if I've written a book or not." He glanced at me and smiled, faintly apologetic but standing his ground. His face for the first time struck me as not really a child's face after all, more adult than his father's. He slid his eyes toward Agaard. "It's not that I want to hurt your feelings."

"Ha!" Agaard said. He spoke loudly, but perhaps only to some voice inside his head.

I lit the pipe and half turned away from the boy, as if to leave. He looked back at me for an instant, as I'd known he would. "You're right," I said, "your own business is your own business. But isn't it odd, not letting *any*one see it?" Somewhat mechanically, like a bad actor, I held my hand out toward him, as if to show him, as you would a dog, that I was friendly. The gesture embarrassed me as soon as I saw it for what it was; but I had no power to take it back.

"It's just a book," the giant said.

"There!" Agaard said, turning to me gleefully. "It exists! He's admitted it!"

I stared at him, then turned and crossed stiffly to the door. Before stepping out into the hall I turned again and said, "I'm glad to have met you, Freddy. Good luck to you— all the luck in the world!"

"Yes sir," he said. "Thank you." It surprised me that he spoke so serenely, accepting it so easily—made me wonder if perhaps I'd gotten closer than I'd imagined. I left, however, having committed myself. After a moment Professor Agaard popped out behind me.

"Well, what do you think?" he said earnestly, much too soon to be out of earshot.

"Very sharp boy," I said at once, slightly slowing my step. "Those constructions he makes are magnificent."

"Oh yes, those," Agaard said.

"And so are the drawings. If his talent as a writer comes anywhere near those other talents—"

Agaard glanced at me, puzzled, perhaps impatient. "I could show you some of the things he wrote when he was younger," he said.

"Oh no—no thank you!" I said rather loudly. "I wouldn't want to look at them without Freddy's permission!"

Poor Agaard was puzzled to speechlessness. We descended the back stairs in silence.

I MOVED AROUND the kitchen restlessly as the old man, scooting back and forth, bending and straightening, put on supper. At one point, abruptly pausing with my back to him, I slipped my pipe into my pocket, thinking of claiming I'd left it upstairs in Freddy's room, giving myself a chance to go back up and talk with him alone. But what would I say? That he ought to get out more? take better care of himself? guard against his father's distrustfulness? The stress of the situation made the pipe trick impossible. To think the thing through, get up my nerve to try it if it seemed right, I needed the pipe in my mouth. I got it out again, loaded it, and lit it.

Agaard was peeling the plastic wrap off a great package of chicken legs. "I hope you like chicken, Winesap," he said crossly. He'd been thinking, had perhaps figured out at last what I'd done to him upstairs.

I nodded and gestured absently. "Yes, fine," I said.

"That's about all we eat around here, chicken and fish and vast quantities of spaghetti. Giants are expensive." He laughed.

"I imagine," I said. I remembered suddenly that I had my paper on Jack and the Beanstalk in my bag in the living-room. I knew intuitively the instant I thought of it that it was the perfect gift for the boy upstairs, though it took me a minute or two to convince myself that I was right. It was true that it had a giant in it, but it had nothing to do with giant-ism, only with the fear of the small and weak in relation to the large and powerful, first in the family, then in the Welsh-English political situation; it had to do with comedy and tyranny, how the joking Welsh Jack-tales made it possible to slip around the mighty political parent unharmed. In a word, it reversed the situation of Agaard and his son—made Agaard the flesh-eating giant, if you will. Perhaps it would make me a villainous guest, at very least ungrateful, giving that paper to Agaard's son; but it was Agaard who'd invited me, presumably to help in whatever way I could, and pre-sumably the decision as to what would be best was mine. I excused myself and went to the front room for the paper. I hesitated for a moment, drawing it out of my bag. It was the paper I'd been intending to read in Chicago; but never mind, I would figure something out—maybe stand there telling jokes, or have a dialogue with the audience. Never mind.

Back in the kitchen, now filled with the smells of squash, potato, and chicken cooking, I said, "I've got a present here for Freddy. You don't suppose there'd be any harm in my taking it up to him?"

"I'll take it," Agaard said. "I've got to take him his sup-per."

"I'd just as soon take it myself, actually," I said, "though of course if you think—"

"What is it?" Agaard said. He spoke into the oven, where

he was bent over, stiffly and awkwardly spooning something onto the chicken.

"Oh, something I wrote," I said, "a little trifle."

Agaard thought about it. Perhaps he guessed what it was that I meant to do. But he said nothing. I took his silence for consent and stepped through the back rooms—he'd left them unlocked—and up the back stairs, moving along grimly, left-foot, right-foot, like a man on a mission he does not entirely approve of. At Freddy's door I paused, listening for a moment, then knocked.

"Yes?" the boy said. He spoke from not far beyond the door.

"Freddy," I said to the doorknob, "it's Professor Wine-sap. I've brought you something."

There was a silence while—frantically, I imagine—he tried to make out what to do. At last he said, "Just a minute," and I heard him coming nearer. One by one, slowly, as if reluctantly, he undid the locks. There was another brief pause; then the doorknob turned and the door swung inward. There he stood, bent over, too tall for the room by a foot or more. He was wearing pressed trousers and a clean white shirt. It crossed my mind that he'd been thinking of coming downstairs; but no, I decided, he'd merely prepared himself in case we should come at him again.

I held out my sheaf of xeroxed pages. "I brought you this," I said. "It's the paper I read the other night at the university. Since you weren't able to be there—" I smiled and tipped my head, trying to show him I was harmless.

He stared at me intently, then abruptly looked down at the paper I held out, and blushed.

"It's for you," I said, and gave the paper a little shake.

"Thank you," he said after a moment, and slowly raised his hand to take it.

"When your father mentioned that you've read some of my work," I said, widening my smile, "it occurred to me that maybe this would interest you. As I said before, we writers have to stick together!" I gave a laugh.

"Thank you," he said cautiously. Then, after a moment: "Did you want to come in?"

Given the way he asked it, I had no choice but to decline. "I'm helping your father with supper," I said, "but thank you for the kind invitation."

He nodded, apparently deciding against pointing out that he had not, in fact, invited me in.

"Well, so long," I said. I cocked my head like a bluejay and gave a foolish little wave.

He seemed to study the gesture, then glanced at my face as if to see if I'd intended the wave to be the childish, self-conscious thing it was. When he saw that I hadn't, he smiled, then tried to hide it, nodding, looking at the paper, then closing the door.

You meddling fool, Winesap! I thought. With a prickling of the scalp I realized that I'd spoken it aloud. Blood stung my cheeks, embarrassment like a child's. I calmed myself. Perhaps he hadn't heard.

Never mind," the professor said testily as we poked at our meal, sitting at the kitchen table. It seemed to please him that I'd failed. He seemed to have shrunk, and grown ten years older, but also he seemed downright delighted with himself, as if he'd discharged some painful responsibility— justified himself and in the same gesture put the guilt on me. We were neither of us ourselves by now, hardly human in fact, prickly and tyrannic as those shadowy powers of the most primitive religions. So much for the noble evolution of the mind!

"That boy needs medical help—immediately," I said—petulant, vindictive. "At very least get him a physical check-up. It's not good, letting him withdraw like that. He'll get peculiar."

"Doctors!" Agaard said scornfully; but he was thinking about it. "You're saying it's too late—is that it?"

"I wouldn't say that, exactly," I said. "It's true, he doesn't care to have his privacy invaded. Sooner or later he's got to get out into the world, you know. You know what Plato says—"

Agaard snorted. "Like his father, you mean. If I don't act soon, he'll be as bad as his father."

I said nothing.

After we'd eaten, he put bread, squash, potatoes, and four large pieces of chicken on an aluminum-foil cooking pan and, holding it in both hands, carried it upstairs. When he came down again, we finished the wine, practically in silence, each of us angry and embarrassed in his own way. He snarled from time to time about this or that, his vituperation striking out in all directions as he tried to make peace by thinking up enemies we both might hate; but it was a paltry effort, the comic bad temper of a Punch and Judy show, and I refused to go along.

At last he took me upstairs, to the front of the house, some distance from where Freddy was, and showed me to my room. The bed had clean sheets and blankets, and someone had dusted, not well. I realized that Agaard had planned from the beginning that I should stay the night. I smiled, rueful, remembering he'd invited me to come around three. The old man had given himself plenty of time to work up his nerve. I had to admire him for the care with which he'd cornered himself—and ultimately saved himself, since now it was all my fault. No question about it, he had an eye for strategy. All those old-fashioned hard-evidence histories of war and intrigue.

Outside the room, wind was howling through the pines.

As he was about to go out the door I said, giving the line one last little tug, "Nobody can live without *some* kind of contact with the world, Professor."

He raised one hand, meaning to interrupt, then changed his mind, too weary of me to argue.

I said, "If you keep trying to manage this alone, there's no telling where it will end. Surely you've considered that yourself. Surely it's the reason you spoke to me last night. You wanted me to come here and judge." I looked at his forehead, not his eyes, my hands in my pockets.

He stood very still, a bent, black-suited old crow, looking at his claw on the doorknob. At last he said, "It's a wonderful feeling, righteousness. I envy you."

I stiffened. "That's hardly fair, I think."

He thought about it, crunching his dentures. "At any rate, as you've said yourself, it was I that lured you here. I get part of the credit." He turned his torso, rolling his magnified eyes in my direction.

"He still needs a doctor," I said sharply.

"Yes, yes." He gave an impatient little wave. "You win, Professor. I agree."

"It's surely not a matter—" I began, but he cut me off.

"You've *persuaded* me, Professor!"

We both stood motionless, in stalemate again. He looked down at the hand on the doorknob, staring at it hard. His voice was cool and level: "You say he must be brought out into the world. Let me tell you what that means. When he was a boy of six he was already unusual. Every single day, week in, week out, he'd come home crying. One forgets what merciless creatures people are. Teachers spanked him to prove they weren't afraid of him. I saw it; they didn't fool me! And don't think a child doesn't notice such things! In the end he hurt someone—not badly, as luck would have it. A terrible little man. A gym instructor." His tone became ironic. "I suppose that's when I myself began to be afraid of him."

I nodded, not certain what was expected. As a kind of stall, I loosened my tie and undid the top button of my shirt. Then I stood once more with my hands in my pockets. I must try not to see it as a fight with Sven Agaard, even if, in a way, it was—historian against historian contending for control of the past. Perhaps I could talk to the boy tomorrow. I should sleep, get it all in perspective, quiet my nerves. I knew how Freddy felt, that absolute safety of books. Living all alone with a man like his father . . . I said, pretending to soften a little, "It may not be as bad as it seems, Professor. We're too close to it right now. A good psychiatrist might settle the whole thing in no time. The boy loves books, paper dragons. . . . All right, why not? He needs to adjust to a few simple chores—proper eating, exercise—" I held out my hands like a lawyer to a sympathetic jury. My voice, against my wish, became as ironic as Agaard's. "He can still have 'the sweet, solitary life' he's gotten used to. A good psychiatrist will convince him."

"Yes, no doubt," Agaard said.

Perhaps that instant we were closer to agreement than he imagined. I was thinking of the glittering lights and the roar of the party last night, the blazing faces as we talked nonsense about the big-foot, honing definitions like childish medieval philosophers, slapping each other's shoulders, laughing at jokes only an ape would think, in the privacy of his tree, to be amusing. We were happy as children, nymphs and satyrs of the Golden Age; yet if it was joy—and it was—it was a fraudulent and ultimately brutal joy: witness the hostility of all those free spirits to an authentic though uncivil intellectual like Agaard; witness the pandering and falsehood of the young man who'd driven me home. In the end, who'd trade a golden imaginary world, Freddy's sad paradise, for such foolishness as that?

For an instant a picture came into my mind. I imagined Freddy Agaard at the same glittering party of university historians—or pseudo-historians—his head brushing sparks off the ceiling, his huge face enraged, his wide hands reaching out to seize people, smash them against walls. I blinked, driving it away. It was vivid, but it was nonsense. I saw Freddy Agaard as I'd seen him an hour ago, flushed and sweating in his walled, locked garden of books, and I winced, shaking my head. No wonder he locked doors. Even if he were strong, he'd be right to hide. Why leave that "green shade," as the poet calls it, for the common, mindless glare? Again, involuntarily, I winced and shook my head. I was sickened by the injustice of things, the doom snapped on him by no one, for no reason, a pairing of genes carried down from the days when, as we read in the Bible, giants walked the earth. But there was nothing I could do. He had cause enough to dislike us, I was ready to admit; cause enough to shrink from us, shudder with rage at our invasions of his sacred grove or sunless cave.

"Well," Agaard said, "good-night, Professor."

I nodded, my head still adrift in mournful images. Then, rousing myself, I said, "Yes. Good-night."

He left.

Knowing there was nothing I could do, no way to alter what I'd already done—much less what Agaard had done before me—no recourse or higher appeal for any of us—I undressed, folded my suit, shirt, socks, and underwear over the chair beside the bed, glanced one last time around the large, dusty room, turned off the light, and crawled under the covers. Still furious at Agaard and conscious of his fury at my failure to help, I closed my eyes. Almost immediately, the house creaked softly, weighed anchor, and began to drift.

WHAT IT WAS that wakened me I had no idea, but suddenly I found myself wide awake, listening.

The room was freezing cold; my breath made steam. Moonlight fell over the bedroom door, slanting from corner to corner across the room from the window to my left—pale, living light, moving on the panelling as if projected through water flecked with fish. Perhaps snow was still falling—I couldn't see from where I sat—but falling softly now, spiraling downward untouched by wind. I could hear it, that unearthly silence of a world deep in white. Every line on the wallpaper—gold and white flowers and birds on a field of blue, I believed, though at the moment everything was a dull, mystic gray—every line of the wallpaper, every crack and flame-image of grain on the door, every hint of a bruise on the glass-knobbed dresser, stood out distinctly. I reached for the chain on the bedside lamp and pulled it. Nothing happened. The lines were down, no doubt. It wasn't surprising, but the fact that the lamp wouldn't work made my fear leap more brightly. I pressed one fist to my chest and held my breath. It seemed not to help.

Still there was no sound. I sat rigid, breathing carefully in and out, waiting.

Then I did hear something, a kind of creaking or scraping noise, that might have risen from under the ground or inside me, a sound I strained to identify—the swing of a shutter on some window in the servants' quarters, the sag of a beam under the weight of snow—anything and everything but what I knew it was: the sound of heavy, quiet footsteps. "Nonsense," I whispered. I remembered how my father would look up smiling in the haylot when he saw me coming cautiously through the twilight with his supper—I was five or six—and how he'd cry out "Applejack!" his name for me then, then and later in fact: to the finish the old man never changed his mind about anything; and he'd open his arms to me, huge, thick farmer-arms, power itself. He'd been dead for ten years now. I heard another sound, the sigh of another floorboard as the giant's foot weighed on it. *It's only Freddy*, I thought, struggling to conjure life's plainness back, the intoxicating rough-hewn serenity of childhood applecrates, cellar doors. But if the boy wasn't dangerous, why was he coming now, in darkness and stealth, in the middle of the night?

It seemed to me that I was thinking as clearly as old Agaard when he plotted out a book, thinking both quickly and with masterful control and precision; I was intellect itself, weighing the possibility of blocking the door with the dresser and bed, surveying the room for weapons—the elegant old hat-rack, the slipper-chairs. I had no inkling that my mind was adrift until I found myself whispering, "Concentrate! Wake up!" I could hear him outside the door now, breathing heavily and slowly.

The doorknob turned; the door cracked open a few inches and quietly swung wide. After a moment his head came down under the lintel, his eyes closed to slits, his cheeks as pale as alabaster, glistening. He was wearing vast, striped pajamas under the monkish robe I'd seen before. He struggled with the door, too low and narrow for him, and at last, silently, he bent down on one knee, and I made out that he was pushing something toward me through the moonlight, some inert gift or offering, the object wobbling in the frail, flecked light, moving in at me as far as his enormous arm would reach. He lowered the object and dropped it on the floor. It struck the carpet with a thump. Slowly, he drew back his hand. After that he rose, stood motionless a moment, then, without a sound, drew the door shut. I heard floorboards creak. He seemed to move more lightly now, as if it had been a great weight he'd carried, that gift he'd brought, the object lying there solemn in the moonlight, mysteriously still and sufficient on the dusty gray carpet—Freddy's book.

II · FREDDY'S BOOK

KING GUSTAV & THE DEVIL

PART ONE

1 IN THE SIXTEENTH CENTURY, when Lappland was almost entirely unknown and Finland was civilization's last outpost, there lived, in the then-insignificant country of Sweden, a knight who was afraid of nothing in the world except the Devil. The knight's name was Lars-Goren.

This knight was not a fool or a superstitious oaf; on the contrary, he was a man of later middle-age, highly respected by everyone who knew him and a trusted advisor to his king, Gustavus I, of Sweden. He'd proved himself a brave fighter against the Muscovites and Danes, Gotlanders and Finns, and many another group about whom history has fallen silent, and he was equally well-known as a just ruler of the humble people who fell within his suzerain. If he had serious faults, neither those above him nor those below him could say what they were.

He was not a man people mocked on first acquaintance. Though everyone in Sweden was tall at that time, Lars-Goren was one of the tallest of the age. He stood eight feet high with his shoes off, and he was three feet wide at the shoulders. He had long, clumsy feet—though he was fine on a horse—and long, strong hands. He was also considered to be of great intelligence, for though he thought slowly, he thought clearly and soundly, so that again and again his opinions were found to be more valuable in the end than the opinions of men quicker and more dazzling. More than once when Lars-Goren had given his advice the king scratched his beard and said, "Why do I listen to these other fools when I could listen to my kinsman Lars-Goren?"

At that period the Devil showed himself in Sweden at least every other day. From time to time in the history of the world, there comes some great moment, sometimes a moment which will afterward be celebrated or mourned for centuries, at other times—perhaps more often—a moment that slides by unnoticed by most of humanity, like a jagged rock below the surface of the sea, unobserved by the ship that slips past it, missing it by inches. At the time of this story, the world was teetering on the rim of such a moment. Immense forces hung in almost perfect balance: the tap of a child's finger might swing things either way. It was for this reason that the Devil made such frequent appearances. He was keeping a careful watch on how his work was progressing.

He had reason enough to be pleased with himself. Magellan had recently circled the globe, opening vast new avenues for greed and war. Europe had more mad kings than sane, and the Devil had both the One True Church and the infant Protestant Revolution in the palm of his hand. In Germany,

the very ideas that had filled him with alarm, when they'd broken out in Wittenberg, were now the occasion of such dissension and slaughter that it was a mystery to the Devil that he hadn't introduced them himself.

But the North, which was the Devil's hereditary home, was of special concern to him. For this there were several sound reasons and one not quite so sound, though more significant to the Devil than all the others put together, and it was this: He felt, every time he went there, something or someone at his back, some threat he could never put his finger on. Sometimes, jerking around suddenly, it would seem to the Devil that he glimpsed it for an instant, but then, as he stared more fixedly, it would resolve itself into nothing of importance—some stooped, bearded peasant cutting firewood or fishing through the ice, some beggarwoman wrapped in foul animal skins and holding out an alms-pan with her ice-crusted, mittened hands. Instantly, whatever it was that he saw would dim and blur, for the Devil was old and, though still far stronger than all the armies in the world, he was sometimes troubled—if he stared at things too hard— by snow blindness.

2 BEFORE GUSTAV'S ASCENSION, Sweden had had no king for a long time, but had been served by regents under the Union of Kalmar, which had made Sweden, Norway, and Denmark one single Scandinavian state. For the most part, this political arrangement satisfied the wealthiest of the Swedish aristocracy—the group that made up Sweden's High Council, or *råd*—since their powerful families had castles and fiefs in all three places and, like medieval magnates everywhere, they swore allegiance, in effect, to no one but

themselves. But to Sweden's lesser aristocrats—men like Lars-Goren—and to her peasants and burghers—farmers, fishermen, artisans, and the miserable creatures who worked in the iron, copper, and silver mines—it seemed intolerable that the fruit of their labor should swell the treasury of a foreigner, Kristian II of Denmark. In secret they called him, not without reason, "cruel and un-Christian old King Kristian." He was, to be fair, a just enough man in his relations with the people of Denmark; but in his relations with Sweden he was the Devil's man completely. And what Kristian did not take from the Swedes, the Pope got. A fifth of all Sweden, including mines, farms, and forests, was in the hands of the Church. The Church, moreover, had armies larger than did the wealthiest of the noblemen. The Swedish commoners' hatred of strangers, whether Germans, Danes, or Romans, came to be as pervasive and numbing as the leaden light.

This mood had been building for a long time. Half a century earlier the Scandinavian Union had staggered, if only momentarily, when a Swedish army made up for the most part of peasants and burghers had chopped up the army of the ruling Dane, Kristian I, at the rebellion of Haraker, and then again, five years later, at the battle of Brunkeberg —the victory celebrated by Bernt Notke's famous carving of St. George and the Dragon, a huge wooden statue representing, respectively, Sweden and her foreign enemies—to this day Sweden's most precious art treasure, now housed in the Great Church of Stockholm. If the wealthier Swedish aristocrats disapproved of what the statue symbolized, they held their tongues, for the regency was to a large extent financially dependent on taxes levied against the commoners— who thus became a powerful force in the Riksdag, or Parliament—and the rich had no wish to take the burden of financing the government on themselves. In any event, despite occasional Swedish victories, the Union was still intact; the rebellious were driven underground. If unrest remained, the Devil saw to it that the rich had their own affairs, all over the North, to attend to.

Sitting with his elbows on his knees on a mountain in Angermanland, frowning to himself, slightly puzzled by how easily things seemed to be going, the Devil moved his enormous wings and fanned the unrest. He needed no divine prescience to know that, whatever the upshot, it must come in the shape of confusion, mad greed, and bloodshed. Only the Lapplanders cowering at his back, wearing horns on their heads and dressed in reindeer skins, so that only a sharp eye could distinguish them from the reindeer that gave them their food and clothes and shelter—or rather, only the Lapps and the reindeer themselves—were aware of that huge hulk perched on the mountain, sending an evil wind across the snows of Sweden.

The unrest he was fanning burst into flame when one Gustav Trolle was elected in faraway Rome to succeed the palsied and half-senile archbishop of Uppsala, recently deceased. As a thoroughgoing Pope's man, Trolle had never been popular with the Swedes—in fact the papal council could have found no one more offensive to them—and the regent of Sweden, Sten Sture the Younger, was filled with indignation when the news of the appointment arrived. To show his anger and scorn of Rome, and also to increase his treasury a little, Sten Sture the Younger—a handsome young man who in the opinion of commoners and lesser aristocrats was the rightful king of Sweden—made so bold as to seize by hereditary right a valuable and strategic piece of property held in fief by the Church, the castle and lands of Almare-Stäket, overlooking Lake Mälaren.

The new archbishop sent a cry for help to Kristian II, the

Danish king, whose army arrived in haste and was at once repulsed—pushed, screaming and flailing its arms, into the Baltic. The Swedish regent called the Riksdag into session for advice on how to deal with Trolle, the offensive new archbishop, for, as Sten Sture said, "what concerns all should have the approval of all"—a phrase which, ironically, he had borrowed from canon law. The Riksdag voted the archbishop a traitor, and in solemn *sammansvärjning*—vowing as one man—they swore on pain of their lives that they would never accept Gustav Trolle as archbishop, and that the castle, with all its contents, should be razed to the ground. It was a grave move, since the razing involved the destruction of relics and the profanation of holy things, not least among them, as luck would have it, the person of Gustav Trolle, archbishop, who was beaten and raped by Swedes overzealous in their service of Truth, or, perhaps, as some said, overzealous in their service of the North's true lord, the Devil.

From imprisonment, Trolle cried out to heaven by way of Rome for vengeance. All Sweden was placed under interdict, and Kristian's war with Sweden received the prestige and appropriate finance of a crusade. Early in 1520 a huge army of mercenaries from Germany, France, and Scotland broke over the Halland frontier into Västergötland and, on the frozen surface of Lake Åsunden, joined battle with Sten Sture's army of lesser knights and peasants. Congealing blood lay thick on the snow and ice; cannon smoke darkened the lead-gray sky. Before it was over, Sten Sture lay half dead, one leg smashed to splinters and pulp by a cannonball. He died two weeks later in his sledge on the way home to Stockholm.

Soon Stockholm fell. In an inquiry set up by Archbishop Trolle, nearly all who'd been involved, and many who had not, were found guilty of heresy; King Kristian took over as Scourge of God, and "the bloodbath of Stockholm" began. On November 8, 1520, between the hours of one and four o'clock, eighty-two persons were beheaded, and many more fell victims in the days that followed. Hundreds of others were publicly broken on the rack. The bodies were burned in three huge pyres on Södermalm hill, along with them the exhumed corpses of Sten Sture and his infant son.

Among those who witnessed the Stockholm massacre—including the Devil, who looked down from a chimney, where he sat disguised as a bent old man in black monk's garb—were the knight Lars-Goren and his young kinsman, a distant cousin in his early twenties, Gustav Vasa, the future king of Sweden. They were wearing round peasant hats and shabby coats, for they were both of the Sture party; in fact Gustav was related by marriage to the Stures and lost in the massacre his father, his brother-in-law, and two uncles. His mother, his grandmother, and two of his sisters—to say nothing of Kristina Gyllenstierna herself, Sten Sture's widow, half sister to Gustav's aunt—were locked in the dungeon at Stockholm castle, awaiting transfer to Denmark, where they could expect eventual execution.

"Surely," said Gustav, his face wet with tears and shining in the light of the funeral pyres, "even for those of us who have escaped the axe, there can be nothing to look forward to but death!"

Lars-Goren nodded thoughtfully, not as a sign of agreement but because it was his habit to nod as if agreeing until he'd thought things through. At last he said, when he saw that there was nothing else to say, "God's will be done."

From somewhere high above him, laughter cracked out like thunder over ice, and he crossed himself.

PART TWO

1 THAT NIGHT as Lars-Goren and Gustav were fleeing
the city, still disguised as peasants, the Devil stepped out of
the narrow alleyway along which they were hurrying and
stood with his crooked legs wide apart, his arms reaching out
like an ape's to the walls on either side, and refused to let
them pass. Gustav was instantly thrown into a rage. He was a
quick-tempered man on the best of days, famous for a farmerish sort of arrogance, and tonight, considering all he'd been
through, it was not surprising that the slightest provocation
should turn him to a madman. Though he was seven feet tall,
he could hardly have believed, if he had stopped to think,
that he was a match for the person who stood blocking his
way, for the Devil, in the shape he had taken on, was taller

even than Lars-Goren. Nevertheless, Gustav put his head down like a bull, raised his fists in front of him, and charged with all his might.

Lightly, so quickly that neither Gustav nor Lars-Goren saw exactly what he did, the Devil sent Gustav somersaulting backward, so that he landed, with a resounding thud, hard on his rear end.

"Your Majesty," said the Devil, "you're too impetuous!" He was standing with his legs wide apart as before, but now his huge arms were folded.

Gustav squinted through the darkness and fog, his expression incredulous and close to tears, then over at Lars-Goren to see if he too was seeing and hearing these remarkable things. As if his legs had gone weak, Lars-Goren was leaning against the farther stone wall, pressing his fingers and palms flat against it. Young Gustav Vasa frowned with such intense consternation it seemed that the heat of his brain might burn out his eyes. With one hand he reached up to his head, confirming that his hat had fallen off, then abruptly he shot his eyebeams back into the Devil's.

"You've got the wrong man," said Gustav. "I'm nobody's king. I'm a goat-farmer."

The Devil laughed. "You're Gustav Erikson Vasa of Rydboholm, kinsman of Sten Sture."

Again Gustav shot a look at Lars-Goren and this time frowned so hard that his lower lip reached almost to his nose. He looked back at the Devil for an instant, then away again, turning over this thought and that thought so quickly and cunningly that the Devil began to smile. Feeling around him on the cobblestones, he found his hat and, as if paying great attention to it, like a slow-witted peasant, pulled it back over his head. Then, clearing his throat, and watching carefully lest the Devil decide to kick him or hit him again, he got up onto his feet.

"I may or may not be this Gustav you mention," he said at last. "But I'm certainly no king."

"Not yet, perhaps," said the Devil, and gave a little bow.

Gustav shook his head and put his fists on his hips, still scowling as if in fury, then looked up hard at the Devil's forehead, not quite meeting his eyes.

"Who are you?" he asked. As he spoke he noticed that the person in front of him had lumps on his forehead, like the beginnings of horns. His heart gave a very slight jump.

"Your friend knows who I am," said the Devil, grinning broadly.

Lars-Goren had his eyes closed, and sweat was pouring into his moustache.

"Hmm," said Gustav, and raised his fingers to his wild, shaggy beard. After a moment he nodded thoughtfully, then squinted, increasingly cunning, at the Devil's large nose. "I warn you," he said, "never underestimate my friend Lars-Goren!" He spoke with great conviction, but then instantly felt a little embarrassed, for Lars-Goren was making an involuntary peeping noise, like a woman who's been whipped; and Gustav said crossly, to hide his embarrassment, "So what have you to say to me?"

"You're heading for Dalarna?" the Devil asked in the tone of a man just making conversation.

"I might be," said Gustav.

"Good. I'll come along with you," said the Devil. "I haven't seen Dalarna in years. We can talk as we go."

"Very well then, whatever you say," said Gustav. He turned to Lars-Goren, who had twisted his face away. The knight's neck was stretched up horribly, like the neck of a man being hanged. "Come along, Lars-Goren," said Gustav gently. "Play your cards right, I'll make you archbishop."

2 As THE THREE walked along, keeping to back lanes and narrow paths through immemorially old, blueblack conifer forests, a darkness where no Danish soldier would dare venture—where for all their pride in their viking heritage, their reputation as drinkers of human blood, no Dane would so much as move his left foot up even with his right— the Devil talked happily, with great animation, of his infinitely complicated schemes. Young Gustav listened in exactly the way the Devil liked, skipping past the trivia, seizing on those slyly planted hints here and there that the Devil's labyrinthine plot might be of use to him, providing him with weapons that might enable him to do what he desired: avenge his kinsmen. As for the kingship, it was an interesting thought, and Gustav Vasa was by no means unambitious, but it was not at all his first thought, at least not yet. His heart was closed like a vise on anger and sorrow. Also, he knew he would do well to move cautiously. Though he was no more afraid of the Devil than he was of God or Death, he was by nature a suspicious man, wary as a wolf, a quality he knew he would need if he happened to become king.

Lars-Goren, for his part, listened in a very different way. Every word the Devil spoke was to him like crackling fire, for he'd read a good deal about the lives of the saints and the martyrs. One had no chance against the Devil, he was convinced, but also, since the Devil had singled them out, he had no choice but to listen with all his wits, in the desperate hope of understanding the enemy and outstriding him. He studied the Devil's limping gait, his way of throwing his arms out wide in a parody of heaven's magnanimity, his way of laying his ears back like a horse and sometimes glancing sharply past his shoulder. As a warrior, Lars-Goren knew weakness and fear when he saw them; but he knew that the Devil was not weak in comparison to them—much less fearful—and Lars-Goren knew, too, as a horseman, that nothing is more dangerous than a powerful creature in a panic.

Lars-Goren, needless to say, was in a panic himself. Stumbling along the path, numbed and blinded by his fear, nearly falling from time to time, clutching his chest with his large right hand to make the hammering of his heart less painful, he tried to think out, slowly and reasonably, what it was that so frightened him. His young kinsman Gustav seemed all but indifferent to the threat of the huge, hump-backed monster lunging through the darkness beside him, occasionally throwing one arm across his shoulders, laughing and ranting like a man who hasn't spoken in years and now suddenly has found his tongue.

"Surely it's not Death I'm afraid of," thought Lars-Goren, rolling his eyes upward toward heaven. A hundred times he'd faced death in battle and once he had very nearly died of a mysterious disease. He'd felt no such fear as this on any one of those occasions. Indeed, lying in his infirmary bed, sick people breathing out their last all around him, more corpses every day, the building full of flies, what he'd chiefly felt was a kind of philosophical curiosity and perhaps a touch of pleasure in finding himself so calm. In the heat of battle, he'd had no time for even that. The horse charging him must be swerved around in time, the sword rightly planted in his antagonist's belly or chest. He had been aware, each time, that this thrust, this leap, this dive into the weeds might be the last he ever made; but his mind was on the thrust, the leap, the dive: the idea that he might die, insofar as it was there at all, trailed behind him forgotten, like the faded red streamer on his helmet. Nor had he thought about death at night when he returned to his tent—except once. Once in the middle of the night a cannonball had crashed through his tent and knocked his cot out from under him—it seemed the same instant, though it couldn't have been, that he had heard the muffled thud of the cannon's exploding black powder. Alarm like a rabbit's had burst in his chest. But even that he had not registered as fear. It had been, he would say, an extreme of startledness, a slam of heart that had nothing to do with his mind, his beliefs and convictions. Afterward— lying on the tent's earthen floor, his two companions bolt upright in their cots, their faces white as moons, their voices booming, blaming it all on Lars-Goren—he had felt his body shaking like a sail in a storm, all feeling gone out of his hands and feet, his heart still thudding hard, only gradually slowing itself. Not even that was, in Lars-Goren's opinion, fear. He experienced the violence in his body as not strictly part of himself, no more essential to his mind or soul than the terror of a horse underneath him or a tremor in the earth. No, in plain truth he was not afraid of death. There were in this world, he knew, men who did fear death—men who froze in the face of it, bending to a crouch, muscles locking, hard as steel, men who belched repeatedly and could not speak—but he, Lars-Goren, was not one of them. If he congratulated himself for this lack of fear, and scorned all people more cowardly, he also knew, in secret, that it was all chiefly luck, some accident of upbringing or blood—his father and grand-father had been the same. Should someone have asked him for the formula for bringing up children just like him, he'd have had to admit he didn't know it.

Neither did it seem to him that his fear was of eternal damnation—hellfire, instruments of torture, and the rest— the things one saw in holy pictures or heard about in stories. Like all Swedes then and now, he was inclined to take the threats of priests with a grain of salt. If hell was as ferocious as the priests maintained, then the justice of God and God himself were in doubt. He had no real question that a god of some kind did indeed exist. His grandmother had been a Lapp, and in his childhood he had visited that queer nomadic people. Second sight was as normal with the Lapps as the ice on their lashes. If a child wandered off and died, they knew where to find it. They saw things thousands of miles away as clearly as an ordinary man sees his fingernails and shoes. Those who had never been acquainted with the Lapps might hotly deny that this was possible, making their faces red, their angry throats swelling up like frogs' throats; and Lars-Goren could not blame them, nor would he labor to argue the unarguable; but the Lapplanders' visions were as much a matter of fact to him as the harsh solidity of their reindeer-horn graveyards. What God had to do with those visions he could not say—nothing perhaps—but whatever reservations his reason might cling to, he accepted, below reason, their premise, a world of spirit—vaguely, God. The Lapps' idea of God, or rather of the gods, might seem peculiar to a Christian; their spirit world was neither benign nor malevolent, at least in the Christian way. It was simply there, beneficial or harmful in about the way wolves or reindeer are, a parallel existence neither loving nor malicious, not even consciously indifferent; a force to be reckoned with, avoided or made use of, like the ghosts in one's hut of stretched hides. Having grown up with the Christian God and stories of His saints, having heard talk of the aloof but concerned everlasting Father from the time he had first learned the difference between Swedish and the various other kinds of noises people made, Lors-Goren had accepted without special thought the Christian opinion that the spirit world was largely paternal and benevolent; and because his father had been the kind of man he was, stern, even fierce, but invariably well-meaning, at least when he was sober, Lars-Goren had glided accidentally but firmly to the persuasion that if hell existed it could only exist because God had gone insane. God might be baffling to a human mind—as mysterious as the beaver-faced Lapps of Lars-Goren's childhood, those midget relatives whose puffy-lidded, smoky black eyes had nothing recognizably human in them, or nothing except affection—but God, if he was sane, was not ultimately dangerous. "Yea, though I walk through the valley of the shadow of Death, I will fear no evil," as the Psalms put it. What in all the earth, or even under the earth, should a just man be afraid of?

On the other hand, it was undeniably a fact that, moving through the darkness with Gustav Vasa and the Devil, Lars-Goren was afraid, as frightened as he'd ever been by night-mares, and his fear baffled him. He clenched his fists and sucked in deep breaths, but the fear would not abate. "Ridiculous!" he muttered through his clenched and grinding teeth. But Lars-Goren's heart went on pounding, pounding, white-hot at the notch of his collarbone. The sound of his heartbeat seemed to thud from the darkness all around him.

3 "THINGS ARE in confusion," the Devil's voice boomed out, "and believe me, the confusion will get worse! That's the kind of time when a man of cool wits can make his fortune!"

"I have no interest in fortunes," Gustav said, then compressed his lips. Perhaps he protested too heartily.

"Yes, of course," the Devil said, throwing his arms out left and right, not in a mood to haggle phrasings. "But I'll tell you this: it's a wonderful moment for *some*body. If not you, then somebody else." He laughed.

They were out of the woods now. Ahead of them lay a village. If there were Danish soldiers there, they were not in the streets. The Devil limped boldly toward the lighted windows, and Gustav followed, too interested in what the Devil was saying to think about his safety. Lars-Goren came twenty feet behind them, trembling and watching like a hawk.

"First of all," said the Devil, his hand on Gustav's arm, his face pressed close to Gustav's ear—though he did not for that reason lower his voice—"you see only the evil, not the good in the bloodbath of Stockholm!"

"Good!" exclaimed Gustav, jerking back his head for a look into the Devil's eyes.

"By all means good!" said the Devil with a roaring laugh. "Think about *this*, my hot-headed little friend: no one in Sweden will be fooled any longer about the character of the Danes! It's not new, this murderous way they have, but people *will* turn their heads—I've watched it for centuries." He shot a look over his shoulder at Lars-Goren, as if measuring the distance between them, and Lars-Goren held back a little. Now the Devil had all his wits on Gustav again. "A hundred times Sten Sture could have seized the advantage and made himself king, but no, he held back, the fool!— contented himself and his thousands of supporters with a miserable regency, played footsie with the Danes, kept his tail between his legs for the highfalutin super-magnates like Ture Jönsson and Bishop Brask. And all for what? For what, my young friend? To be killed and buried and dug up and burned like a dog on a garbage dump—with all his friends!"

Gustav stopped walking and turned to the Devil, angry enough, by the look of his expression, to try one more time to knock him down.

"Now now!" said the Devil quickly, raising his hands in surrender. "No offense! Mere facts! He acted in good faith—

he took his little share and left the Danes and super-magnates their big one. I admire him for it, to a certain extent. All the same, the Danes showed their colors—you can't deny that! We all deplore the bloodbath, that goes without saying. But now that it's happened it's no use whimpering and turning our faces to the wall. We have to look at where it leaves us."

Gustav grunted, carefully noncommittal. His cheeks twitched, and it was clear that he kept his temper only by strong self-discipline.

They were passing a small inn, and when the Devil noticed, happening to glance in the window, he said, "Ha! Here's an inn, and not a Dane in sight!" In fact there *were* Danes in sight, Lars-Goren would have sworn, but the instant the Devil spoke, they vanished. The Devil proposed that they stop and have a tankard at his expense, and he would tell young Gustav his mind.

When they were seated and served—the Devil so large, hunched over the table, that his stiff gray cowlick brushed the beams of the ceiling—the Devil continued: "Where it leaves us is this: King Kristian's whole effort in the Stockholm bloodbath was to make certain nobody was left to oppose him. All the best men of your beloved Sture party he murdered by the axe and the rack. We can grieve that fact— that's only right and human—but also, if I may say so, we can *use* it."

Gustav studied Lars-Goren, who sat in the corner, his hands over his face, his eyes peeking through the cracks between his trembling fingers. At last, looking back at the Devil, Gustav said, "Speak on."

"Gustav, my friend," the Devil said, interlacing his fingers and smiling kindly, "the Stures have no one left but you, if you reveal yourself to be willing—though they hardly know your name as yet. And they have no one strong enough

to oppose you in the unhappy event that Sture's widow should escape execution and try to claim the leadership."

Gustav thought about it, then warily nodded. In the shadowy corners of the room where the people of the inn cowered, keeping as far as they could from the Devil, a few began to whisper. "Speak on," Gustav said again.

"In Denmark, King Kristian has troubles of his own," the Devil said. He leaned forward, smiling, lowering his voice, meeting Gustav's eyes with his own small fiery ones. "He's at odds with his barons." The Devil had a tendency to spit as he spoke. Gustav Vasa drew his face back. "There as in Sweden, Germany, or France," the Devil continued, "it's the commoners who pay for the government. For that reason Kristian has wooed his commoners, giving them all sorts of privileges and liberties—he even allows them their Lutheranism, even shows an inclination to practice it himself, to the horror of the aristocracy and the Church. He's weaker than you think, my dear Gustav! And the commoners aren't all. He's grown friendly with the Dutch, hoping for more profitable trade than he can get with the Hanseatic League. The Germans don't like that, needless to say—especially the Germans of Lübeck, since Lübeck stands to suffer most if the Dutch get their deal. You, now, have friends in Lübeck, I believe." He raised his eyebrows.

"That may be," Gustav said, "and again it may not be. I could say I'm no fonder than the next man of Germans."

Suddenly the Devil's red eyes flashed. "Don't be coy with me, Gustav Erikson! I see everything! Everything! You were captured by the Danes in Sten Sture's war. You escaped from prison and fled to Lübeck. You think I'm so old and blind I *miss* these things?"

"That may be," Gustav said more meekly, still cautious and suspicious.

"Very well," the Devil said, and calmed himself, glancing

around the room. "The Stures can't oppose you—at first, I predict, they'll take you as their own, thinking they can govern you and dump you when they please—and Lübeck, your good friends in Lübeck, will finance you."

"And where do I gather my army?" Gustav asked. He asked it so off-handedly that Lars-Goren knew he'd been thinking about it.

The Devil raised his mug and drank, then wiped his mouth. He smiled. "You're on your way to the mining community of Dalarna?"

Gustav thought about it, then nodded. "Dalarna," he said. He turned to his kinsman Lars-Goren. "What do you think?" he said.

Lars-Goren closed the fingers he'd been watching through and lowered his head a little, his lips trembling, saying nothing.

"What is this dependence on cowards and fools?" the Devil asked, lightly sneering. "You can see very well he's too frightened to add up six and seven."

"You're wrong," said Gustav. "He's a slow thinker, but very accurate."

"Pray you don't need his opinion when your house is on fire," said the Devil, and grinned. Then, before Gustav's eyes, he turned into a great swirl of gnats and, little by little, dispersed and vanished. He had forgotten, apparently, that he'd promised to pay the bill.

4 IT WAS a long way to Dalarna, the restless, everlastingly troublesome region of the mines. Again and again they were almost caught by the prowling Danes. Twice when they walked into the houses of old friends, the Danes sat waiting,

with the friends hanging dead from the beams of the room, like hams; and each time it was only by miracle that Gustav and Lars-Goren were able to escape. Indeed, the near-captures were so frequent that Lars-Goren grew suspicious. Except if the Danes had captured some Lapp and made him work for them, only one person in the world could know who they were and where they were going, and that person was the Devil. Lars-Goren scowled thoughtfully, riding in the covered cart he'd crept into with his kinsman Gustav, who was asleep. Lars-Goren turned over thought after thought, slowly and carefully, like a man sorting boulders, trying to make sense of what was happening. Lars-Goren's fingertips no longer trembled, his heart no longer pounded, but even now, with the Devil far away, he felt a steady chill of fear. He did not like Gustav's strange cooperation with the Devil, but he did not waste time over annoyance at what Gustav was doing. He set down in his mind, as something he must think about later, the question of why Gustav was doing what he did, that is, the whole matter of understanding Gustav, to say nothing of the somewhat larger matter of understanding all human beings who take favors from the Devil. Even Lars-Goren, slow and meticulous as he was about thought, could make out at once that the initial fact was simple: by chance he had met and befriended Gustav, and now, whatever he might think of Gustav's ways (he had, as yet, no firm opinion), the Devil had entered the scene, and where the Devil was involved, Lars-Goren had no choice, as a knight, and a father of small children, but to involve himself also.

And so, setting aside all questions of whether or not his young kinsman was right, Lars-Goren worried questions more immediate. The main question was this: did the Devil have some plan far more devious than the plan he'd spoken of? Had he lied to them? That is, had the Devil some plot which depended on the capture or murder of Gustav and Lars-Goren, a plot which with luck Lars-Goren might help Gustav sidestep? Or was the Devil simply crazy, revelling in confusion, urging everyone around him to frenzied activity, having, himself, no idea under heaven what the outcome would be, merely hoping for the best, like an idiot chess-player who occasionally wins by throwing away bishops and queens and confounding his foe?

Lars-Goren brooded on this, riding in the hide-covered peasant-cart, looking down at the pale white blur of his kinsman's face.

At last the cart stopped, and after three or four minutes the humpbacked driver raised the edge of the hide that served as their tent-flap and peeped in. "Dalarna," he growled in a voice oddly muffled, and he closed the flap again. Gustav opened his eyes and, gently, Lars-Goren put his hand over Gustav's mouth, lest the young man forget and cry out, and all be lost.

5 NOWHERE IN SWEDEN was life more grim and unappealing than in the dale of Dalarna. The mountains, high and brooding and disfigured as the Devil himself, gazed down as if vengefully, strewn with slagheaps, pocked with holes like a carcase full of maggots, irregularly shorn as if sick with the mange, the lower slopes crawling with stooped men and animals—pit-ponies, draught-horses, oxen, dogs, and mules —not one of them, man or beast, uninjured—or at least so it seemed to Gustav Vasa, standing bent over like a peasant in line with Lars-Goren, waiting to see the German who did the hiring. There seemed to be no Danes anywhere. Here and

there patches of smoke rose and flattened, black against the gray of the clouds. Workmen moved past the hiring line, endlessly laboring back and forth, pushing wheelbarrows or pulling at their sullen mules, some with heavy wooden boxes on their shoulders, some bearing crudely hacked mineshaft timbers, some rolling barrels or carrying buckets of gray water. One had no fingers, another a wooden leg; all of them had scars, barked knuckles, scabs and sores.

"Behold the army of King Gustav," he whispered to Lars-Goren, and grimly smiled.

Lars-Goren said nothing. They came to the German's crude table.

"Nimps?" said the German.

"Lars-Goren Bergquist," said Lars-Goren.

"Erik Bergquist," said Gustav with a smile.

The German smiled back. "I don't beliff you," he said, "but no matter, I write dem down." He was a short, stocky man, shaved and trim as the Germans always were, even in the country of the mines. When he looked up at Gustav, something made him pause and look closely. "You come to make big revolution?" he asked, then quickly raised his hand, palm out, and smiled. "Never mind! Good luck! We hev new revolution in Dalarna every Tuesday. Tenk Gott for revolution! Otherwise we all go crezzy."

6 THERE WAS THAT NIGHT, as there was almost every night in Dalarna, an open-air meeting, with beer-drinking and speeches. It was run, though crudely, with all the stiff formality of the annual *Ting*. To Lars-Goren's vague distress there was still not a Danish soldier in sight—at least not one in uniform—but gradually, as the reason came clear to him,

his distress gave way to amusement. For all the wooden politeness of the meeting, the concern for proper order—each man rising and speaking in his turn, and speaking with as much moderation as he could manage—the miners were a fearsome company, not to be trifled with. No Dane, once the miners had found him out, would have lasted a minute in the riot the discovery would have unleashed. On the other hand —as the Danish rulers were undoubtedly aware—whatever the pent-up fury of the miners, there was not much to hear at an ordinary meeting in Dalarna. A man stood up, black-bearded, big-bellied, and harangued his fellow miners about foreigners and Lutherans. He pounded his fist on an imaginary table, his eyes bulged with anger, spittle flew glittering from his mouth past the high, smoking torches. The Germans —there were many of them here in Dalarna, most of them owners, officials, or engineers—nodded solemnly, as if in complete agreement, though in all probability every one of them was Lutheran. Another man, a Swede with long blond hair and eyes sunken in like the sockets in a skull, raised his arms for recognition, to answer the big-bellied man with the beard. "Don't be fooled!" he cried in his thin, woeful voice. "Whatever people say, there's a lot we can learn from the Lutherans!" The Germans, as before, nodded solemn agreement. The Swede gave the old and familiar arguments, how the peasants on Church-owned land were for the most part tax-exempt, and the Church owned a fifth of Sweden; how a churchman or even the servant of a churchman, if he committed murder, could be tried only in the churchmen's special court; how the bishops in the Riksdag and råd had been keeping the government weak at least since 1440, though they themselves dealt in land and trade, even fought wars against their neighbors, like any other nobleman; how the bishop of Skara could produce thirty armed horsemen for knightly service, while even the richest of the lay magnates could bring out only about thirteen. "The True Church," cried the Swede, shaking his finger at the sky and almost weeping, "is not the bishops but the whole community of the faithful! Let the True Church—the people—get the wealth of the Church, not the bishops!" The men of Dalarna applauded him and shouted encouragement, raising their steins. A bald, nervous German with a rounded back and twitching, pink eyes was granted recognition and spoke against the Lutherans and, especially, against all Germans. "I am one of them!" he cried. "I look in my own filthy soul, and let me tell you, I am horrified!" He began to shake all over. "A German who has got no authority outside him is worse than a filthy beast!" He shook both fists.

Before he knew the reason—perhaps it was the smell, like the stink of a goat—Lars-Goren felt his heart turn to ice. When he swivelled his head around, he saw the Devil standing in the shape of a crow on Gustav Vasa's shoulder, whispering in his ear. Gustav scowled, his hand on his bearded chin, then slowly raised his eyes to the platform.

The men of Dalarna knew at once, when Gustav began to speak, that this was no ordinary ranter and raver but a man who, if he survived, might change the world.

Lars-Goren could never remember later what it was, word for word, that his kinsman said in that famous speech. Whether it was the Devil's inspiration or his native ability, never before tested, Gustav addressed them with force, not in grand phrases but like the commoner he was. He spoke of the bloodbath, how the axe had fallen smoothly, without clumsiness or hurry, indifferent as the knife of a Copenhagen housewife chopping mushrooms; how after each stroke, as the head fell away toward the sawdust, shooting out its spiral of blood, the headless body jerking, clutching at the air with its white, blind fingers, the axeman drew his axe back and wiped it with his cloth, looking out over the crowd as if wondering what time it was, then leaned the axe against the sawhorse beside him and crossed another name off, while his two assistants dragged the body away, pulling it by the shoes, and then led up another man, as polite and unhurried as assistants to a rich, fat Copenhagen tailor, and helped him kneel at the block; and how then the axeman dusted his hands, spit on the palms, and casually reached over for the axe.

"How can one reasonably hate such people?" Gustav Vasa asked. He held his arms out, innocent as morning. He was indeed, there on the platform—still and calm in the churning torchlight—the kind of man one could easily imagine one's king. Nothing, he said, could have been more logical, impersonal, and efficient than the Stockholm bloodbath. Supremely efficient! No question about it, they were much to be admired, these Danes! All their enemies in the party of the Stures they'd removed at one fell swoop, and without a trace of risk! No new leader in the party of the Stures could arise now to trouble them, because no Sture kinsman who'd ever shown the slightest sign of talent had been left among the living. Though the widow of Sten Sture had been spared, she would prove no exception: she would certainly be executed, quietly, in Denmark, for as everyone knows, and as history has shown repeatedly, no tyrant is safe until the last pretender to the throne he has stolen has been slaughtered. No Sture money could be turned to financing revenge for the bloodbath and the horror that attended it, because the estates of the dead—all the wealth of the Stures—had reverted to the Union crown, that is, to Kristian of Denmark. And the wealth of Kristian and his friends would increase. All bureaucratic positions once managed by Stures here in Sweden, from Kalmar to the Pole, would be managed, henceforth, by

loyal Danes. Perhaps, Gustav said—showing his large and perfect teeth in a smile—perhaps some members of his audience might be imagining they could still look for help from the democratic Lutherans, especially those of the German port of Lübeck, Sweden's main contact with the League. Alas, an empty dream! Though a Lutheran himself, for all practical purposes, Kristian of Denmark was switching his trade from the Hanseatic League to the Netherlands. Ask any merchant from Muscovy to Spain! Lübeck, for all her wealth and beauty—for all her seeming power—would soon be no better than a ghost town. Gustav's voice began to tremble with emotion. Lübeck's halls would soon be empty, her spires stripped of bells. For the overworked, overtaxed miners of Dalarna and for their German owners, officials, and engineers, the last reasonable hope lay in three great piles of blowing ashes on Södermalm hill. The victory of the Danes was complete and elegant. How, he asked again—his voice trembling more—could anyone reasonably hate a race of men so efficient?

The men of Dalarna stared, hardly knowing what to think, stunned by his carefully marshalled, gloomy arguments. The rounded German with the twitching eyes sought recognition, but they ignored him. The Devil, now disguised as a half-wit peasant to Lars-Goren's left, stood grinning, his blear eyes glittering. He seemed to have forgotten his position in all this. He rubbed his hands, his head thrown forward, enjoying the suspense and the victory sure to come, grinning and eager as the humblest of mortal partisans. Lars-Goren's wits reeled, and sweat ran down his face, but it struck him that, if only he could make himself think clearly, he had, there beside him, a clue to how the Devil might be beaten—possibly forever! He knew, even as the notion came to him, that of course it was absurd; yet the strange conviction persisted, scorn it as he might.

The crowd began to whisper, its anger building, and at the last possible moment Gustav Vasa broke his silence. "Men of Dalarna," he said, "I have told you no reasonable man can hate the Danes, much less dream of beating them. But I do not come before you as a reasonable man. I come as the last, wild hope of the Stures, a Sture myself and a man with powerful acquaintances in Lübeck, men who owe me favors and have even more need of me than you have—more need, as they know themselves, than has all of Sweden!" The shock his words gave them seemed to pass through the crowd in waves, like wind over wheat. "Is it possible?" they said to one another. "Is he mad?"

Lars-Goren began to feel troubled. It was not so much that Gustav was lying a little, though he was, of course—he was not quite as close to the Stures as he pretended, nor did anyone in Lübeck owe him favors. Neither was it, exactly, that for a man in such a passion, Gustav Vasa spoke remarkably well-turned sentences. One fights as one can, Lars-Goren told himself. A man in a fury makes use of his fists in the best way his training makes available to him; so why should Lars-Goren object if his kinsman Gustav used careful rhetoric? Nevertheless, Lars-Goren felt distressed, looking up at the platform from his place beside the Devil. Like torches at a stage play, flickering on the sweatbeads of an actor playing Christ, throwing up a shadow on the wall behind him, so the torches around the platform gleamed and danced and raised shadows over Gustav. Like an actor's lines, not like real, direct feeling, the well-turned cries of Gustav's anger rang out over the crowd and rebounded from the mountains. Even the answers of the crowd sounded staged: *Is it possible? Is he mad?* The smudged faces, swellings, and wounds of the Dalesmen—real as he knew them to be—looked like putty and paint in the torches' red glimmer, and even the Devil, with spittle on his lip, seemed all at once, to Lars-Goren, like a child in a costume. All the world had gone unreal, mere foolish play—a shoddy carnival, a magic show; and remembering those who had died in Stockholm, those real severed heads, mouths working in the dirt, those real bodies stretched and torn apart on the rack, Lars-Goren began to be filled with frustration and anger that it should all come to this.

"My name," Gustav Vasa was saying on the platform, "is Gustav Vasa! After my old friend and wealthy, staunch supporter Bishop Brask, who was spared because of his clerical status and his pretended friendship with that filthy pig Gustav Trolle, archbishop, I am the last close relation of Sweden's fallen hero, the man who should have been our king, Sten Sture the Younger!" He lowered his eyebrows, smiling like a demon, and ground his right fist into his left palm, waiting while they roared their pleasure; then he spoke again. This time Gustav made no secret of his strong emotion. He told them of the death of his father and uncles, the imprisonment of his two lovely sisters; told them—almost gently, though his voice clanged out like a Swedish iron bell and tears streamed down his cheeks—that *he*, for one, could still unreasonably find it in his heart to hate the efficient and elegant Danes. *He*, for one, could dream of overthrowing them, dream of sending those noble old sea-kings out to sea for the rest of their days—let them settle in China! He said: "'And where will this Gustav get his army?' you ask." He raised both hands, pointing. "You," he screamed, "will be my army!"

The Devil, in his excitement, was sobbing and, at the same time, dancing. From every quarter of the crowd rose a roar of approval. Everywhere, miners were kissing each other.

At just that moment a man came running up the hill from the village. He pushed into the crowd, trying to reach the platform, shouting something to everyone who would listen. When news of what the man was saying reached the Devil, his hair stood on end and his eyes rolled in fury and confusion. Then, collecting his wits, the Devil made a rush—roaring and swinging his fists to make a path—pressing to the platform, where he whispered in Gustav Vasa's ear. Together, they melted at once into the crowd and hurried to the darkness beyond the farthest reach of the torches. As well as he could, Lars-Goren followed. He caught up with them at the nearest of the pit-barns, climbing onto horses.

"What is it? What's happened?" Lars-Goren called out, keeping clear of the Devil, trying to look only at his kinsman.

"It's Brask!" Gustav answered. "Bishop Brask and his men! Somehow or another they've got on to us! Grab a horse, Lars-Goren! If they've heard about me and what I've claimed for them, they've probably heard that you've been with me!" He shouted to his horse, wheeled, then galloped off, the Devil galloping right behind him, his black cape flying. As quickly as he could, Lars-Goren caught a horse for himself and set out after them, but as luck would have it, he was too far behind and got lost in the woods. When he found them—or, rather, found Gustav Vasa but not the Devil, sitting at his campfire beside a high mountain lake—Bishop Brask and the noblemen of his party had already caught up with him. Their horses were coming from the woods toward Gustav just as Lars-Goren came toward him from the opposite direction. When Gustav saw them he leaped up in a fury, then at once sat down again and began to bang the earth with his fist, crying without shame, like a schoolboy, swearing his heart out.

7 BISHOP BRASK was a tall, bald-headed old man,
lean and straight of back, with heavy-lidded, pale blue, near-
sighted eyes and fingers so stiff and thin that, even in their
gloves, it seemed that a strong wind might break them off like
twigs. He wore a stern black cloak over his purple outfit, a
wide-brimmed black hat with a blueblack feather, and high-
heeled boots from Flanders. His attire was like a king's, by
Swedish standards, though Sweden was of course not Germany or France, and in fact when the bishops of Europe
were called together he always made a point of not going,
lest his poverty be revealed.

He sat on a black horse in skirts and blinders—a sleek,
fine animal by the name of Crusader, the old man's most
treasured possession. It was dancing a little now, twisting its
head, trying to understand the acrid smell of Gustav Vasa
but not giving the question its full attention, trying to work
the iron bit out of its mouth, drooling and giving its head
quick sideways snaps. Bishop Brask drew the reins in more
tightly and pretended not to notice. He stared down gloomily
at Gustav, waiting for him to finish. The bishop's men sat
waiting a little behind him, chins lifted, hands folded on the
pommels of their saddles, their capes thrown back, like aristocrats posing for a painting.

Lars-Goren got down off his horse, tied it to a tree, and
walked toward Gustav. Abruptly Gustav looked up at him,
then over at the bishop, and stopped swearing.

As if it were a signal, the bishop got down off his horse
and gave the reins to his man. He came toward Gustav, stepping warily, like a man who disliked having to walk on dirt,
and he worked the tight leather gloves off his fingers as he

came. When he reached Gustav, he gave an ironic little bow surprisingly like the Devil's and said, "I understand we're in some way kinsmen."

"That may be," said Gustav.

The bishop raised the tips of his fingers to his chin and seemed to muse for a moment, as if his speech were off-the-cuff, though everyone present was aware that it was carefully planned. "Come, come," he said, "there are hardly so many of us left that we can afford to be unfriendly." Slowly, his frown became a not entirely unpleasant smile, and he stretched out his hand.

Gustav Vasa stared up at him in amazement, prepared to be furious if the thing should prove a trick, then abruptly and heartily rose to his feet to shake hands. The firmness of Gustav's grip made the bishop wince—it looked a little like a sneer of rage to Lars-Goren, but Gustav seemed not to notice. When he had retrieved his hand, the bishop closed it inside the other, as if to keep it from further damage, and changed the sneer to a smile.

"So," he said, "you made a great impression on the Dalesmen, I understand."

"I told them what I think," said Gustav guardedly.

The bishop nodded and moved closer to the fire to look into it and warm his hands. "An interesting speech, by report anyway. You're quite right, of course. The party of the Stures is finished if it doesn't find a leader." He glanced at Gustav, a look simultaneously baffling and direct. Partly, Lars-Goren thought, it was a look of appraisal such as duelists give one another before they fight; but there was more to it than that. Lars-Goren couldn't make out quite what.

"I realize," Gustav said, meeting the bishop's eyes but keeping his voice polite, unassertive, "there are richer and more powerful men than me still living and loyal to the

Stures. Yourself, for instance, or the magnate Ture Jönsson. But you're a bishop, and as for him, with all his holdings in Norway and Denmark—"

Brask waved his hand impatiently, cutting him off. "Yes, yes, all true," he said. "The miners of Dalarna, Kopparberg, and so on—they've never been fond of churchmen or the very rich. You're the kind of man thàt appeals to them. One of themselves, more or less." His lips twitched slightly. He controlled them at once. "Our interests aren't exactly identical," he said. "They want a king. That's not exactly our first priority. But on the other hand, they want a Sture as king; and for our own positions, our little advantages—" He gave a slight wave with his right hand, disparaging the little advantages he enjoyed, the castles and lands he held by favor of the Stures. "We like to see the Sture party reasonably strong. A young man like you, with a gift for persuading the populace and a willingness to do a little fighting if need be . . ." He bent his head and tapped his chin with one finger. "It would be awkward, of course, if you yourself should decide that you ought to be king."

Gustav laughed as if nothing could be farther from his mind.

Brask smiled to himself. "By rights, you know, there are people much closer to the throne than you are—if there should have to be a throne."

"I'm their servant," Gustav said, and gave a stiff bow, like a farmer.

"Yes, I'm sure," the bishop said. He turned around to warm his back for a while. Over his shoulder he said, "It's a tiresome business, isn't it."

"Tiresome?" Gustav echoed.

"When I was young," said the bishop, "I was a great reader of books. They were my chief pleasure—my very life,

I would have said." He shook his head, ironic. "But books are expensive, and you'd be surprised how easily they burn, if the fire gets hot enough. And so one involves oneself in money-grubbing and politics, even war. For the luxury of reading the gentle thoughts of Plato or St. Ambrose, or sharing the pastoral meditations of the Emperor who turned his back on Rome to run a chicken farm—for the serene pleasure of musing at one's ease on the glorious illustrations of the Arabs or the masters of Byzantium—one turns one's whole attention to manipulating fools full of bloodthirst and ambition, making them and, when the time comes, breaking them, crushing underfoot all that God and the philosophers have stood for. It's a tiresome business."

"I can see that, yes," said Gustav. He stood looking at the ground, marking it with the side of his foot.

The bishop nodded and for a time seemed lost in thought. His men on their horses sat as still as the trees behind them.

Abruptly, the bishop said, "You're right about Lübeck. Their money's the key. Personally, of course, as a Christian bishop sworn to stamp out heresy, I can't in good conscience have dealings with the Lutherans, though I'm acquainted with a Jew, in a business way. . . . And you're right about Dalesmen; there's the heart of your army—though what they want in the end—taxation of the Church, seizure of Church property, equal say with their betters . . . Theoretically, in other words, you and I are in quite violent opposition."

Gustav nodded, slightly smiling.

The bishop's hand had wandered inside his cloak while he talked. Now, swifter than a striking snake, he drew his sword and slashed at Gustav, aiming straight at his neck. Gustav jerked up his arm to block it—blood rushed down his forearm—and in the same instant he drew his own sword, amazement on his face, and lunged. The bishop lightly side-stepped, released his sword, and threw up both hands. "A test!" he cried, "don't kill me!" Gustav hesitated, and the bishop lowered his hands. "You're a quick thinker," he said, "and you're clearly no coward." He smiled. He waved in the direction of his men, and one of them got down from his horse and hurried over to them, bringing liniment and bandages. With a bow almost humble he went to work on Gustav's arm. Lars-Goren, who had drawn his own sword, slipped it back into its sheath and drew nearer. Meanwhile, the bishop said, "Very well, you shall have your revolution. I'll support you, have no doubt. Not openly, of course. But then, neither will Lübeck support you openly. It would ruin their chances of wooing Denmark back from the Dutch."

Gustav gave a cry of pain and raised his fist to hit the man tending him, then thought better of it.

Bishop Brask lifted his sword from the ground where he had dropped it, cleaned the blood off the blade, and put it back in its sheath under his cloak. "Sooner or later, as you know," he said, "our theoretical opposition will become actual. I'll be sorry to see that happen. I love grand ideals—eternal friendship, loyalty, all that. In that respect we're very different, I suspect. Except for a dedication to survival, you have no principles at all. It's odd that the Devil should have chosen such a man; but then, he's a fool." He shrugged.

"For a man of principle," Gustav said crossly, "you certainly have your little ways."

"I think you haven't quite understood me," said the bishop, "not that it matters, of course; not in the least. You see—" He put on a look so baffled and ironic, above all so extreme in its admission of absurdity—like the expression of a poisoner when he sees that, by carelessness, he's drunk the wrong wine—that Lars-Goren for an instant felt pity for him. "You see, betrayal of ideals—" He waved vaguely, as if dismissing their pity. "Betrayal of ideals is a great sin and a torment. But what you do, that's merely savage, merely bestial. Who blames a dog if he eats cow dung? We merely look away in disgust. Dogs will be dogs. But if a man eats dung, and not from madness, which makes him just an animal again, but for some considered purpose not central to his survival but pursuant to his comfort or luxury—*then* we look away with a vengeance, my friend"—he raised one stern finger—"not in disgust but in scorn!"

"Yes, I see," Gustav said. If he saw, he was not impressed.

"Perhaps you do, perhaps you don't," said the bishop. "It's not important, of course. You do what's natural to you, widowing young women, burning down perfectly good buildings. And I, I cunningly support you as long as you're useful, shifting money and men to your side, providing you with maps and equipment, castles to hide in, information on the enemy's activities. I have seen to it already that both Dalarna and Kopparberg are armed and equipped, waiting for your command. I will support you, as I say. And then, of course, when you're no longer useful—" He closed his eyes for a moment and tipped his head up, then opened them, staring into the lead-gray sky. "Such a stupid waste," he said. "The whole business. I wonder which of us God finds more uninteresting!"

For the first time, Lars-Goren spoke. "Why do you do it then?" His voice broke out louder than he'd intended, sharp as iron striking rock. Gustav gave a start, but the bishop moved only his eyes, studying Lars-Goren. Then, losing interest, he looked away again and lowered his head until his chin was near his chest. "Why do I do it, you say." His face moved painfully from one expression to another, like the

face of an actor constrained to say an overfamiliar line from
a too-well-known play. "Why not?" he said at last, and
grinned bitterly. He glanced at Gustav's bandaged arm,
nodded to himself, and, without another word, turned
abruptly to walk toward his horse. Now as before, he walked
a little mincingly, as if he hated the uncertainty of the grip
earth gave, hated getting soil and bits of leaf on his shoes. His
man gave him a leg up, then went over to his own horse and
mounted.

The bishop scowled, made a kind of *tsk tsk*, then looked,
full of gloom, at Gustav and Lars-Goren. "Time for the exit,"
he said, "the interesting farewell gesture, the parting bit of
wit." He slung his jaw sideways—exactly as the horse was
doing again, trying to be rid of the bit—then breathed deeply,
shaking his head. "You know"—he nodded to Gustav Vasa
—"you, in my position, would simply turn your horse and
gallop off, not true? Man of affairs, much on his mind, no
time for entrances and exits; you simply come and go. How I
envy you!" He looked up at the sky again. It seemed to have
gone darker, affected by his mood. "Is Bishop Hans Brask
not ten times busier than Gustav Vasa? Yet always, always
the intolerable burden of style! Always the cool eye drifting
toward the murder!—excuse me, I meant *mirror!*" He looked
flustered, almost shocked. "Stupid slip," he muttered. He
glared at Lars-Goren as if the whole thing were his fault.
"Stupid," he whispered, his face dark with anger, and
abruptly, still blushing, he turned his horse toward the woods
and galloped off. After a moment his men wheeled around
and followed. A little foolishly, as if unable to think what
else to do, Gustav Vasa waved.

8 So it was that Gustav Vasa became, first, regent, then king, of Sweden. To set off the revolt of the Dalesmen of Dalarna, he scarcely needed to raise his hand. Rumors fanned by the Devil's huge wings were already widespread of Kristian's intention of putting all Swedish mineral exports in Denmark's control, and there were rumors, too—most of them well-founded—of atrocities committed upon peasants and country priests by the Danish soldiery. On the off chance that anyone alive in Dalarna had not yet heard the rumors, Gustav seized the Lutherans' printing press at Uppsala and turned it from the printing of Bibles in German and Latin to a different and highly original purpose, propaganda. It was a stroke of genius, that unprecedented use of the new machine. Even in France there were men who gnashed their teeth in envy, wishing they themselves had been the first in the world to think of it.

The miners of Kopparberg soon joined the uprising, then all of Bergslag, then farmers and lumbermen from the areas surrounding; and since Kristian's government officials in Stockholm were too busy squabbling among themselves to come up with effective counter-measures, the rebellion gathered momentum. In April 1521 the rebels were able to defeat Kristian's forces at Västerås; in May they captured Uppsala. With the speed of an army on sailing sleds, Gustav pushed eastward to the sea to win a port through which supplies could reach him from abroad, and by the beginning of summer his army stood outside Stockholm. Now Hans Brask, bishop of Linköping, and Ture Jönsson, governor of Västergötland, came openly to his support. It was through their influence that he was elected regent in August 1521.

Kristian of Denmark fumed, pacing, wringing his hands, and swearing; but for the moment he was helpless. For three months he'd been visiting the Netherlands, playing high politics with his Hapsburg relations, pursuing his plan of shifting all his business from the Hanseatic League to the Dutch, where the profits would be greater. He wrote furious, imperatorial letters, the Devil sitting at his elbow, giving him advice, but the letters did no good. By Christmas, most of Sweden was in the hands of the insurgents. "Never mind," said the Devil, his huge, crooked hands calmly folded on the table, his head bowed low, so that Kristian could not see his expression. "Take what they will, these lunatics," said the Devil, "it will all melt like snow."

"Like snow, you say," said Kristian. Even with the Devil, he had a way of staring with one eye wide open, so blue it looked like glass, the other eye closed to a slit. He drummed his dimpled fingers on the table.

Solemnly, the Devil nodded. "You forget, my friend," he said, "we have on our side the most brilliant general in the world, the magnificent Berend von Melen!"

"Ah!" said Kristian of Denmark, raising both eyebrows and beaming with pleasure. "Ah yes, the German!" He had met this Berend von Melen only twice, and both times had judged him, after careful thought, to be insane. Kristian had been delighted. He had never been much of a warrior himself, and the stories of vikings he'd heard in his childhood had convinced him that only the insane made good soldiers.

As it happened, and as the Devil was well aware—unless it had briefly slipped his mind—at just the moment when the Devil was giving consolation to Kristian, Berend von Melen was formally switching his allegiance to Gustav Vasa. All that now stood between Vasa's peasant army and complete victory were the fortresses of Stockholm, Kalmar, and Älvsborg. With the army he had at hand he knew he could not take them, for it was largely an army of volunteers, most of them unpaid, always anxious about their crops and families, eager to go home; but Gustav was by no means out of cards. By April, in return for trading privileges, the two nearest cities of the Hanseatic League, Lübeck and Danzig, were covertly supporting him, sending privately funded armies. By October Lübeck was a formal ally. Gustav was now in control of the sea and able to blockade Stockholm; on land he was now strong enough to invade the Danish provinces of Blekinge, Skåne, and Viken.

Kristian, walking with the Devil on the battlements in Copenhagen, wept and wrung his hands. "What a fool I was, listening to the Devil," he said. "I've lost my kingdom and, for all I know, my immortal soul as well!"

The Devil shook his head as if bewildered by it all. "Who knows?" he said. "Maybe something will turn up."

He knew pretty well what it was that would turn up. At that very moment the Danish nobility, alienated by Kristian's legislation on behalf of the peasants and burghers of Denmark—and certain great lords of the Danish church, shocked at Kristian's flirtation with the Lutherans—were secretly meeting with Fredrik of Holstein, brother of the Holy Roman Emperor, Charles. By the end of their meeting, they had elected Fredrik their king.

"I'll fight him," said Kristian, when he heard the news. "Nobody's king of Denmark till he's sitting right here on this throne, and there's no room for two!"

"That's the spirit!" the Devil said eagerly, and ground his fist into his hand. "We'll fight him!"

One eye wide open, the other almost shut, Kristian looked at the Devil and slowly raised his hand to his mouth. He began to smile like a man who's lost his senses, like a poor, doltish peasant when soldiers come and murder his parents and take away his horse. The Devil narrowed his eyes to study him more carefully, feeling—for some reason he couldn't quite get hold of—a mysterious alarm. There were tiers of candles behind the king's left shoulder, and as the Devil stared intently, trying to make out Kristian's expression and fathom what it meant, the king's whole body became, because of the brightness of the light, a blur, a figure as intense and undefined as a sunspot. The Devil, with a feeling of inexplicable dread, looked away.

Kristian had been fooled for the last time. With his family, dressed in the humblest peasant garb, he fled that night to the Netherlands.

9 DENMARK was now in great confusion, struggling with government by a foreigner. The multimillionaire merchants of Lübeck met in secret, smiling and nodding their round, plump heads, the Devil inconspicuously seated in their midst. To Fredrik, they would promise their full and unstinting support, they agreed, beaming happily. To Gustav Vasa they would promise the same. Let the stronger dog kill the weaker, or let each dog rule his own yard, growling at the other.

Bishop Brask, when he received the secret messenger from Lübeck, smiled bitterly, showing his long yellow teeth. He went for a walk to get himself in hand, then sent the same messenger to bring him Gustav.

"My friend," he said to Vasa when he arrived, accompanied by Lars-Goren, "it seems you've been made king by the Germans." He stood grimly smiling, letting the words sink in. When Gustav showed nothing, as if the news were already old and dull to him, the bishop continued, "It's a curious turn of events, as you must know. You're not the person we'd have chosen, if we'd had any say in things. By 'we' I mean—" He turned away toward the great dark arch of the fireplace, as if embarrassed. The room they met in was comparatively small and gloomy, a mere closet if set against the great halls of Paris or Vienna. They were alone, the three of them, except for a round-backed old monk in the corner, reading a book and muttering to himself in Latin. Gustav Vasa sat on a small wooden bench, his hat over his knees, his gloved hand lying on his swordhilt. He seemed much changed by his experience as head of the rebellion. He'd hardened everywhere—every muscle turned to cable, his skin dark as leather and so tough it seemed unlikely that even a dagger could puncture it—but hardened especially around the forehead and eyes. His expression was like that of a man listening for something, listening so intently that he had nothing left over for what was happening around him, not even the strength or interest to raise an eyebrow. His eyes were serene but as hard as blue steel. He was slightly drunk, just noticeably sullen. They'd stopped at an inn on their way to their meeting with the bishop.

Bishop Brask had changed too, but in a different way. He looked older by fifteen years than he'd looked that day in Dalarna when Lars-Goren had met him, or so it seemed to Lars-Goren.

The bishop cleared his throat and continued, looking out at the night, "King Fredrik has hinted that he may release Kristina Gyllenstierna, Sten Sture's widow." He glanced at Gustav Vasa as if to see if he'd heard the news already. Gustav showed nothing. The bishop frowned. "Fredrik knows her claim's better than yours—not to put too fine a point on it. No doubt it's occurred to him that her presence in Sweden would rouse supporters."

Just perceptibly, Gustav nodded.

"You, of course, would be one of the first," Bishop Brask continued. "You're a reasonable man, a just man. You'd hardly deny that her claim is superior to your own."

Gustav said nothing.

The bishop stretched his neck, adjusting the sagging flesh to the high, tight collar. "Your stance, of course, would have a good deal of influence. You're a national hero." Again Brask threw a look at Gustav, then quickly looked away. He interlaced his fingers in a gesture curiously meek and pious, then turned once more to the window. "However," he said, "what's right and just is apparently not the point—as usual. The Germans prefer you to Kristina. You've made certain agreements with them. The point is simply this." He sighed heavily and for an instant seemed to lose his thread. Abruptly, he continued, "It would please King Fredrik no end to see us tear ourselves apart in civil war. The Germans wouldn't like that, of course. Who would? except Fredrik? We can't move an inch without the Germans. We all know that. And the terrible truth is, even with the noblest intentions in the world—not that I accuse you of any such thing—" He smiled to himself. "Even with the noblest intentions in the world, you might be pushed, one way or another, into pressing your claim. These things happen. Someone might persuade you that you're the better choice, might stir up your powerful patriotic feelings; or you might perhaps, on some sudden impulse . . ." Slowly, he turned back to Gustav. "The point, as I was saying, is: I'm not in a position to back losers, even if I like them. So you win, it seems." He smiled again. "It's an interesting life." He could hardly have spoken with more weariness and despair if he were saying, "All the world is a grave."

Gustav Vasa was frowning with that farmerish look he

was fond of putting on with those who thought of themselves as his superiors. Lars-Goren, standing at the door, stared hard at a tile halfway between the bishop and himself. His kinsman Gustav sat in the periphery of his vision, yet Lars-Goren saw his expression clearly. It was, if one saw past the peasant mask, the look of a guard-dog, a look so ferociously focused on one thing that it might have been mistaken for madness.

"I don't ask to be king," he said. "I don't want anything to do with your plots and schemes."

"Of course you don't!" said Bishop Brask, quickly and reassuringly. He gave a weary little wave. But Gustav was in no mood to be patronized. He stood up, clenching both fists. "My dear bishop," he said, barely controlling himself, "for all your vast experience and learning, you don't know anything. I fight your wars, I pull in the help of the Germans, I out-fox von Melen himself and bring him over, and you want some fine lady to be ruler of the Swedes. Have her! Good for you! Just don't waste my time bringing me to hear your reasons!"

Bishop Brask sadly shook his head and rubbed his hands together. "Come, come," he said, a kind of whine in his voice, "you're too hard on me! It's quite true that you wouldn't be my first choice as king, but you *are* my choice. Why be difficult? I'll tell you what it is that I mind most about seeing you chosen. Shall I?" He looked over at Lars-Goren as if asking for his permission too. "What I mind most—on your account as much as mine—is that it will change you from an animal to a man."

"The day that happens, the Devil will convert to Christianity," said Gustav.

Abruptly, loudly, the monk in the corner of the room began to laugh. They all knew the voice; it was the Devil. Lars-Goren felt a weakness coming over him.

"I've gone about this very badly," said Bishop Brask, wincing and looking hard at Gustav. His voice, to Lars-Goren's surprise, became a pitiful old man's. "I've been a good ally to you, Gustav, surely you'll agree. I'd hoped that if I spoke with you frankly, laid my cards on the table—no tricks, no cunning manipulation—we might become friends."

"We'll see," said Gustav.

"Yes, we'll see, of course."

As Gustav moved toward the door, the bishop caught his arm and leaned close, timid and confidential. "Make no mistake, your troubles are just beginning!" he said. "You'll need every friend you can get! Surround yourself with men who have proved you can trust them! Remember your own!"

Gustav seemed to think about it. "I'll do that," he said. "Good-night."

"Good-night," said the bishop, his fragile old fingers snatching at Gustav's hand to shake it. As Lars-Goren followed, the bishop caught his hand too and shook it heartily. "Good-night, my friend," he said to Lars-Goren, eagerly fixing him with his eyes. "Good-night and God bless you!" As they walked down the stairs he called from the landing, "Well, good-night then!"

"What do you make of it, Lars-Goren?" Gustav muttered at the door.

"I'd say he's as good a man as any to nominate a king," said Lars-Goren.

Gustav nodded. "And after that?"

"He'd like some high office, that's clear," said Lars-Goren.

Gustav waited, frowning impatiently.

"He might be a fine and Christian man," Lars-Goren said, "if he had nothing to think about but books."

"Appoint him to nothing whatso*ever?*" said Gustav.

"All I really said—" Lars-Goren began.

"Incredible suggestion!" said Gustav; suddenly smiling, he hunched forward, and lightly tapped his fingertips together near his nose.

On the sixth of June, Gustav accepted the crown. Eleven days later, the Danes in Stockholm surrendered. It turned out afterward that the messenger from the merchants of Lübeck had had the papers of surrender in his pocket when he'd come to Bishop Brask.

"Goat-farmer," said the Devil, "you've done well for yourself. I'm sure Mother Sweden can look forward, now, to years and years of peace."

"That may be," said Gustav, and glanced at Lars-Goren, who stood gray as ashes, carefully not looking at either of them. It crossed Gustav's mind that sooner or later, he must drive his friend the Devil out of Sweden.

PART THREE

1 WHILE GUSTAV began the work of setting up his
government—a task as exciting to him as planning and carrying out the revolution, for he had high hopes: he knew himself no fool, knew to the last detail what was wrong in
Sweden and what he, as king, could do about it; knew, moreover, that he had a gift for inspiring those around him, so
that surely his government must prove a masterpiece of sorts
—Lars-Goren, for his part, turned his mind more and more
to the question of understanding and outwitting the Devil.
He was not free, during the first few weeks, to leave Gustav's
side, since Gustav insisted that he needed his advice; but as
soon as the new king felt he could spare him, Lars-Goren bid
farewell to his friends at court and started north to his home

in Hälsingland, to visit his wife and children, find out how his estate was maintaining itself, and give himself the leisure to read a little, and think.

It was the middle of summer when he started on his journey. Goats stood on the roofs outside the walls of the Stockholm fortress, nibbling grass and moss and looking down with malevolent eyes at every carriage that passed. Boats filled the harbor, mainly German, Polish, and Russian, for the Swedes were at that time passive traders; they waited for the buyers to come to them. It seemed a sensible policy, though Gustav Vasa would later change it. Sweden was relatively poor and small, and shipping was expensive, not only because of the cost of boats, equipment, and sailors, but also because of the cunning and skill of the pirates who preyed on shippers. A few great rulers of that day and age—like Ivan the Terrible, Henry VIII, and the Holy Roman Emperor—could afford strong navies to defend their coasts and seaways. But for lesser monarchs—even Fredrik of Denmark—who had to scrap with their magnates for wealth and manpower, the cost of such policework was prohibitive. For all Lars-Goren knew that morning, half a dozen of the gray, high-masted ships he looked down on now might be disguised privateers.

Imperceptibly, the city changed to farmland. No one riding Lars-Goren's road north could have said where one left off and the other began. Even at the heart of the city there were goats and gardens; but at some point there began to be more cows than goats, and the gardens became fields. Lars-Goren, lost in thought, hardly noticed the change, merely felt a slight lifting of the heart that meant he was in country a little more like home, though home was still provinces away. By the time he reached Uppsala, after riding for days—gangling and vague-eyed, arms and legs loose as a straw-

man's, his beard as thin and curly as brown moss—he was in
the heart of the farmland, the beginning of the region that
paid its taxes in butter and hides and gave the kingdom its
most important exports, all that could be wrung from a cow,
from the horns to the tail. Though by knightly privilege he
could have slept where he pleased, he put in at a hostel in the
shadow of the clumsy, towering cathedral where the archbishop Gustav Trolle had inadvertently put Sweden on the
road to independence. Before dawn, he was on the road
again.

He travelled through fields and forests and spent the second night in Gästrikland, bordering Dalarna. There he slept
with peasants, a chicken on the bed beside him, queerly
friendly though also cautious, as if the chicken possessed the
soul of a cat. He had nightmares which he couldn't quite
remember in the morning. He would have thought he'd forgotten them completely except that at the mention of
Dalarna, to the west of him and not on his way, he got a brief
flash of imagery, possibly prophetic, he thought. Lapps with
torches (somehow he saw this while lying in the snow-
covered grave they attacked) were digging up his body. He
saw this with his food raised halfway to his mouth, then remembered no more and finished eating.

Soon he was in the pitchdark forests of Hälsingland,
veering west of the principal city of his province, Hudiksvall,
heading toward the fields and streams of his family estate.
When he emerged from the darkness to the light of the fields
it was like being reborn, he thought, and thought, the same
instant, of Bishop Hans Brask, who would have winced at the
neatness of the symbolism. The image of Bishop Brask—
sitting on his horse as he'd sat that morning beside the lake in
Dalarna, about to dismount and have a word with Gustav
Vasa—was so sharp and real that Lars-Goren reined in his

horse. It seemed to Lars-Goren that he and the bishop had made a long, hard journey. But there was no one there, just fields of new-mown hay, a small village in the distance, a crooked wooden steeple rising above the other village rooftops.

"Bishop Brask," he said aloud, as if the man were still there.

A shudder passed through him and he tried to remember what he'd been thinking, all this way, but all that came into his mind was light and fields, a dark, dead tree somewhere in one of the forests he'd passed, beside the road, also one toothless old woman who had waved and smiled, then crushed her hat down under one hand and vanished into the weeds.

With his knees he started the horse forward again. He began to pass the huts of the people who owed their allegiance to him. Small huts, well kept, better than most, he would have said; but then, the war had never come to Hälsingland, and though the sons of these peasants had fought with Lars-Goren, they had been lucky from the beginning: all but a few hundred had come home without a scratch, as if the Devil, for some reason, had decided to leave them alone.

Toward dusk, Lars-Goren reached the village closest to his own estate, and here, unaccountably, he found himself full of dread. He tried to think of what he would say if someone hailed him, and his distress increased. But tall and erect though he was, no one noticed him. And so, long after sunset, he came to his home estate. Though summer was at its height, the air was frosty. The fields lay perfectly still, bathed in mist, nothing stirring but rabbits and a fox and what might have been a deer. On the hill overlooking the river, his castle stood unlighted, as if everyone had died. He knew, of course, that that was nonsense, an idle nightmare rising and sinking again in an instant. Nevertheless, he swallowed hard, like a man full of fear and remorse. The horse, called Drake, or Dragon, looked back at him. He patted its neck. They moved on and came to the plank road, loud under his horse's hooves, that rose abruptly to the castle gate.

At the gate he reined up his horse and sat for a while, like a man coming back to his sanity. He knew now why the castle was dark. There were no dangers here, no passing strangers. His people had simply gone to bed. He looked at the stones of the castle wall, docile and familiar yet unearthly in the moonlight, moss-hung, mysteriously alive, as it seemed to him, not stones but something stranger, perhaps a towering stack of sleeping sheep. He looked at the planks of the huge oak lift-door, built by his grandfather, heavy not for defense against enemies but to carry the weight of carts. At last he got down from his horse to go to the door and bang the knocker.

2 HIS WIFE, LIV, stood in the kitchen cooking for him —"No need to wake the servants," she had said, but he'd known what she meant. She would rather be with him alone after all this time. Around her, except where the fireplace-glow reached, the stone walls were gloomy and dark, a world paradoxically intimate and foreign after all he'd seen in Stockholm. He sat at the heavy pine table, far away from her, where they could watch each other. The room had no windows. In winter, that region could be bitterly cold. The red light from the fireplace where she cooked flowed over her and threw a tall shadow on the wall to the left of where Lars-Goren sat. His wife's long hair, yellow-red and translucent as cloud-berries, was tied up in a bun.

At first she asked him questions, which he answered briefly and negligently, much as he'd have answered some stranger at court to whom he was obliged to be polite though neither had any great investment in the other. Then, noticing what he was doing, he tried to answer more expansively, telling her about Gustav, what life was like in Stockholm under the new regime, how the city and the people there had changed since she'd seen it last. She listened as if with interest, occasionally asking about some family they knew; but they both sensed that it was not yet time for details, or sensed that he couldn't yet give her the details most important to him, above all the stories of his encounters with the Devil himself. They let the conversation die, he by pretending to sink into thought, she by working more actively at the fireplace. When the silence grew embarrassing, she took up her part.

She told him, as she worked, who had died, who had married, which children had been ill. Her words were brief and clipped, with long pauses between them. Sometimes she would turn and look at him for a moment. Occasionally she smiled, but it was not the smile he remembered. Then, gradually, as the foodsmells grew thicker and sweeter in the room, both of their hearts seemed to warm a little. She filled a dish from the kettle and brought it over to the table, checked the beer-pitcher to see that it was not yet empty, then sat down across from him to watch him eat. When he bowed his head to pray, she also bowed. Afterward he said, "One of these days—"

She nodded.

He regretted that she'd nodded. He would have liked to try to put it in words. But since she'd given him no choice, he began to eat, shaking his head and saying nothing.

Then, forgetting that he'd decided to say no more, Lars-

Goren said, blurting it out with great urgency, like a child, "I always feel guilty, coming through the villages when I've been away so long." His wife was looking down at her pale, folded hands, her eyes unusually dark under the half-lowered lids. He sipped his beer, spilling a little of it down his beard and quickly wiping himself, then leaned forward on his elbows, looking at her forehead, and continued, "I feel even guiltier coming here."

She raised her eyebrows as if questioningly, though still she kept her eyes on her hands.

He began to nod thoughtfully, his lower lip over his upper, his eyebrows low. At last he brought out, his voice oddly thin, at least in his own ears, like the bleating of a sheep, "There are evils in the world that a man can't take the blame for, evils that nobody can do anything about—my going away, I mean. Not being here to see the children grow up."

The softness of her voice startled and unnerved him. "I know."

He thought of touching her hand, then thought better of it. "Surely it's the truth—at least I think it's the truth—that when a man in my position . . . having people who depend on him, the country not safe unless he goes out and does what he can to make it safe . . ." He closed his eyes for a moment, feeling hollowed out and helpless, like a child who's been caught in a lie, though Lars-Goren was not lying. "If I could stay here all the time, the way a husband should," he said, "if I could watch over the peasants, see to their welfare, settle their disputes—" His fingertips were trembling.

"Hush, Lars-Goren," she said, "eat your supper." She was looking at him now, her eyes a faded blue, beautiful, like ice come alive. As if she'd come to some decision, she reached out and touched his left hand. "I know how it is," she said. "You do what you have to do. I'm glad you're home."

Lars-Goren closed his hand tightly around his wife's hand, small and strong, and his head swam with thoughts he had no words for. She rose, with her hand still in his, and as if at a signal, he too rose. "That's all you want to eat?" she asked, eyes widening in surprise, as if she didn't know—and perhaps indeed she didn't—that it was she who had given him the signal to rise and come with her.

"No," he said, "it's good, but I've had enough."

She led him to the beds of the children, one by one, and at each bed he stood for a long moment gazing at the face he knew as well as he knew his own heart yet at the same time seemed not to remember. It had been more than a year, and the changes in his children were so mysterious and painful— or the fact that he hadn't been there to watch them change was so painful—that he felt again, more strongly than before, that helpless hollowness of a child in despair. Holding his wife's hand, bending forward to see, he wore an expression of fear and foolish eagerness, a face prepared against the chance that the child should awaken and discover him standing there.

As he stood beside the bed of his elder son, Erik, what he feared came to pass. The boy frowned in his sleep—he had a long, angular face with wide, sharp lips like Lars-Goren's— his mouth moved, almost spoke, and then all at once his eyes were wide open, staring straight into his father's. His head raised a little from the pillow. "Pappa?" he asked. He was twelve, a large, broad-shouldered boy, his shoulders blue-white in the light from the candle in Liv's hand.

"Erik!" Lars-Goren whispered, bending closer, smiling.

He couldn't tell whether the expression on his son's face was joy or panic, or so he would have said. In the dark part of his mind from which dreams come, he knew the whole truth: what he was seeing was terrible love and pain, the exact hollowness he was feeling himself, the woe of the child who has no hope of being loved, who feels deservedly betrayed and abandoned. Lars-Goren bent, thinking of seizing his son in his arms, but the boy had changed greatly, there was fuzz on his upper lip, and at the last instant Lars-Goren's heart shied, and instead of seizing him he merely reached out clumsily and touched his shoulder. Now, in spite of the remains of his smile, the look on the boy's face seemed almost entirely panic.

Quickly, his mother said, "Go to sleep, dear. Your father will be here in the morning. You can talk to him then."

Erik's eyes flew to his mother; then he let his head fall back on the pillow.

"Good-night, son," Lars-Goren said. Already he was beginning to back away.

"Good-night, Pappa," said the boy.

The rooms now seemed larger, more foreign than before. As they moved down the hall toward their bedroom, candlelight flickering on the walls, his wife said, "They talk of you all the time, Lars-Goren." She gave his hand a squeeze.

Like a man standing back from himself, he watched how his heart gave a leap at those words. He shook his head, grieving and rejoicing, and opened the bedroom door. When they'd entered and he'd closed the door behind them, she turned to face him, smiling. He took the candle from her, seizing it awkwardly, so that he burned the palp of his thumb on hot wax and very nearly let the candle fall, then composed himself and set the candle in the holder on the table beside the bed. She waited. He returned to her and took both her hands, studying the smile. After a moment, for the first time since he'd arrived, they kissed. The feeling of strangeness and guilt fell away; he understood by sure signs that, odd as it might seem, he was the joy of her life, as she was of his. He held her in his arms, bending down so awkwardly that he was tempted to laugh at the absurdity of things—this huge man, this small woman—and he pressed his cheek to hers, then bent down more and kissed her shoulder.

When his wife lay asleep in his arms, he stared at the ceiling, not thinking but floating in the sensation of being home. It seemed a long, long way from where the Devil schemed and plotted. Indeed, it was hard to believe in the Devil's existence, here in his own long bed, with his wife. Yet the Devil was real enough, he knew, somewhere far away— or maybe not so far away. He thought of the toothless old woman who had smiled and waved, then fled, and the shadow of movement that might or might not have been a deer. As he drifted toward sleep, he thought briefly of the distance he'd felt between himself and his children, even between himself and Liv; thought of how he'd failed to take his son in his arms, and how he'd hoped no one would see him as he passed through the villages in his keeping. Not that one could call that the Devil's work, exactly. He struggled to rise back out of sleep and think, fight off the fear surging up in him, but someone was muttering, an old Lapp with brown eyes, beating with his fingertips on a drumhead on which lay three stones.

3 IN THE MORNING, Lars-Goren looked through the records of his glum old groundskeeper, veteran of many wars —an exasperating man when he got off on his exploits—and reviewed the accounts of the village managers. By ten he'd talked with all his lesser officials. When he'd approved or

disapproved the peasant requests that had been set down in writing to await his return, dealt with small complaints and one slightly larger one, the request of some villagers that a certain old woman be burned for witchcraft, a charge they supported with positive proof, Lars-Goren announced his intention of riding out for a first-hand look at his villages and lands. He invited his twelve-year-old, Erik, and his ten-year-old, Gunnar, to ride with him. His wife and the cook prepared a lunch for them, on the chance that they should find nothing to their liking in the peasant kitchens or the village inns; and the groom brought around three horses and gave Gunnar a leg up. "I'm all right," the boy protested, but only for show, accepting the help. Gunnar was red-headed and freckled, still chunky and dimpled like an infant, and though his grin boasted confidence, he was secretly afraid of horses, as all of them knew. Erik sat very tall, comfortable in the saddle, and watched his younger brother's struggles with friendly detachment and the patience of an adult. Lars-Goren, covertly watching his elder son, felt a shower of pride and felt, at the same time, even more remote than he'd felt last night in Erik's bedroom. Somehow without Lars-Goren's help, or so Lars-Goren imagined, the boy had become all any father could have wished. It crossed his mind that Erik would soon be old enough for war. Hastily, to distract himself, Lars-Goren glanced behind him, making sure that Lady, his spaniel, was not too close to the horses' hooves.

Seeing him turn to look at her, Lady yapped officiously, then growled low in her throat and feinted at the fetlock of the horse's left hind leg and yapped again, showing her master in her own way that she had everything in hand—have no fear! she was paying close attention! Lars-Goren laughed at the dog and at himself, then glanced at Erik and saw that he was smiling. "How I love that boy!" he thought; then, glancing at Gunnar, seeing how he was still smiling with pretended confidence, a dimple cut deep into his right cheek, but his pupils cocked downward, exactly like those of a colt in alarm, Lars-Goren corrected himself, "How I love all of this! Erik, Gunnar, my wife, my girls, the peasants who look to me for defense, this glorious land—!"

Now everything was ready. His wife and two daughters waved to him from the arch. Lady stood poised, looking up at him, meaning to take her first step the same instant his horse did. He made one last check, glancing at the cinch-straps, his younger son's two-handed grip of the reins—he held them high over the withers and sat unnaturally erect, like a circus performer. Then, since all was well, Lars-Goren leaned slightly forward and, as if part of one motion, quick and sure—quicker than Gunnar had expected, judging from his face—the horses and dog began to move. At a half trot Lars-Goren's horse Drake, one ear cocked back in case Lars-Goren should whisper, led them down the hill and, at the faintest suggestion of a signal from Lars-Goren, angled through a break in the hedge, took an easy little ditch (Lars-Goren glanced back at Gunnar, whose eyes briefly widened in alarm, but all was well), and headed crosslots through the fields in the direction of the nearest of the villages.

The sun was high, the day warm. In the second field they came to, peasants were cutting and shocking rye, working, as always, in their dark, heavy clothes, dark round hats or ker-chieves, working quickly, as they never did at any other sea-son, since the weather would allow them only three or four weeks to get the grain in the bins, the hay harvested, and the land reploughed. Lars-Goren rode straight to where a group of them were loading up a wagon. They stopped their work as he approached and straightened up to greet him; a few raised their arms in a two-handed wave. It was as if he hadn't

seen them in years, he thought. After months of war and
weeks of Stockholm, they were like apparitions from another
century, black-garbed and wrinkled, even some of the
youngest of them toothless, their smiles open and innocent.
Even their language was at first strange to him, though he'd
heard it all his life. But almost at once, almost as soon as he'd
registered it, the strangeness fell away and he was one of
them.

An old man with a gray moustache and beard put his
hand on the side of Drake's neck. Lady, wagging her tail,
stood close to the peasant and looked up at Lars-Goren making sure it was all right.

"Good to have you back, sir," the peasant said.

"Good to see you well," Lars-Goren answered.

The old man smiled and looked over at Erik, then Gunnar. "Big boys," he said, and shook his head as if the fact
saddened him.

"They've grown, all right," said Lars-Goren. "And how
are yours?"

The peasant's smile came back, wide and toothless. "Six
grandchildren now," he said, "all strong as oxen, two more
on the way. So far, all boys!"

"God keep them!" said Lars-Goren, with more feeling
than he understood.

Tears came suddenly into the peasant's eyes. "And the
same to you and yours!" he said. He gave a pat to the horse's
neck as if to end the conversation.

Lars-Goren glanced at Gunnar. The boy was watching
with great curiosity as an old woman with hands so stiff they
would hardly bend stood dabbing at the corner of her mouth
with the end of her black kerchief. What Gunnar was thinking Lars-Goren couldn't tell, but he saw that the old woman's
legs were shaky; she was too old and weak to be working in

the fields. Lars-Goren threw a questioning look at the peasant he'd been talking with.

"It was a hard winter," the old man said with an evasive smile. "The Devil is always busy." Again he gave a pat to the horse's neck, and this time, to make sure the conversation was ended, he turned away.

"Well," said Lars-Goren, looking from the old man to the rest of them, "God be with us all!" Without another word, he swung his horse around and started at a trot down the field in the direction of the trees and the village beyond.

When they reached the road into the village, his son Gunnar came up beside him. "Pappa, what happened to the old woman?" he called out. His chubby, freckled face hovered between expressions, as if at a signal from his father he was ready either to laugh or show concern.

"Trouble of some kind," Lars-Goren said. "They keep these things to themselves, if they can. Maybe she had a stroke, maybe her son turned murderer. If it's bad enough, sooner or later we'll hear."

"But aren't we supposed to take care of them?" Gunnar asked. When Lars-Goren said nothing, the boy demanded, "Aren't we supposed to be like God to them?"

Lars-Goren glanced up. Though the sky was clouded over, the light was intense.

It was Erik who spoke, riding a little behind Gunnar, to his left. "Even God they'd never ask for help," he said.

Lars-Goren glanced back at him. Erik was staring straight ahead, like a knight, or rather like some image of a knight that Lars-Goren had somewhere seen but couldn't call to mind.

"It's true," Lars-Goren said, half to himself. "They're stubborn. They serve us, they treat us with a certain respect; if war comes, or plague, they're willing to depend on us. Otherwise, our hands are tied."

"You mean even God's hands are tied?" asked Gunnar. As if without knowing he was doing it, he lowered his left hand to the pommel of the saddle, making himself more secure.

Lars-Goren smiled and gave no answer. They were entering the village now, Lady trotting out ahead of them, guarding her party against ox-carts, stone fences, and cats.

4 WHILE THEY were eating their lunch in the church garden, they talked with the village priest, whose name was Karl, an officious little man with large gray eyes and a face like a woman's, a flatterer and a liar from the day he was born—for which he despised himself, but no matter how he tried he could never improve. He sat on a headstone across from them, his plump hands folded on his knees.

"Yes, yes," he said, "all's well! No problems!"

Whatever the situation in the village, that was always his claim.

"We had some trouble with wild dogs; in fact a child was killed, the wall-eyed boy that used to tend the horses."

"Yes. I remember."

"It was a pity. Terrible. But the situation's well in hand now."

He cocked his head with the meek expression of one of those saints in old paintings. "It's good to see you back," he said. "You know how people talk. 'That's the last we'll see of Lars-Goren,' they say. 'Now that he's a friend of King Gustav, we'll drop from his mind like last year's toothache!'" Father Karl rolled his eyes up and smiled like a baby. "They say, 'Lars-Goren's become a Lutheran now.' 'Oh?' I say. You can imagine how it makes me laugh—Lars-Goren a Lutheran! They say, 'He's become a great lover, down there in

Stockholm.' 'A lover, you say!' I tell them, and laugh to myself. 'That's not the Lars-Goren *I* know,' I say to myself. I could tell them a thing or two about Lars-Goren, God be praised; but what's the difference, it does no harm, all this chatter of empty-headed fools!" He opened his hands as if granting all gossips his mercy.

Lars-Goren's son Erik sat staring at an arrow-shaped headstone with interlocked snakes, his face slightly pale with anger. Gunnar from time to time glanced at his brother as if trying to decide what expression he himself ought to wear.

"Ah well," said Father Karl, "there's always unrest, even here in Hälsingland. There's always gossip and lying and idle speculation, especially when the lord is away, you know, and people have time on their hands. I let it go, for the most part. When the moment seems right, I put a word in." He smiled, his eyelids lowered, and glanced at Lars-Goren, too good a friend to ask for thanks.

Lars-Goren knew well enough that it was all lies and flattery, Father Karl's childish way of showing loyalty and affection by making others seem less devoted; but he said, just to be on the safe side, "What kind of unrest do you mean, Father?"

"Ah, the usual, you know—" He threw his hands up and gave a laugh. "New governments are always a problem, of course. Where will they get the money to keep things going, you know? Where will they get leaders, with all the old ones killed off in the war or the bloodbath of Stockholm or fled away to Germany? The Lutherans are everywhere, needless to say. And who knows, some of them may even be close to the king. Will they argue that the holdings of the Church should be seized? Will they raise the peasants' taxes, or take them from the fields for the army? Such are the questions people ask in their drunken foolishness." He blushed slightly and threw a glance at young Erik, then leaned toward Lars-

Goren, confidential. "You see, it's hard to worry about someone you never met. King Gustav's a mystery. The villagers and peasants have never laid eyes on him. But Lars-Goren, now, there's a face and figure they can call up in their minds, a man they can brood on and speculate on: 'What will he do? What will he think? How might he betray us?' That's why they gossip, you see. Testing each other out, each man trying his fears on the others, watching for an answering spark of doubt." He shrugged sadly and looked at his knees.

Suddenly Gunnar said, "I don't believe you!" His eyes were large and fierce, his freckled face red.

Lars-Goren shot him a look, and Gunnar closed his lips together.

"Of course you don't, my son! And I don't blame you in the least!" The priest smiled with childish eagerness. "Who can believe these people we've known all our lives to be evil? And indeed they're not! Just childlike, that's all! There's no evil in their hearts! No, no, nothing like that! They babble without thinking, these poor ignorant peasants, no more evil than the flowers in this garden!" He shook his head sadly, holding out his hands, then folding them in his lap again. "That's the Devil's way, you know. Make use of whatever lies at hand. It's not the people who are wicked, they're just little children, like all of us." He shook his head again and put his fingertips together as if praying. "God have mercy on us all!"

Lars-Goren and his sons had finished eating now. Fruit-flies and garbage-bees hovered over the remains, which Lars-Goren had placed on a stone for the priest to clear away. Lars-Goren said, "Thank you for your company and advice, Father Karl. I'll think about these things, you may be sure." He moved, with Erik and Gunnar behind him, toward the stone archway that opened onto the street.

"The pleasure's all mine," said Father Karl, hurrying up

beside him. "You mustn't take these things too much to heart," he added. "I may exaggerate the danger. Needless to say—"

"I understand," Lars-Goren said, and nodded.

At their approach, Lady jumped up from the shade where she'd been lying, awaiting their return, and came trotting to push her head into Lars-Goren's hand, then turned away again, wagging her tail and urging them to hurry. Villagers on the street stopped walking to look at Lars-Goren and his sons. They smiled, silent as stones, but what they were thinking not even the Devil could have said.

Behind them on the cobblestones, Father Karl said, making Lars-Goren pause, "I understand you've become good friends with Bishop Brask."

Lars-Goren turned, his lips slightly puckered. "I've met him," he said at last.

The priest nodded, avoiding Lars-Goren's eyes. "It's a dilemma," he said, and nodded. "One would have thought he'd have gotten some high office in the government, after all his help."

Lars-Goren waited.

"But of course he's a difficult man, that's true too. I met him once myself. Who can say which way he'd be more dangerous to the king—as an official or as a man embittered by the king's ingratitude."

Lars-Goren smiled half to himself. "You hear a good deal, here at the edge of the world," he said.

"Well, yes. He's a churchman, of course. We have mutual concerns, although naturally—"

Lars-Goren nodded. Erik was giving his brother a leg up, Gunnar smiling grimly, as if waiting for the horse to shy or maybe rear up and strike at him.

"Thank you again," Lars-Goren said, dismissing Father

Karl with a nod and getting up on the horse. It was mid-afternoon and he had three more villages he was hoping to visit before nightfall.

As soon as he saw that his sons were ready, he set off at a canter, his horse's hooves striking sparks from the stones. When he looked back, Father Karl was on the steps of the church, waving after him with both arms, in the style of a peasant. A few villagers had come out into the street to watch Lars-Goren ride off. They too raised their arms. Gunnar was riding with one hand clenched tight on the pommel, his head too far forward, close to the horse's flying mane. Erik rode beside him, watching him. Lars-Goren reined in a little, surprised at himself, trying to make sense of the anger that was flaming in his chest.

5 IT WAS DUSK when they came to where the witch had been burned. They could see the smoke and bright embers from a mile away. From a half mile away they could smell the charred flesh and bone. Neither of his sons said anything. The horses became skittish, and the dog, catching the uneasiness of the horses, kept closer to Lars-Goren's side. In the west, the clouded sky had become brighter but no redder. It glowed like the blade of a knife in a strong, clear light. Black specks—vultures—floated around the smoke. There were no longer any people, though as Lars-Goren and his sons approached nearer they found the hoofprints and ruts left by a large crowd. He slowed his horse to a walk as they went past. Drake moved carefully, with his gray ears cocked toward the embers, his muscles tensed, prepared to shy off to the left at the first sign of life from the neighborhood of the smoke. One ember fell from the beams that supported the sagging black

remains; it struck lengthwise and broke, shooting sparks, but the horses only flinched a little, waiting for worse.

When they were almost past the place, Erik reined up his horse and sat looking. Gunnar rode a few steps more, then stopped his. Lars-Goren continued—stubborn as one of his own peasants, he thought—then abruptly changed his mind and stopped. He refrained from looking back. At last he heard his sons' horses coming up behind him, and with his knees he edged Drake forward again.

As he came even with Lars-Goren, Erik said, "When I become lord here, there'll be no more burning of witches."

Lars-Goren said nothing.

"Did you hear me, Father?" Erik asked.

"In that case," said Lars-Goren, "I must see that you never become lord here."

The rest of the way home, they rode in silence.

6 Lars-Goren knew it was his imagination—there had been nothing visibly human in the black remains—but he carried with him all that night, both awake and asleep, an unsettling image of the witch's face, for some reason the face of the old peasant woman he'd seen that morning in the field of rye, though he knew it had not been the same old woman. She stared straight ahead of her, with an expression he could not fathom, as if she were looking at something no one else could see, perhaps a steel-bright light like the light he'd seen in the clouds as he rode home, but a light that came not from the clouds but from everywhere at once, as if the whole physical world had vanished, consumed by that terrible brightness. In his dreams he saw the burning they'd been too late to witness, saw how the long gray hair sparked and smoked and ignited, how the heavy black peasant clothes smoldered, then

flamed like burning leaves. Sweat broke out on the face, and the flesh became puffy and dark, then burst open, dripping blood and fat. Even as he dreamed, he understood why it was that her expression never changed—showed no pain, no rage, no fear of the Lord, only that terrible, mystical blankness like indifference: he was seeing not the burning of a living witch but his memory of those burning corpses on Södermalm hill.

When he awakened in the morning he was weak and heavy-limbed, as if he hadn't slept at all. The bed beside him was empty, and he somehow knew at once that Liv had risen hours ago and gone down to help with breakfast and start her day. From somewhere outside, beyond the windowless stone walls, came the sharp sound of iron striking iron—someone shoeing a horse, perhaps, or clumsily hammering the iron band on a cartwheel. He sat up and put his legs over the side of the bed, his flesh still numb, shivers running up and down his back as if he'd caught an ague. For a long time he sat staring at the wall, hardly knowing what he was thinking, rubbing his hands and his arms against the cold all around him, though his breath sent out no steam; then, awakening again, he got up and began to get dressed.

Downstairs only his daughters were still indoors. His elder daughter, Pia, just turned seven, fixed him breakfast, while the younger, four, sat at the table beside him, watching him with tightly folded hands.

"You slept late," Pia said, bringing him eggs and bread, buttermilk and honey. She had her mother's face except that her hair was dark brown and her smile was more furtive. She walked already like the over-tall girl she was becoming, her head slightly ducked, eyelids lowered, apologetic.

"Your mother should have gotten me up," he said.

Pia nodded, nervously smiling. "She said you had bad dreams."

Little Andrea's eyes winced narrower, shooting him a look. Lars-Goren turned to study her. More than the others she was a stranger to him, self-sufficient and mysterious, watching like an enemy spy. He smiled as if hoping to soften her judgment of him. Her expression did not change.

Lars-Goren looked back at Pia and said, "I hope my tossing and turning didn't keep her awake?"

Pia shrugged, drew back the chair across from him, and sat down. Like Andrea, she folded her hands.

Abruptly, Andrea asked, "Are you going to take us to see the dragon?"

Chewing, Lars-Goren looked at Pia for an explanation.

"King Gustav's sent the statue of St. George to Hudiksvall," she said. She glanced at him, then down again, and busied herself tucking a strand of hair behind her ear. "He's sending it to every great city in the kingdom, so they say. It's to celebrate our victory and independence."

Lars-Goren considered. "Do you know what that means —'independence'?" he asked.

Again she shrugged, ducking her head. There were moments when, at seven, she seemed as wise as a woman, but just now she looked embarrassed and frightened, like the child she was. "It means everyone's happy," she said.

Lars-Goren nodded. "So we hope," he said. He remembered his son Erik sullenly riding from the place where they'd burned the witch.

"Will you take us?" Andrea asked again. She tipped her head to one side, not so much pleading as scrutinizing, reserved.

"Whatever your mother says," he said, and raised the bread to his mouth.

"That's what she said you'd say," said Andrea, whether with scorn or satisfaction he couldn't make out.

"Tell her we'll go then," said Lars-Goren, "if she hasn't changed her mind."

Outside someone was again banging metal against metal. The sound was too irregular to be the work of a hammer, and the sound was sometimes loud, sometimes lighter, a mere clink. Abruptly, it broke off. He scowled, still trying to guess what it was, but no answer would come to him, and at last he put it from his mind and finished eating. Then, just as he was rising from the table, it began again. He hurried to the door and down the hallway, Andrea coming after him, keeping her distance.

When he emerged into the castle yard he discovered that the day was bright and hot, the sky so blue one could hardly have believed that yesterday there had been heavy leaden clouds. Chickens scattered in front of him, cackling in indignation, startled by the suddenness of his coming through the door. Lady leaped up from her nap in the sunlight and trotted over to him, looking up at him for instructions. A bent old man looked up from the corner of the bailey where he was working, poking mortar into the stones, and he smiled, slightly raising both arms, like a fighting-cock proffering for attack. Again the sound that had been puzzling Lars-Goren stopped. He looked around. Andrea stood a few yards behind him, on the castle steps, the thumbs of both hands in her mouth. He held out his hand to her, inviting her to walk with him. Solemnly, she shook her head. He smiled and shrugged, then turned away, casting in his mind for the direction from which the sound had come. Now the sound began again, and Lars-Goren, with the dog at his heel, went striding toward the castle's northwest corner. As soon as he'd rounded the corner he stopped and stood motionless, instinctively raising one hand to Andrea behind him, commanding her to silence.

Two men, helmeted and muffled from head to foot in

protective ropecloth, stood slashing at one another with blunted two-hand swords. They struck with such ferocity, such murderous solemnity, without yells or grunts, it seemed that even muffled as they were they must certainly kill one another with their unwieldy, archaic swords. Now Lars-Goren saw what he had missed at first: his son Gunnar crouched just out of range of the flying swords, watching with eyes full of fury and fear. "To the leg!" Gunnar screamed, and the smaller of the swordsmen, seeing the opening at the same instant, came down with so violent a flat-sided blow to the flank of his opponent that the leg went flying out from under the man, turned in grotesquely, as if broken at the knee. "Break!" screamed Gunnar. "Break! *Break!*" The smaller of the swordsmen broke and stepped back, dropped the sword, threw off the helmet, and ran to the man who lay rolling on the ground and moaning. Lars-Goren's dog rushed in, barking officiously. When the victor pulled down his mask, Lars-Goren saw what he'd by now suspected: it was Erik.

Erik reached down to help the man on the ground, who seized the muffled arm and clung to it, wailing "Good hit! Never mind!" then at once went back to moaning and clutching at his leg.

Lars-Goren moved closer, Andrea beside him, taking his hand as if unaware that she was doing it. "Hush, Lady!" he said. The dog barked once more, then controlled herself. When Erik looked up, his face showed nothing, no shame, no pride, no fear—nothing whatsoever. Gunnar moved back a little, as if expecting a blow. The man on the ground was tearing at his mask now, no longer moaning. "It was the boy's idea, sir," he said, eyes bulging, full of tears. Lars-Goren recognized his groundskeeper.

Lars-Goren nodded. "Let me help you inside," he said. He let go of his daughter's hand and bent down to his groundskeeper, feeling for the break in the bone. So far as he could tell, there was none, but he'd be able to tell for certain when he got him stretched out inside. He put his hands inside the groundskeeper's armpits, helping him to his feet.

"I told him nobody fights with these old-fashioned swords anymore," said the groundskeeper. He bit his lips and winced. "But you know these boys!" he said. "Violent! Violent!"

Lars-Goren put his arm around the man's thick waist and steadied him as he hopped on one leg toward the door, the dog coming carefully beside them, eager to be of use. The groundskeeper's face was ashen.

Erik hung back, picking up the groundskeeper's sword, then his own. Gunnar and Andrea came a little behind Lars-Goren, watching him and staying out of reach.

At the steps, Lars-Goren half turned and looked back at his children. Erik, loaded down with the two swords and helmets, met his eyes, as expressionless as before. "Get cleaned up," said Lars-Goren coldly, as if wearily. "This afternoon we start for Hudiksvall, to see the dragon." He gazed a moment longer at his son Erik, then turned his attention once more to the wounded groundskeeper.

"They have their own ideas, these young lords," said the man. His smile was half fearful, half cunning. Tears streamed down his cheeks. "They're the Devil's own henchmen—no lie, sir!" Quickly, as if afraid he'd offended, he added, "But he's brave as the day is long, that Erik! Brave and good-hearted as a saint, sir, that's no lie!"

7 AT NOON on the following day they arrived at Hudiksvall. There was no stable anywhere, as they learned from visitors pushing back from the heart of the city, and at

last, full of misgivings, Lars-Goren left his animals with a rabbit-toothed old peasant who'd roped off a field at the outskirts of the city, a field so crowded there seemed no room for the horses to lie down. The city too was crowded, so packed with visitors there was hardly a place to stand, and the crowd was so noisy Lars-Goren and his family had to shout into one another's ears to be heard. Andrea rode on Lars-Goren's shoulders, solemn as a viking on watch. Lars-Goren's wife came just behind, pressing close to Lars-Goren, her hands clamped tightly around the hands of Pia, on her right, and, on her left side, Erik, who held tightly to Gunnar's right arm. "Do you see it?" yelled Gunnar, as if furiously angry, "do you see it yet?"

Then at last Andrea cried out, "There it is!" and a moment later Lars-Goren saw it too, a huge, shabby canopy that bore the arms of King Gustav.

"We're almost there!" he called out, and twisted around to make sure that his wife was still behind him.

The closer they came to the statue, the quieter the crowd became, as if somewhere in the vicinity of the dragon and saint some accident had happened, some trampling or stabbing so terrible that a hush of dismay went out around it. But as they pressed still nearer, they discovered that the cause of the silence was not what they'd imagined; it was the statue itself that made the crowd forget its voice.

Lars-Goren for one had seen the statue before, but never with people all around it like this, looking up as if entranced. It was as if, without the people, the statue was incomplete, unreal as a miracle in a grotto where there is no human eye to witness it. Gustav's soldiers stood every six feet around the statue, but no one gave them reason to raise a finger. For all the pressure of the crowd farther back, it was as still and calm here by the statue as the eye of a tornado. Peasants, burghers, knights in fine dress stood motionless, gazing up, some of them weeping, hardly bothering to dab away the tears. Lars-Goren looked at them and felt a ringing in his heart that he could hardly put a name to, whether pain or awe or love or something else—though certainly part of it was love, he knew, love for Sweden and all her bright, wind-bitten faces, long or short, fat or thin, light or dark—and love for faces he would never see again, the faces of those who'd died in Sten Sture's rebellion, on frozen Lake Åsun-den, in Execution Square in Stockholm, and later, in Gus-tav's revolution. Lars-Goren too was now weeping, hardly noticing, unashamed.

For a long time he hardly glanced at the statue itself, but looked instead at the people—first at strangers, then at his wife, then at his children. When he did turn at last to the statue, the sight struck him like a fist. Where Bernt Notke got the massive blocks of wood—to say nothing of the skill at carving, to say nothing of the vision—God only knew. Every notch and curl sang and glowed. The dragon impaled on St. George's lance seemed to writhe in agony, eyes violently roll-ing, tail slashing, gleaming talons slicing at the belly of the trembling horse. But none of these did Lars-Goren see that instant.

What he saw was the blank, staring face of the knight, gazing straight forward, motionless, as if indifferent to the monster, gazing as if mad or entranced or blind, infinitely gentle, infinitely sorrowful, beyond all human pain. I am Sweden, he seemed to say—or something more than Sweden. *I am humanity, living and dead.* For it did not seem to Lars-Goren that the monster below the belly of the violently trem-bling horse could be described as, simply, "foreigners," as the common interpretation maintained. It was evil itself; death, oblivion, every conceivable form of human loss. The knight, killing the dragon, showed no faintest trace of pleasure, much less pride—not even interest.

He saw again the face of the witch above the churning flames in his dream, the dead swelling faces on the pyres of Stockholm, his son's cold stare. "When I become lord here, there'll be no more burning of witches."

Though it seemed to make no sense, Lars-Goren heard himself saying—his hand on his son Erik's shoulder—"Very well, you shall be lord here."

He looked down at Erik's face, to see if he'd spoken it aloud, as he imagined. His son, in alarm, looked up at him, as if he thought his father had gone mad.

"Very well," Lars-Goren said, and nodded.

His son met his eyes, but his face now showed nothing, as blank as the face of the knight staring straight into the sun.

8   ON THE NIGHT before the day he was scheduled to leave, Lars-Goren sat at the fireplace with his family, Andrea on his knee, Gunnar on the bench beside him. Pia sat across from him, on the bench beside her mother. Erik moved restlessly in the shadows behind them, as if the room were too small to contain his ambition and desire. Lars-Goren was talking of his visits, as a child, to Lappland.

"Strange people," he said, "if one can really call them people." He felt embarrassed and disloyal and quickly made an effort to explain. "They're people, of course," he said, "as human as any of us. They love their children, love their incredible white country and their reindeer. The Lapps work and play like the rest of us, and they're religious, just as we are. That's not what I meant."

He explained, as well as he could, what he meant. His wife gazed into the fire, half smiling, her hand on Pia's arm.

Perhaps the reindeer were the secret, he said. The reindeer gave the Lapplanders everything they had—food, clothes, shelter, love-tokens, even the devices of their religion. In Lappland nothing grew but what was food for reindeer, so the Lapps ate virtually nothing but the reindeer themselves, blood and meat and the marrow of their bones. For houses and sleds they used reindeer bones, horns, and hides. Perhaps for that reason after all these years the minds of the Lapps had come to be partly reindeer minds, preternaturally alert to every change in the wind, alert to mysteries no ordinary human being could grasp. But that too, he realized, was not exactly what he meant.

"It's something about the simplicity," he said, "the absolute simplicity of the landscape, the light, the inescapable concern with necessities, nothing more."

Lars-Goren fell silent, staring into the fire. Here too, in Hälsingland, life was simple, he thought; or simple enough. His daughters would grow up and marry neighboring lords, his sons would take care of his villages and lands, oversee the planting and harvesting, building and razing.

Now his son Erik came to the glow of the fireplace and, after a moment, sat down on the floor beside Gunnar.

Pia said, "I wish you could stay with us, Pappa."

Lars-Goren looked at her, then at his wife. "I wish I could too," he said. "Soon, perhaps."

Now he was thinking again of the Devil, how on the night he'd sought them out he'd told Gustav his infinitely complicated schemes, and how Gustav had listened in secret fascination, fitting his plans into the Devil's complexity. He saw the jumble of bodies on Södermalm's pyres, the clutter of leaflets blown like leaves through Stockholm's streets, after Gustav seized the Lutherans' printing press and made it his voice.

"Are you all right, Lars-Goren?" his wife asked.

Only now did he realize that he'd covered his eyes with his hand. "I'm fine," he said.

"We should all go to bed," she said, but without full conviction.

"Not yet," he said.

For another half-hour they sat staring into the fire, six glowing shapes like one. At last his wife rose and came to touch his shoulder. He nodded, took her hand, and stood up, lifting Andrea and carrying her, asleep, on one arm.

When Lars-Goren looked in on him, saying good-night, his son Erik said, "Father?"

Lars-Goren waited, standing beside the bed.

After a moment, Erik said, "The trouble is, it's not possible to be like the Lapps." His head was raised slightly from the pillow.

Lars-Goren put his hand on the boy's white shoulder. "No, I know," he said. He leaned down and kissed the boy's forehead. Then he went to his wife.

"I must think about this queer streak of fear," he thought, for it was creeping up on him again, he found, now that he was going back. "If I'm not afraid of death, and I'm not afraid of hell—" But he could push the thought no further. To the marrow of his bones he was a reasonable man, yet here, real as life in his mind's eye, was this saurian being with the goatish smell, this idiot god, by all evidence, who could make him tremble where he lay.

"Suppose the world makes no sense," he thought, "no sense whatsoever. Suppose good is evil and evil is good, or that nothing is either good or evil." It was a thought that should have alarmed him, he told himself, but though he played with the idea, trying to feel alarm, he saw that the more he played with it, the more he felt nothing whatsoever. "Perhaps it's this that makes a monster like Bishop Brask,"

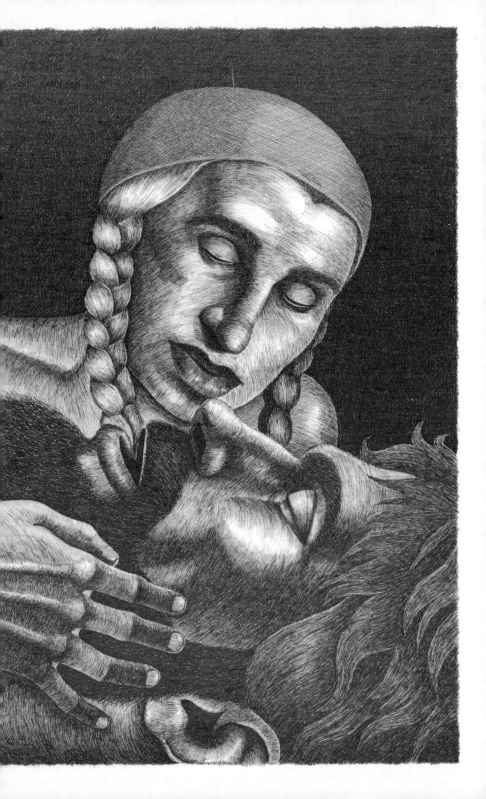

he thought. He concentrated on the idea of Bishop Brask, cut off from heaven by boredom and despair, a man who no longer had feeling for anything except, perhaps, style. He, Lars-Goren, could become a man like that. Surely, *that* was evil, *that* should make him tremble! But he felt no slightest tingle of alarm.

Beside him, lying on her back, his wife asked softly, "Lars-Goren, what are you thinking?"

"Shall I tell you the truth?" he asked.

When she said nothing, he said, "I'm afraid of the Devil." He told her what had happened, and how he'd felt an overwhelming, senseless terror.

She rolled over in the darkness and put her bare, soft arms around him. "Perhaps it's only rage," she said, and kissed his cheek.

"Rage at what?" he asked, drawing back a little. "Do I seem to you a man of senseless rages? Rage at what?"

"Just rage," she said. "Is it so terrible to feel rage for no reason?"

The thought was comforting. Instantly, he began to think of reasons for his senseless rage.

PART FOUR

1 LONG BEFORE he came to the dales of Dalarna, Lars-Goren heard rumors of the trouble there. The Devil was everywhere, gleefully whispering into the miners' ears. Sometimes he was seen at public meetings, ranting in the torchlight in the shape of a hunchbacked country priest or a twisted old copper hauler. Sometimes he appeared in the darkness of the mines themselves, dropping insinuations about Gustav's ways.

As soon as he arrived, Lars-Goren sought out the cheerful little German who'd done the hiring when Lars-Goren and Gustav had come here first. He was now much risen in the world, part-owner of the mine.

"Iss a sad bissness," the German said, shaking his head,

smiling brightly. "But vat you going to tell dem, dese miserable people?" He winked merrily and offered Lars-Goren a beer.

At the meeting that night, there was no trace of the careful order that had before been so conspicuous. They shouted one another down, sometimes threw things. Scuffles broke out here and there in the crowd, and gradually it came to Lars-Goren that Germans were as rare here tonight as Danes had been the last time he'd visited. No wonder, for the talk was all of foreigners, and how Gustav's government had no Swedes in it, to speak of—only Germans, Russians, and Danes.

Suddenly his back turned to ice and he realized that the man at his side was the Devil.

"Well, well, Lars-Goren!" said the Devil, in a voice like an old woman's. "How things change, from time to time! But have no fear, my friend, don't be fooled by appearances! I'm as much on your side as I ever was!" Torchlight glittered on his corpse-pale skin and on his mouth, where there were droplets of blood.

"I'm sure that's true," said Lars-Goren, just audibly. "I'm sure you've never changed sides." He began to back away.

The Devil's head shot forward, grinning. "Don't fool with me, Lars-Goren," he whispered, *"for the sake of your children!"*

Blindly, crazily, Lars-Goren began to run. The Devil was right beside him, like a floating fire. Lars-Goren ran so hard he thought his heart would burst, but still the Devil was at his elbow. "Christ save me!" Lars-Goren shouted. Suddenly it was dark. He was lying in his bed in Stockholm fortress.

2 "AH, AH!" sighed Gustav, pacing before the window, pulling at his knuckles. He looked fifteen years older but tougher, leaner, more leathery than ever. His beard was like a wild man's, glittering in the sunlight; his eyes, for all his troubles, seemed filled with some crazy joy. Abruptly, he came bounding toward Lars-Goren's chair. "Anyway, now you're back," he said, seizing Lars-Goren's shoulders, "you can shatter all my plans with good advice!"

Lars-Goren closed his eyes.

"Here now!" Gustav shouted. Lars-Goren opened his eyes again. "Here now, my dear friend and kinsman! No napping!" He snapped his fingers. His eyes, peering into Lars-Goren's, went suddenly unsure, then evasive, looking past Lars-Goren's ear. "Very well!" he said, and turned away as if angrily, storming back toward the window, into the light. He clasped his hands behind his back and nodded, then laughed. "How simple it all seemed to us when we were poor young idealist fools!"

Lars-Goren for a moment put his hands over his eyes.

"Ah, ah, ah!" groaned King Gustav in sudden agony. He stretched out one arm and clenched the fist. "I meant to make Sweden magnificent," he said. "I knew what to do, how the government should run, how it could benefit the people." He jerked his head around and stared at Lars-Goren, sunlight behind his head so that Lars-Goren saw only the outline, like a burn. "But it hasn't been so easy to put Sweden on her legs! Not so easy, believe me! I was called to rule a country shattered and disorganized by political uncertainty, exhausted by her war of liberation, also bankrupt. And who was to help me with the heavy work of government, from the highest ministerial positions to the work of local sheriffs? All our best people had perished in the bloodbath of Stockholm —not just people who knew the ropes, I don't ask that; I mean people with the simplest kinds of skills, such as reading and writing! Just reading and writing! Is that so much to ask? But there was no one—anyway, no one Swedish, no one I could trust. In such a case, you take your ministers where you find them!" Again Gustav laughed. Smiling, more sour than the Devil, he raised his left hand, fingers spread, to count on them with his right index finger. "My first chancellor is none other than Erik Svensson, toady to King Kristian of Denmark—a double-dealing Swede who's already changed sides twice! My second minister is Master Lars Andreae, one of the men who gave the verdict that led to the bloodbath. Ha! My archbishop of Uppsala, Johannes Magnus, is another of the same, even fouler than Master Lars. And then there's that cabbage-eater Berend von Melen, Kristian's former general, now husband to my cousin, God help me, and illegally (between you and me) made a member of the råd. There's the cabbage-eater count John of Hoya, married to my sister—God help me again!—to whom I've given, again illegally, the castle and the fief of Stegeborg. I've even made overtures to that bitch Gustav Trolle. I say 'bitch' of course only because he's dared to turn me down. My peasants—the poor devils who died for all this—and especially the peasants of Dalarna, God knows—they don't altogether understand these things."

King Gustav stopped, legs wide apart, before Lars-Goren's chair, and smiled as if with satisfaction, his eyelids trembling. "But all that's nothing," he said. "Take the matter of taxes. Most of Sweden's paid no taxes since long before Sten Sture's rebellion. Poor bastards, they have little enough to give, God knows—and they're the very same people whose sons I saw butchered in the war. Nonetheless, what am I to do about my loans from Lübeck, eh? What am I to do about piracy, or repairing the fortresses and docks we blew up? What am I to do about the crippled and the starving? Eh?

"Starvation, that's another thing!" King Gustav clapped his hands. "Whether or not it's the work of my old friend the Devil, ever since the day I took the crown we've been having the most incredible bawl of bad weather! The peasants are down to eating bark-bread. They're calling me 'King Bark'— it's a fact! No doubt they're right; if I were a proper king I'd raise my hands against the snow and the snow would turn away and say 'Excuse me, sire!' I'd sing out for rain and the rain would come in gushes. 'Oh, yer *welcome*, sire!' But I'm the only king they've got, as they know, or rather as they *should* know. They don't. No, they don't, not at all. That's another of my troubles."

He was standing bent toward Lars-Goren's chair, his hands on his knees, his bearded face thrust forward. "Kristina Gyllenstierna's on the move—Sten Sture's widow. She's sending out letters for help in all directions—no doubt you've heard. She's even written to the king of the pirates, Sören Norby. On which subject more later. Also she has her various old friends, like Bishop Brask. They've found plenty to work with, no lack of grievances to nurse: the dearness of the times, the lack of salt, the no-good coin—I've been minting pure cowshit, I readily admit it. I've analyzed the riches of Sweden, and that's our best product. Where was I? Ah yes—the grievances. They say I'm plundering the True Holy Church—which I am, so I am. They also say I've murdered dear Kristina's son, someone named Nils—which is an absolute lie; I think so; to the best of my knowledge pure slander." King Gustav smiled. "So you see, beloved kinsman, I could use a little clever advice."

Lars-Goren sat perfectly still, dizzy.

"I know," said Gustav, wheeling away, throwing out his hands to each side, furious, "no doubt it all seems simple to a man like you! You haven't heard the half of it."

At that moment Berend von Melen broke in on them.

3 "FORGIVE ME, Your Highness," cried von Melen, thumping his chest with his right hand, "I was told you were alone!"

"No reason you should doubt what you're told," said Gustav, turning from Lars-Goren angrily. "Everyone in Sweden believes whatever stupid foolishness he's told."

"My dear King Gustav!" said von Melen, stiffening, pretending to be insulted beyond measure. Now his arms were at his sides, his right boot thrown forward, the toe cocked out— the stance, it seemed to Lars-Goren, of a comic dancer. He was balding, clean-shaven except for a small jut of beard like an Egyptian's. His shoulders were narrow, his belly like a globe below his hollow chest. Except for the pomp of his beribboned chest and the stiffness of his posture, no one would have thought him a military man, but he was said to be an excellent fencer.

"Never mind, never mind," said Gustav wearily. "I snarl to keep in practice. You've met my friend and kinsman Lars-Goren?"

Von Melen bowed deeply, like a performer. He made an effort to seem unimpressed by Lars-Goren's great size and breadth, but even in the middle of his sweeping bow, von Melen kept his eyes on the knight. Lars-Goren half rose from his chair, nodding back, then sat down again.

"So tell me, what wonderful news have you brought me?" asked Gustav.

"Not news, exactly—" von Melen began, glancing at Lars-Goren.

"I thought not." King Gustav waved his hand. "Go on."

Von Melen clasped his hands behind his back and stood cocked forward, head tipped, eyes narrowed to slits. "It's a delicate matter," he said cautiously.

Again Gustav waved, this time impatiently. "Delicate matters are Lars-Goren's specialty. You may speak out as freely as you like."

"Very well," said von Melen, and began again. "As you're well aware, you've received great benefits from the remains of the party of Sten Sture." He waited for acknowledgement from Gustav. None came. Von Melen cleared his throat, professorial, and continued: "These benefits you haven't always been diligent to repay. I might mention, for example, Sten Sture's chief chancellor and factotum, Bishop Sunnanväder. What have you done for this man who was once the most powerful lord in all Sweden, a prince of the Church, and a man on whom your election very heavily depended? You invite him to celebrate High Mass on your entry into Stockholm, and you toss him the bishopric of Västerås—a crumb! Or again I might mention Knut Mickilsson, dean of Västerås—another who took a prominent part in securing your election. Again and again you've passed over him as if he'd died in the bloodbath."

"That's a pity, yes," said Gustav ambiguously.

Abruptly, like an actor at his important moment, von Melen drew a paper from the pocket of his coat. "Let me read you what they're saying in Dalarna these days." He adjusted his spectacles, held up the paper, and read. " 'All those who faithfully served the lords and realm of Sweden Gustav has hated and persecuted, while all traitors to the realm, and all who abetted the country's cruel foe King Kristian, and who betrayed Herr Sten and all Swedish men, these he has favored.'" Crisply, he lowered the paper, then folded it and put it in his coat.

"You're not going to leave me the paper?" Gustav asked.

"Surely, if you like." Von Melen got it out again and handed it to Gustav. "There are thousands more just like it. As you see, they've copied your use of the printing press."

"Yes, naturally. They're slow, but they learn." Gustav glanced at the paper, then carelessly stuffed it in his pocket. "So, von Melen, what is it precisely that you're after, generously bringing up the names of these nincompoops who'd turn on me in an instant if Fredrik should release Kristina Gyllenstierna?"

Berend von Melen smiled with raised eyebrows and pursed lips. When he thought the expression had made its effect, he said, "I of course come to you as your friend and now cousin by marriage. Also, of course, I have some very slight concern about myself. That letter against foreigners— that filth so typical of the Dalarna mentality—has dark implications. It places Sten Sture and his party on one side, and on the other side you and all of us who have so loyally served your country though not in fact born here. If Kristina should be released, as Fredrik threatens, and the peasants and burghers should join in league with the remains of the party of Sten Sture—'the international magnates,' as you call them . . ."

Gustav nodded and cut him off. "Yes, yes, enough." He scowled. "I'll give it some thought."

"Meanwhile," said von Melen with an apologetic gesture, as if sorry to trouble His Majesty with more—and again he showed his peculiar, prissy smile—"if you were to ask me to visit Dalarna, with a small, discreet army, nothing of the sort that would suggest, you know, oppression—"

Gustav scowled more darkly and glanced at Lars-Goren. Lars-Goren looked at his hands, then, drawing out his knife, began cleaning his fingernails. Von Melen watched in disgust.

"You must admit," said Gustav, "it's an interesting thought."

"Not a very wise one, I think," said Lars-Goren. He avoided looking up.

"Not wise?" snapped Gustav, flushing a little, as if the idea had been his own.

Lars-Goren shrugged. "Why send a foreigner to Dalarna, where foreigners are hated? Send him, say, to Gotland—to Visby, say, where the pirates hide between attacks on the merchant ships of Lübeck. Wipe out Sören Norby and his privateers, and—who knows?—perhaps Lübeck will be inclined to grant us an extension on the war-loans."

"Ha!" said Gustav, clapping his hands and whirling around to face von Melen. "You see how ingenious we are, we Swedes? You, a German, will fight for a cause of importance both to Sweden and to Germany! You'll win yourself great honor. I think so! Ah, what a day this is for you, von Melen!" In his delight, King Gustav seized von Melen's arm. "Go prepare! Get whatever you need—don't be cheap!" He added quickly, "Don't be *too* cheap."

Von Melen's mouth worked, twisting as if by itself like a snake, hunting for objections. "As you say, Your Majesty," he brought out. His tiny blue eyes looked hard at Lars-Goren. After a moment he said again, "As you say." He brought himself to attention as if at some inaudible command from Gustav, turned sharply, and marched out.

Gustav moved quickly to Lars-Goren and bent toward him, his hands on his knees. "You're good," he said. "I wish I had ten of you!" Then he laughed. "Poor von Melen! How can he plot against my government with Sten's bishops when he's sloshing around off Gotland?"

Lars-Goren laughed too. It was pleasant, this scheming

and counter-scheming. Who could deny it? The sound of their laughter set off curious echoes. He glanced around the room.

4 PLOTS AND COUNTERPLOTS, thrusts and counter-thrusts—ah, what a moment it was in the life of the Devil! He was everywhere at once, passing out leaflets—attacks on both sides—in Dalarna and Småland; conspiring both for and against the Dutch with King Fredrik and the tsar; stirring conflict in Stockholm between the city authorities and the pigs and chickens that roamed freely in the streets, the wolfpacks that crept along the hedges. Above all, he paid close attention to Sören Norby and the Stures.

"My friend," said the Devil, appearing to Sören Norby in the terrifying guise of Sten Sture's ghost, "you are my last resort now—you and your courageous pirates!"

Sören Norby sat bolt upright, his gray eyes as wide and glittering as coins. "Who are you?" he shouted. He shot his right hand under his pillow for his knife.

"I," intoned the Devil, "am the ghost of Sten Sture the Younger, foully murdered by King Kristian of Denmark and now betrayed on every hand by my own Swedish kinsmen!" He stretched out his arms, his charred remains still smoking in the tatters of his windingsheet.

"The hell you are!" Sören Norby yelled, leaping up onto his feet on the bed, the knife in his right hand, his left hand stretched out, fingers splayed wide, ready to fight.

"Hear my words, Sören Norby," intoned the Devil, the sockets of his eyes staring emptily through the smoke. "Look down at this child beside me, this innocent torn from life!" Little by little, like the master illusionist he was, he revealed to Sören Norby's horrified eyes the smoldering remains of the infant Sture who'd been exhumed and burned with Sten at Södermalm. The trick was so masterful, as it seemed to the Devil—and the pirate such a stupid and sentimental fool—it was all the Devil could do to keep from laughing. "Ah yes," thought the Devil, "you swat them as a cow's tail swats flies when they're just a little older, but a poor dead infant—how the sight moves you!" Nonetheless he kept his face morose, his tone sepulchral. "Look on these ruins of my child and take thought on my second son Nils, who still lives! I make you his guardian and protector, Sören Norby, and in payment of your kindness I promise you this gift—" With a pass like a magician's he showed a vision of his widow Kristina Gyllenstierna, stark naked on her pallet in her prison cell in Denmark.

"My lord," breathed Sören, for the corpse of the infant and the nakedness of Sten Sture's widow had persuaded him, "I am not worthy!" He sank to his knees and wiped his eyes with his forearm.

5 FROM THAT moment on, Sören Norby was like a wildman in his support of the party of the Stures. He sent letters to Denmark, asking for an audience with King Fredrik, which he received. His plea for Kristina's freedom was so impassioned that Kristina gave him a ring and said she hoped he would think of her as his dear, dear friend. As soon as he was back in Gotland he wrote more letters, one of them to Bishop Brask, telling him of his vision of Sten Sture's ghost, and all that Sten Sture had said to him, and how he, Sören, had visited King Fredrik in Kristina Gyllenstierna's behalf, and how the king had listened with interest. Now, to Sören

Norby, Gustav Vasa was the Devil incarnate, renegade to the cause of Nils Sture, Sten's son, and except for the love of Kristina Gyllenstierna, Norby desired nothing in the world with more ardor than he desired King Gustav's fall. All this, too, he set down in his letter to Bishop Brask, with more in the same vein, and numerous expressions of his respect and good wishes for the bishop.

Bishop Brask held the letter at arm's length, staring in disbelief.

"Bah, he's a madman," said the Devil, seated at the bishop's elbow. With Brask he was by now so thoroughly comfortable that he made no effort to disguise his appearance, merely scaled it down so that it fit inside the room—hairy-rooted horns, face like an idiot's, flesh soft and scaly as an enormous, fat snake's. He sat with his dark, matted legs crossed, jiggling one hoof. His pitchdark wings, when he half extended them, covered all the wall like a curtain.

"Not mad, I think," said Bishop Brask irritably. "Misled, no doubt—no doubt by someone we know." He said no more, at least nothing more aloud. It was true that the Devil could sometimes read one's mind, that once he'd gotten into you there seemed to be no shaking him; but at least one could in some measure limit the monster's conversation. That, thought Bishop Brask, was the real horror. Never mind the everlasting fire or the imps with forks. He could bore you, bore you to the ninth pit of madness, and think then of something still stupider, stupidity so deep it was unanswerable, a matter of awe, even terrible worship. Oh yes, Bishop Brask understood the Devil. Perhaps he could even outwit him, he sometimes thought, if he could summon up enough of his heart's former warmth to make it worth it; but that was something he was in no mood to expect. It was a curious venom, the poison that flowed from the Devil. Say that all human life is idiotic, all human feeling an absurdity, effect without due cause; say that to weep at the death of one child after the deaths of a million million children—centuries of corpses, centuries of mothers gone berserk and wailing, each father turning sharply, heart leaping, at the voice he's mistaken for his own dead child's—say that all this is a shameful humiliation, an outrage not to be put up with; say that love and sorrow, considered from the peak of the mountain of eternity, are as paltry and insignificant as the wild, ravished hymning of blueglinting flies on the four-day-old corpse of a mongrel. Say these things, yes, say all this once, thought Bishop Brask—say it once with conviction—and how are you to rise without revulsion to even the emotion of a heartfelt objection to the death you've just swallowed? Dry as a spider, the old bishop listened to the desiccate kiss of his rhetoric, the grotesquely chiming rhymes: *conviction, revulsion, emotion, objection.* How was he to feel anything worthy of even the debased coin "feeling," he asked himself, limited forever to the predictable trapezoids of his mind's drab spiderweb, language? *Coin* or *coign*, he thought, and furiously glanced at the Devil.

And so, in secret, in company with the Devil, he sailed to Visby, on the island of Gotland, stronghold of Norby and his pirates.

6 Snow FELL softly over the ship and into the water. Sheets of ice, heavy with snow, lay all around him, and more snow lay heavily on the yardarms, the poop and the forecastle, the decks themselves. The sky was brilliant, so charged with light that only with one's eyes closed to slits could one see anything at all. Bishop Brask, in a fur coat white with

sticky snow, and a wide fur cap even whiter than his coat, stood gazing morosely toward the faint shadow he knew to be Gotland, in the distance. They seemed to be making no headway at all. For all he knew, they might die here, not that he cared. The Devil lay below, fuming and restless, eager that the ship get moving again. Bishop Brask, just now, had no time to think about the Devil. He was pondering a curious impulse that had come over him, an impulse so strong and so remarkable in its way that it seemed to him astonishing that nothing had come of it. In his cabin, an hour ago, he had thought of writing a long letter to Lars-Goren Bergquist, a letter which would explain to the knight exactly what Bishop Brask thought of life and how it was that he had come to his opinions. He had written, with great firmness and elegance: *To Lars-Goren Bergquist, Knight. Dear sir.* Then he'd stared at the paper, as white and empty as the world around him now, and had struggled desperately to overcome his sense of the absurdity of the gesture, break past the thousands of reasons for saying nothing—the futility of expression, even will, the certainty that his words would be misunderstood or, if somehow understood, used against him, the firm knowledge that words, however elegant and true (if such things were possible), could hardly undo the past, that in any case Lars-Goren was his enemy, not his friend, and would have no choice, as servant of King Gustav, but to twist the words the instant he read them, lest his strength as an enemy be weakened.

The attempt to write had come to nothing, of course. It was not that fact that he brooded on now, but the odd fact that he had wanted to write at all, that somehow, below reason and contrary to it, the childish impulse to tell the truth was still alive in him, that indeed he still believed, in some back part of his brain, that there existed some truth to tell.

"I was out of my mind," he said, too softly for anyone to hear. He shuddered, thinking of the dangers he'd have opened himself up to if he'd written that letter. It was the Devil's work, he thought; but at once his heart jerked back from that idea, though he could not, when he tried to think it through, make out why. Was it the miserable cold that had sent him this lunatic impulse? he wondered. Or the universal whiteness that made nothing more important than anything else?

He was so deep in thought that he at first hardly noticed when one sailor, then another—darting white shadows in the general whiteness—began to shout and point to starboard. As more and more of them came out on deck, some of them pushing roughly past him where he stood, unable to distinguish him from less important white shadows, Bishop Brask rose sufficiently from his half-dream to realize that something was afoot. He moved toward the rail where the others were, and at last he saw what the shouting was about. A great fleet of rowboats was coming toward them, making its tortuous way through the breaks between ice-sheets.

"It's Norby and his pirates!" someone shouted, seizing the bishop's arm. "We're rescued!"

Baffled, Bishop Brask stared hard in the direction in which the man at his side was pointing. He understood only now—and even now without particular emotion—that they had in fact been in serious danger. It was obvious of course, once one bothered to think about it. The huge, clumsy ship was ice-locked. It hadn't moved all day.

All around him sailors and passengers were shouting, "God bless Sören Norby!"

Considering the conditions, the boats were approaching with remarkable speed, he saw now. When they reached the ice in which the ship was wedged, Norby's men climbed out of their rowboats and came precariously on foot. Sören

Norby was at the head of the party, shouting and waving, grinning like a fool. The ship's captain ordered ropes thrown over the side, and in no time Norby's pirates were aboard the ship, holding out fur-mittened hands to the fur-mittened hands of the sailors and passengers, joking in loud voices, and at last helping the ship's people down onto the ice and guiding them over to the rowboats that would take them to shore. The snow fell still more heavily. Bishop Brask could no longer see even the rowboats, much less Gotland. Two pirates helped him down to the ice, careful and respectful young men of maybe twenty. Holding him by the armpits, they led him in, he hoped, the right direction, all three of them taking small steps, shielding their eyes against the light.

How they reached the rowboat Bishop Brask was unable to remember later; all his mind retained was the cold and the whiteness and the blur of fur-wrapped oarsmen as white as the rest. A kind of thudding broke through his gloomy thoughts, a thudding different from that which had risen from the sides of the rowboat as it labored through the ice, and looking up he was dimly aware of pilings and a dock, mittened hands reaching down to him, and high above the shadows of people the shadows of towers, walls, and trees, the white-masked face of Visby.

Then he was seated in the great roaring hall of Sören Norby, every wall piled high with plunder, not treasure-chests and ingots but bedsteads, ornamental chairs, fine tables, sacks of grain, machinery, bundles of clothes, iron weapons, great cylinders of rope. Such was the booty Norby's pirates had taken from the ships of the Dutch and Germans, Poles and Russians.

"Magnificent, hey?" a voice boomed in his ear.

When the bishop turned, half in a daze, glancing first at the hand on his shoulder, then up at the face, he saw that the man who'd addressed him was none other than Norby. He'd thrown off his coat and stood, wide-shouldered and jubilant, in a short-sleeved burgher's shirt, grinning like a boy. Bishop Brask smiled faintly. "Magnificent, yes," he said.

"Come," said the pirate, "first a bit of food and wine, then talk!" He lowered his hand to the bishop's elbow, as if he thought him a feeble old woman, and helped him to his feet. "I have with me other friends from Sweden," he said, "gentlemen with whom you're acquainted, I think." He led the bishop into a high, narrow corridor and down it to a smaller chamber where in the fireplace flames licked eagerly at a great stack of logs. Three men were waiting there, two in humble monks' garb, though they did not carry themselves like monks, and a third man the bishop knew at once that he'd seen somewhere before, perhaps often, though at first he couldn't place him. This third man stood staring out the window, dressed in fine clothes and a long, dark blue cape. None of them turned as Sören Norby led Brask to a chair and brought him wine. When the man in the cape finally did turn, he did so with the cool, mechanical elegance of a figure in a masque—the figure of Death, perhaps, or the Devil in one of his more flattering representations.

"Berend von Melen!" Bishop Brask exclaimed, then instantly calmed himself, for it was a matter of policy with him that he never show interest or surprise. Though he had indeed been considerably surprised—not at von Melen's duplicity, of course, but at the speed with which Norby had arranged all this—Bishop Brask was sure that he'd shown very little, no more than what they'd surely interpret as a flicker of interest.

"Bishop Brask," said von Melen, and slightly bowed. Now Hans Brask recognized the two dressed as monks—two of the most important members of the party of Sture, Bishop

Peder Jakobssen Sunnanväder and Master Knute Mickilsson, both of them passed over, like Brask himself, when Gustav had chosen his ministers. They all shook hands.

Sören Norby was beaming. "Poor Gustav!" he said.

Beware of underestimating Gustav, thought the bishop, but he merely let out a little smile and said nothing. Sunnanväder and Mickilsson were careful not even to smile.

Sören Norby closed the doors to the room, and the talk began. Bishop Brask registered it without interest. All conspiracies were curiously similar, he'd observed long since. Always a few foxes, always a few geese. Now Norby was in the role played once by young Gustav—the man of feeling, radiant with self-confidence and unthinking love of justice. He was a handsome young man, far more handsome than Gustav, with a better sense of humor (insofar as the young can ever have a true sense of humor, he thought), and a far more ingratiating smile. At the biceps his arms were as thick as a normal man's thighs. Muscle-bound. Not a good quality in a swordfight. But Norby was no duke, no aristocratic duelist, but a pistol man, knife-fighter, boxer. He would do.

The plot was uninteresting, though serviceable. Von Melen would come and pretend to attack Visby, put on a fine show but in the end see Sweden's navy to the bottom of the sea. Sunnanväder and Mickilsson would strike at Gustav from within, from their base in Dalarna, with armies and leaflets. Ah, always leaflets! thought the bishop. The world would never again be the same, now that leaflets had been invented and firing them off had been refined to a science as precise as the firing of cannonballs. "Poor Gustav," as Sören Norby called him, had invented the weapon that would sooner or later be the death of him—no doubt also the death of distinguished prose. It was ironic; if he could work himself up to it, the bishop would even call it sad. Gustav, like the

Lutherans, had thought leaflets the weaponry of Truth and noble sentiment. So Sören Norby seemed to think them, too. None of the bishops disabused him.

Very well, very well. Bishop Brask sipped his wine, then sat toying with it, watching how it caught the light, breaking it to pieces. Kristina would be released—Fredrik had as much as given Norby his word—and of course it stood to reason. Norby would be regent of Sweden until Nils reached majority, when Nils would become regent, and thus the Union of Kalmar would rise out of Södermalm's ashes, with Denmark at its head, as in former times. To clinch the arrangement, and safeguard Nils' position, Kristina and Norby would marry—a state both of them desired, Brask knew. He'd lived long enough to recognize a man in love when he saw one, not that it made his old heart leap. That Kristina should not feel the same was unthinkable. As flies beget flies, love begets love—the thought had no particular disrespect in it, nor did it enter Brask's mind as an expression of distaste. All of us live on illusion, so long as we can afford it. Hans Brask, in his youth, had been an avid reader of poetry, and not a casual, indiscriminate reader. He knew the difference between Dante and Petrarch, the *Song of Roland* and some foolish French tale. He had wept, in his youth, at the story of the saintly Jewess Teresa of Ávila; he might weep again now if he had time for books. "Faith," he'd once written, "is creating what we cannot see." It had a fine ring to it, and in Latin an excellent pun. But faith was for a man in his study, a dreamer, or for a man who had no other options, such as a farmer planting seeds.

Forgetting himself, Bishop Brask heaved a sudden sigh. Bishop Sunnanväder glanced at him with a look of concern. Brask knew well enough that the concern was, like everything else, policy. He waved his hand vaguely and smiled.

"It's nothing," he said. "Just thinking of the snow." Bishop Sunnanväder glanced at the window, a great blank of white, and his expression changed to cunning. He was a fat man, professionally meek and jovial, a man who always cried at church music—cried genuinely, perhaps, as Brask cried genuinely over poetry—but he was not as good an actor as he no doubt imagined; the look of cunning was always waiting at the edges of his face, prepared to leap out and seize his features.

Norby, for his part, had no time for these delicate dramas. He said, "King Gustav counts heavily on the friendship of Lübeck, but he's in trouble there. Fredrik of Denmark is no fool, believe me! It was Kristian's policy to shift trade to the Dutch, but now Kristian himself is in the Netherlands—he and his supporters. Why should Fredrik serve the friends of his enemy? Everything has changed before his eyes, but poor Gustav doesn't see it!" Norby laughed. "I rob the ships of Lübeck, but I never kill a soul. They expect me—they know when I'm coming. We have an arrangement. I take their goods, I very carefully store them, I prevent them from reaching their Swedish destinations, but when the wind changes—"

"That's good! That's very good!" said Mickilsson, eyes widening. Clearly it came as a complete surprise to him. Troublesome, troublesome, thought Bishop Brask. It was all very well to work with innocents like Norby, but to conspire with fools was a dangerous business. However, he let his face show nothing.

Long after all that needed saying had been said, the meeting of the conspirators dragged on. It was the weather, perhaps, the snowy day outside as bleak as their prospects if the plot should fail; here inside, the immense warm fire, comforting as victory. And so they talked and talked, repeating themselves. Gradually Bishop Brask stopped listening entirely, brooding on dangers more remote.

Gustav Vasa would of course destroy the Church; it was a foregone conclusion. He had never claimed he would do otherwise. Already he was hinting that the portion of tithe which was allotted to the running of parish churches should be diverted to the pay of his soldiers. To Bishop Brask himself he had written, "Necessity overrides the law, and not the law of man only, but sometimes the law of God." And already his minister Lars Andreae had proclaimed, on Gustav's instigation, the Lutheran doctrine that the Church, properly considered, was made up of the whole community of the faithful, so that the wealth of the Church was in fact the wealth of the people. Already he had turned the printing press at Uppsala to the production of a Bible in Swedish, and, adding insult to injury, had ordered Bishop Brask himself to help with the translation—an order Brask had had no choice but to obey. But what would they gain, overthrowing Gustav Vasa? Now King Fredrik too, it seemed, was warming to the merchantmen of Germany, Luther's right arm. Bishop Brask began to see more clearly, staring down thoughtfully at his amber-red wine, the strategy of the Devil —and its futility. Keep everything in confusion; that was the Devil's way of doing things. Baffle and madden the enemy and hope for the best. And if the Devil was as powerless to control things as he seemed, what could the best be, Brask thought, theological, but the will of God? The bishop kept himself from frowning, not wishing to draw attention. Did he believe, he wondered, in "the will of God"? Like a reflex, a soul-crushing weariness came over him. What did it matter what he thought, after all? Life would go on, or would go on until it stopped. If the will of God was inescapable, like the fall of the stones in an avalanche, then it was clearly no business of his. Let the chips, the boulders, the castles fall where they may. He closed his eyes.

He dreamed he was standing before the Pope, who was for some reason enormous, clothed in the brightest red velvet. The Holy Father was raising a silver chalice, holding it carefully between his thumb and first finger, his smallest finger affectedly extended, his face not a man's but a woman's, elaborately painted. When he'd sipped, he began to set the chalice down, holding it out over Bishop Brask's head and lowering it slowly, as if he did not know that Brask was standing there, about to be crushed. "Father!" Bishop Brask squealed, his voice no louder than the hum of a mosquito. Now a great shadow had fallen in a circle around him from the base of the chalice. Just before darkness engulfed him, he saw, high above the Pope's head, a great circle of blinding light descending like a ring of blue-white fire. The circle seemed as large as the whole world, and it was speedily growing larger, like a planet on collision course with Earth. Bishop Brask jerked suddenly awake, spilling a little flutter of wine. Otherwise, he showed no sign that he'd fallen asleep. Something had crashed, the same instant he awakened. It was a glass Sören Norby had thrown, in high spirits, into the fireplace.

7 BY THE SPRING of 1525 the conspiracy was all but crushed. No one in Stockholm was much surprised, least of all Bishop Brask, who had read the signs well enough and soon enough to keep himself clear of suspicion. Von Melen, called home from the fiasco at Visby, prudently avoided Stockholm and went to earth in his castle of Kalmar.

Gustav Vasa shook his head in disgust, pacing, as he

seemed always to do these days, venting his anger on the huge, patient figure of Lars-Goren and, across the room, Hans Brask. "The fool!" he said, shaking his fist before Lars-Goren's face. "Does he think I don't know what he's been up to?" He whirled away, pointing fiercely at Bishop Brask, who sat waiting as patiently as Lars-Goren to learn why he'd been called. "God send me an enemy worth my trouble!" shouted Gustav. "Fools, maniacs! It's like living in a house full of flies."

Bishop Brask sadly nodded.

"Pah," said Gustav, turning away from Brask as if he too were one of the flies. "Who is his houseguest there at Kalmar? Who sleeps in his fluffy German bed and eats his cabbage? Nils Sture! None other! Heir to the family's pretensions! And by miraculous coincidence—" He turned his back on both of them and stared out the window, breathing deeply, trying without success to control his rage. "By miraculous coincidence this great patriot von Melen is also putting up, as his beloved houseguest, none other than what's-her-name, daughter of Sören Norby. A pretty match, eh? Nils Sture and Norby's daughter? He's a matchmaker, von Melen. His heart rules his head. That's it, yes of course! Behind all the schemes he's a softy, yes that's it!" He spat like a farmer, indifferent to the splendid furnishings. "You know what I would just once like to see in this world?" he asked furiously, stabbing the air with his finger. "I would like to see a little pure unmitigated evil! Yes! Not stupidity, not snivelling little plots and counterplots, not jockeying and jostling—pure outrageous evil!"

He crossed quickly, stooped over, knees bent, to Brask's chair. "I met the Devil once," he said, pointing at the bishop's nose. "I was interested. I was excited! 'Ha,' I thought, 'by God it's the Devil himself—no joke! *Now* you're in trouble, Gustav Vasa,' I thought. 'Now you'd better keep a sharp eye out!'" He paused, drew his finger back. More softly, he said, "You didn't know I'd had meetings with the Devil, eh?"

"I thought perhaps you might," said the bishop. He glanced at Lars-Goren, whose presence made him strangely uneasy. Lars-Goren showed nothing. If the bishop had somehow revealed himself—he had no idea whether he had or not—Lars-Goren was carefully not showing it.

"Well, I did," said Gustav. Again he turned away, petulant now. "All in all, he's proved a disappointment."

"So we've all found," said the bishop, taking, as he knew, a risk.

But Vasa was in no mood for subtle innuendoes. "Very well," he said, "I'm disappointed. Everything in life disappoints me, that's the truth, but the Devil most of all, lording it over us, wasting our valuable time. I'm not a man to sit quietly and endure a thing like that!"

Lars-Goren glanced at him, perhaps in alarm.

"First I'll kill Norby," Gustav Vasa said, fixing his gaze on a spot high on the wall. Abruptly, he glanced at Brask. "You've heard, I suppose, that he's escaped to Denmark?" He hurried on without waiting for a response. "To Denmark —where else?—where he's collected another fleet. God knows how he does it! Well, I'll sink him, that's settled. I don't know how yet, but sure as I'm standing here I'll sink him! And I'll get rid of von Melen and his high-minded friends, all these plotters and meddlers, silly-brained impediments, always crossing me, always bothering me, getting in my way for no good reason—I'll wipe them off the slate!— and then, gentlemen—" He paused significantly, looking first at Brask, then at Lars-Goren, raising his fists slowly, his eyes like two shining steel rivets: "Then we drive the Devil under the ground!"

Lars-Goren's hands clenched on the chair-arms, and his

eyes opened wider. Bishop Brask faintly smiled, slightly blanching, and sadly shook his head.

Gustav Vasa brought one hand to his chin and looked soberly at Bishop Brask. "Lars-Goren doesn't worry me," he said, after a moment. "Lars-Goren is afraid of the Devil, as is right. He'll be excellent. I think so. But what about you?"

Bishop Brask went on smiling, shaking his head, the spotty skin of his face sagging heavily. "Maybe you can do it," he said at last. Just perceptibly, he shrugged his narrow shoulders. "But tell me. Does it matter?"

8   PLOTS, COUNTERPLOTS; the Devil was so busy he could barely keep track. By means of agents, Norby's trusted friends, he lured Sören Norby into secret alliance with the Netherlands and his former lord, Kristian, and managed to put Gotland back in Norby's hands. He persuaded the Lübeckers to try to seize Gotland, since Norby had betrayed them and would certainly continue to do so, for love of King Kristian and hatred of Gustav, chief buyer of Lübeck's goods. He persuaded King Fredrik to defend Norby's stronghold and to grant him the town of Blekinge as a life-fief, a base in immediate proximity to the Swedish border and within striking-distance of Kalmar. At once, again at the Devil's suggestion—and it seemed reasonable enough, for whatever the nobility of a man's ambition, he can do nothing without wealth—Sören Norby resumed his indiscriminate attacks on shipping—German, Swedish, Russian, even Danish. Again and again, with elaborate apologies, he sent back to those he pretended were his friends, such as Fredrik and the Lübeckers, whatever booty he'd taken "by mistake"—but it was never all there. "The fools," said the Devil gleefully, disguised as an old friend, "they'll never know the difference

—take my oath on it!" In August 1526, a combined Swedish-Danish fleet sent most of Norby's squadron to the bottom: Norby himself escaped by the skin of his teeth to Russia, where at the Devil's instigation he refused to take service with the tsar and was thrown into prison. There, one day when he was walking along a road in company with other prisoners, carrying his pick—for Norby's punishment was work in the salt mines of the tsar—the Devil himself visited him in the form of a mule.

"Sören Norby," the Devil whispered through the mouth of the mule, "don't lose heart! All is well!"

Norby's eyes widened and his knees went weak. "God in heaven!" he whispered, "do mules now speak Swedish?" All around him, prisoners moved away from him a little, supposing the man to have gone mad.

"I'm your faithful old helper," said the Devil, and made the mule's mouth smile. "I've been with you from the beginning, and I'm with you yet."

"Then you're the Devil!" said Norby, and this time he spoke aloud, so that the prisoners around him were more frightened than before. "Get away from me! Go!" He burst into tears and, without thinking, took a swing at the mule with the flat of his pick-axe.

"You there!" someone shouted in Russian. It was the guard, just a few feet behind him. "Leave that mule alone!" He brandished his long, narrow club as a warning.

"You see?" said the mule pitifully, pretending to be in pain. "You see what comes of senseless violence? Now use your head, and put your pick on your shoulder, and listen like a creature of reason."

"Never!" whispered Sören and, balancing the pick in the bend of his arm, put one finger of each hand into his ears.

"What kind of fool are you, trying to block out the voice of the Devil with your fingers?" the mule scoffed. "Plug your

ears with pebbles if it pleases you, and sing at the top of your voice to drown me out. I'll still be heard!"

Norby saw it was true and only from stubbornness kept his fingers in his ears.

"Fredrik's brother the Holy Roman Emperor will save you," said the mule. "He's begun negotiations already!"

"You're a liar," said Sören Norby. "What's it to Fredrik whether I live or die?"

"It's not for Fredrik that the Emperor's doing it," said the mule slyly. "It's to annoy the tsar, and to gain your services for his Italian war, and also to please Kristina."

"Kristina," said Sören Norby, and began to weep again. "Would that I'd never laid eyes on her!"

"Maybe you'll change your tune one day," said the mule with a smile. Abruptly, the mule's whole manner changed; he was merely a mule again, walking along the road with his burden.

"Monster! Unholy deceiver!" whispered Norby. But then he began to think that, all in all, what the mule had said was not unreasonable. He glanced around at his fellow prisoners —stupid idiots, hopeless from the day they were born, one no different from the other, none of them like himself. "The Emperor must know he could hardly find a better man," he thought. "If I serve him well, and show the Pope I'm no Lutheran, who knows? I may one day be king of Sweden!" He walked with more spirit now, and the prisoners around him hung back farther.

As for von Melen, after various machinations in which the Devil was always his eager advisor, he at last escaped by guile to Germany, where he at once began to work for a new alliance with his former master, King Kristian. To be on the safe side—for as a general he knew the wisdom of the groundhog, who always has two or more escape routes—he made himself also a servant of the Elector of Saxony, sworn enemy of King Kristian and the Dutch. He had misgivings, of course, for if either lord should learn of his attachment to the other, von Melen would be in trouble. His misgivings grew to fears and eventually to terrors, so that wherever he went he kept his hands clasped tightly together to prevent them from shaking. One night when he was lowering his knife to cut into the trout on his plate, the trout's eye rolled to meet his, and the trout's mouth opened.

"Von Melen," said the trout, "you're a stupid man!"

Berend von Melen stared in horror and disbelief, but his anger was even greater than his alarm. "What?" he cried. "What did you just say?"

"You're a stupid man," said the trout again, as placid and indifferent as when it was swimming in the stream.

"Stupid trout," hissed von Melen, glancing past his shoulder to be sure no one was watching. "If you think you're so smart, how come you to be dead and cooked?"

"That may be," said the trout. "I may have made one small mistake in my life, but it's nothing like the big mistake you've made!"

"Ha?" said von Melen. He drew back his knife, deciding to let the trout speak on.

"You're a doomed man, trying to serve two masters as a general," said the trout. "Sooner or later their wishes will conflict. However, if you took a different road, you could please them both and be as safe as a fox in a tree."

Von Melen scowled. "How?" he said. "Explain."

"Write!" said the trout, and gave von Melen a cunning smile. "You're a stylist as well as a famous man. You have all Europe's respect. Turn these things to advantages, then."

"Write what?" von Melen asked. He bent down toward the plate. "Poetry? Autobiography?"

"You see?" the trout said. "I told you you were stupid! Write about Gustav Vasa! Vilify his name! Both Kristian and

the Elector will be delighted—you'll be a hero on both sides."
The trout looked pensive, then at last heaved a sigh. "But of
course, if you think you're not up to it—"

"Not up to it!" cried von Melen, and leaped up from the
table. "Not *up* to it, you tell me, you stupid little trout!" He
was so excited by the idea—for his hatred of King Gustav
was boundless—that he forgot about supper completely and
started for the door. With his hand near the doorknob he
abruptly paused, turned around, and went back to the table.
"Stupid trout," he said, "you shall see how I write!" And
without noticing that the eye of the trout had filmed over he
snatched up the plate and carried it with him to his study,
where he set it on his writing desk, near enough to watch
him. For the rest of his life, von Melen blackguarded Gustav
Vasa throughout Europe, comforting his enemies, thwarting
his policies, fomenting conspiracies, piling lie on top of lie or,
when Vasa made mistakes, trumpeting the truth. He became,
from all his writing, as bent-backed as the Devil. His eye took
on a glitter, his mouth became parched and cracked. The fish
on the plate beside him rotted away to dust.

9 PLOTS, COUNTERPLOTS; one would have thought
even the Devil would eventually have tired of them, but he
did not. For this he had one main reason: something was
afoot, he could feel it in his bones. He brooded; he travelled
far and wide, spying; even at the houses of the very poor he
would sometimes crouch at the window, listening; but all to
no avail. Of one thing the Devil grew increasingly sure: the
trouble was in Sweden.

Once, in the trivial, insignificant city of Härnösand, close
to the southern border of Angermanland, he saw, just at
sunset, a crowd gathered around a tent which bore the shield

of King Gustav. He compressed himself into a pigeon and walked inside. Slowly, carefully, avoiding people's feet, he made his way to the exhibit at the center of the tent. No one was saying a word; everyone was looking in the same direction. He followed the people's gaze and saw a large wooden statue—a knight with his lance through a dragon's neck. The Devil felt suddenly hot all over, he had no idea why.

"Very well," he thought, "say the dragon refers to myself, and the knight has vanquished me." He blinked, then flew up onto a crossbeam to think the matter through. "Why should this hopeful little fantasy alarm me? Am I dead because a silly piece of wood is dead?" He cocked his head thoughtfully. "No," he decided.

"Does the knight who might kill me exist, is that why I'm afraid?" Again he considered the question with care and, at last, with a quick little side-to-side jerk of his head, said, "No." He began to concentrate on reading the minds of the people. To his astonishment, nothing came. Was it possible? he wondered. Was everyone in the crowd thinking *nothing? Nothing whatsoever?* Now the crowd began to shift, and he began to get things. A child had wet its pants and was worrying, thinking it might be spanked. An old man had an itch on a part of his back he could not reach. A man with his arm around his wife was looking at a woman not far off, his mistress.

In disgust, the Devil flapped his wings and flew away through the opening in the tent, changed at once to his own form, and, on his huge, dark wings, soared high into the night. It crossed his mind that the way to be safe was perhaps to kill everyone in Sweden. It was an interesting idea, but it immediately slipped his mind.

He flew to Stockholm, to watch the mock triumphal entry of Sunnanväder and Master Knut. Perhaps he would speak to them, he thought—give them a little false encouragement.

Or perhaps he might whisper to the crowd, pass out leaflets, start a riot, and set them free.

Sunnanväder and Mickilsson had fared no better than Norby and von Melen. "Fly to Trondheim!" the Devil had whispered in their ears when the army of Dalarna had surrendered. Little did they know—though the Devil knew—that the archbishop of Trondheim was one of the silliest men who ever lived. They took the Devil's advice, crossed the Norwegian frontier, and found shelter with the archbishop, who was pursuing political objectives of his own and thought the fugitives might perhaps prove useful. He met them at his door, a candle in his hand, his white hair flowing nearly to the hem of his nightgown, and kissed each of them on both cheeks. All that winter the archbishop treated his guests like princes, sitting up half the night with them, arguing fine points of theology and politics, giving them great feasts on holy days, introducing them proudly to every stranger who landed at that frozen outpost on the edge of the Arctic Ocean. When summer came, he imprudently delivered up Master Knut on the rash supposition that he would be tried in Sweden by an ecclesiastical court. He was tried by the råd— the king himself served as prosecuting counsel—and was speedily condemned to death. In September what had happened to Master Knut somehow slipped the archbishop's mind and he delivered up his second guest to Gustav. Sunnanväder, too, was at once condemned to death.

So now they entered Stockholm on the backs of asses, Sunnanväder wearing a floppy straw crown and carrying a battered wooden sword such as children might play with, Master Knut in an archiepiscopal mitre made of birch-bark. The crowd laughed and shouted, for here in the capital, the people were all solidly on the side of the king. A mangy dog ran up to bark at the animal on which Sunnanväder rode. Suddenly what came out of its mouth was not barking but speech. "Never mind!" yelled the dog. "They laugh now, these morons. Let us see who does the laughing tomorrow!"

Sunnanväder, weeping, did not bother to look down. Mickilsson, riding beside him, opened his mouth in astonishment. When he could speak, he said, "Peder, am I dreaming?"

Sunnanväder wept and said nothing.

When the parade of humiliation was over, they were shipped unceremoniously, like animals, to Uppsala for beheading.

"So much for my human enemies," said Gustav when the second head fell.

Lars-Goren said nothing, and the king turned to look at him in a way that commanded speech. "There are always more," Lars-Goren said. At the last moment, a strange, rapt expression had come over Knut Mickilsson's face. Lars-Goren's mind would not let loose of it.

"Nevertheless," King Gustav said, "the time has come to seek out the Devil."

Lars-Goren looked down at the severed head in the sawdust. "Surely he's here," he said.

Gustav's look became sharper. "In me, you mean? Speak plainly, old friend and kinsman!"

Around the steeple of the church, sparrows flew crazily, unwilling to rest. Lars-Goren pointed up at them. "In the birds—in you—in the cobblestones under our feet, perhaps. Who knows where the Devil ends and the rest begins?"

King Gustav's frown was dangerous. "You have your orders," he said, "you, my best friend, and Bishop Brask, my best enemy. You'll manage. I think so."

Quickly, for fear that he might begin to make threats, King Gustav turned on his heel and hurried away.

PART FIVE

1 BECAUSE IT WOULD be useless to try to flee to Europe, especially for Lars-Goren, who had no friends there, Lars-Goren and the bishop fled north, on the pretext that there, where his home was reputed to be, they were most likely to find the Devil.

It was a bitter trip for Lars-Goren. They followed the same route he had taken in happier times, when King Gustav was newly crowned and full of high hopes and idealistic plans for Sweden. It was almost the same season as when he'd ridden north before, to be united again, for a little, with his family; the summer was just a little farther along—there was fog in the valleys, mornings and evenings, and some-times, as they passed through open farmland, a sharp smell of autumn. Sometimes tears filled his eyes as he rode, his thoughts dwelling on his wife and children, his household servants, and his peasants. Even the foolish flattering priest whom he'd visited on his last trip and whom he'd known since childhood, Father Karl, who was always trying to advance himself by making up stories of what others had said—even that man Lars-Goren remembered fondly now. "I'll miss him," he was saying to himself. For he knew he could hide only so long at his own home castle. Gustav, in his present tyrannical mood, would be sure to hound them. Gustav's plan might be mad—so Lars-Goren believed it—but the king was perfectly serious about it. After a time, their failure to report success in their struggle with the Devil would turn the king against them, and all the force of his frustration would come down on their heads. It was a strange thing that a king should have such a power—that the people should voluntarily grant him such power—but it was a fact of life, clearly, and had been so for centuries, all over the world. Thus in time Lars-Goren would become a danger to his household by being there; to save them, he would have no choice but to press on, God knew where. His responsibilities would fall to Erik. "God bless him," Lars-Goren thought. Bishop Brask glanced at him, then tactfully looked away. They rode on, moving toward Uppsala, in silence.

In this cloud of gloomy thoughts, Bishop Brask was something like a lightshaft of relief. He was not a man Lars-Goren greatly liked or even admired, though he was clearly no fool; but he was at least a distraction, a point of interest. For hours at a time he would ride without a word, lost, perhaps, in his own gloomy thoughts. He rode with his back very straight, like a man in pain, or like a prisoner riding with a rope around his neck. He seemed to look neither to left nor right nor off into the distance, but only at his horse's

ears. His attire was elegant, like a rich lord's, yet when one
looked more closely, as Lars-Goren had ample occasion to
do, it was not all it might be: the collars and cuffs had been
shrewdly repaired; the cloth stretching over his knees was
thin, no more substantial than a fine lady's hankie. He rode
the same horse he'd been riding when Lars-Goren had first
met him beside the high mountain lake in Dalarna, the splendid black stallion he called Crusader; but the horse was old
now, and though he still habitually fought the bit and sometimes rolled back his eyes, recalcitrant, there was no longer
spirit in the horse's rebellion; it seemed more crotchety, like
the fussing of an old man no longer aware that he's fussing.
He snatched leaves from the branches of trees as he passed,
and Bishop Brask, each time, would give a perfunctory little
jerk at the reins; but neither of them was any longer interested in the struggle. When they cantered, even for short
distances, the bishop's horse breathed harshly and took crafty
advantages, favoring his forelegs as he came out of jumps,
breaking stride for swamp-ground, throwing his head for
leverage as they climbed steep hills. As if respectfully, Lars-
Goren's horse Drake held in a little, though Drake, at ten,
was at the height of his powers. Crusader was perhaps six-
teen. The bishop found excuses, perhaps without knowing it,
for moving his horse no faster than he had to, and Lars-
Goren, half-unconsciously, fell in with this. It was only when
he realized that they wouldn't reach Uppsala until the middle
of the night that he saw clearly how slowly they'd been moving, and the reasons. But no matter, he told himself. There
might come a time when speed would make a difference, but
except for Lars-Goren's strong wish to see his family, there
was no great hurry just yet. At times, as if to distract Lars-
Goren from the slowness of the pace, the bishop would look
over at him with his milky old eyes and speak.

Once he said, "I've been interested, watching this hobby of the king's—breeding livestock. I visited one of the farms, outside Vadstena. He's a fascinating man, King Gustav. One wonders how much he understands, how much he merely acts."

Lars-Goren raised his eyebrows, waiting, inviting more. The bishop for a moment sucked his lips inside his teeth, looking down at Crusader's mane; then he continued: "It may be more important than people think, this business of breeding livestock. It's been a favorite occupation of kings for centuries, clear back to the Greeks, and as I once mentioned in one of my books—perhaps you've read it—'what kings do for sport will in the end stand the world on its ears.' Heaven knows what I meant, exactly, but in this case it may well apply." He nodded thoughtfully, smiling a little, as if the conversation were ended.

"I'm not sure I follow," Lars-Goren said.

For a moment Brask said nothing, musing in private. "Just this," he said at last, as if reluctantly, already slipping toward boredom. "If you look at it philosophically—not just at how breeding can produce a particularly meaty strain of pigs or an extra-large bull, not just at how, in the short run, a wolf can be transformed in just a few generations to a domestic hunter . . . if you look, instead, at the long-term implications. . . ." He compressed his lips and looked suddenly cross. "The Church, if it were paying attention—which it never does, of course—would be shocked to the soles of its boots by this breeding of livestock."

They rode awhile in silence, Lars-Goren, for his part, pondering why it was that the bishop had such difficulty bringing himself to put his thoughts into words. It was not for lack of thoughts; Lars-Goren had known that since the first day he'd met him. But words seemed to come from the bishop's heart as if weighted by fieldstones. Even to say, "Good morning," it seemed the old man had to take a deep breath, overcome inertia.

There was a whir in the grass to the right of them, and a flock of partridges flew up, wings roaring. As if the noise and sight had renewed his strength, the bishop asked rhetorically, "What does it suggest, this stock-breeding? It suggests that, given enough time, we could transform the world, change every tree, every flower and insect. Mate the dogs with long noses, generation on generation, and in time you have a species of long-nosed dogs. Is it that that draws kings to the sport of breeding stock? Have they seen to the heart of the mystery? have they noticed that they're on to the fundamental secret of God? You look at me in alarm, Lars-Goren, as if you think I've gone mad. I haven't. Nothing like that. But think: suppose it's the same with ideas, governments, even virtues? Surely it's that that these kings have guessed, though if you asked them they might not understand it."

"You've lost me," Lars-Goren said.

"No matter, just an old man's nonsense," said the bishop. After a time he said, "Put it this way: We hear the expression 'Might makes right.' Suppose it's true—I mean *profoundly* true. Suppose there is in fact no good in the world except *that which survives.* We create a horse stronger than other horses, put him in a field with those lesser horses, and he kills them. They're dead forever, then—unable to throw their line. Suppose it's the same with governments. Create a form of government more effective than all others, in due time it will destroy or at any rate outlive all the others. What more could any king ask when he dies than to be remembered as the man who created such a government as that?"

"Yes, interesting," said Lars-Goren.

Bishop Brask nodded, his face slightly glowing, as if even

he were for a moment interested. "And ideas," he said. "What of ideas?" His face took on an apologetic look, as if not by his will but by its own accord. "I've been working, as you know—" He gave a little shrug, then forced himself to continue, "I've been working on Gustav's translation of the Bible into Swedish. One encounters some rather peculiar problems. It's nothing new, you understand—nothing I'm the first man in the world to discern. Alcuin, Grosseteste, Bacon—they were all on to it, though their conclusions were perhaps not exactly the same as mine. The Hebrew's not all of a piece, that's the heart of it. The language and ideas change not by decades but by centuries. In a single sentence the language may jump hundreds of years. You follow my drift?"

Lars-Goren considered, then shook his head.

"What I'm saying is, Holy Scripture grew. Like a plant. Like a horse. It *changed*, sometimes drastically. There seem to be startling cuts, shifts of opinion—as if God's spirit, dictating, kept changing its mind."

"Possibly you've made some mistake," said Lars-Goren.

Bishop Brask looked at him. "No," he said. "It's no mistake."

"And what do you make of it?" Lars-Goren asked.

Bishop Brask stared hard at his horse's ears. "I think the whole book is a record of trials and errors," he said.

"You sound like a Lutheran," said Lars-Goren.

For a time Bishop Brask said nothing. Then: "No, worse."

Darkness was falling. They were still a good twenty miles from Uppsala. Lars-Goren urged his horse to a brisker pace. As if without noticing, the bishop did the same.

2 THEY SLEPT that night in one of the elegant stone houses in the garden of the cathedral, a walled-in park with trees and headstones, some of them old arrow-shaped viking stones. The night air was heavy with the scent of horses. It crossed Lars-Goren's mind—an idle thought, but one not a little distressing to him—that here in the walled cathedral garden they were "in sanctuary." Theoretically at least, no sheriff or general from Gustav's government could touch them. It wouldn't be a bad place to live out one's life, all things considered—heavy-beamed old trees, a creek with clean-swept bridges, statues here and there, lit by flickering torchlight, some of them finer than anything at the palace in Stockholm, if Lars-Goren was any judge.

An old serving man opened the door for them and bid them come in. Behind him in the darkness, people were moving about, lighting candles, stoking the fire, softly calling to one another. It was queer, all this fuss for two more or less unimportant travellers, Lars-Goren thought. He soon discovered they were not as unimportant as he'd imagined.

Four priests came forward and greeted Bishop Brask with great respect, almost fear, as if to the clerics of Uppsala he was of a rank with the Pope himself. Some knew him, it seemed, for the force and cunning of his political activities, some for his scholarship. The young priest who was placed in attendance on them, rousted out of bed, puffy-eyed with sleep, was, it turned out, one of those involved with the bishop on the Uppsala translation project. He could not seem to do enough for his master, and though he was solicitous, too, about the welfare of the king's advisor Lars-Goren, one could see at a glance that in the priest's eyes—in all the priests' eyes—Lars-Goren was a humble commoner in comparison with the bishop.

Bishop Brask was gray with weariness and walked slightly tilted, as if his back were hurting him. He seemed to want nothing more than sleep; yet at the priests' urging he seated himself compliantly and drank a glass of brandy, then another and another, and talked at length, mainly with the young man involved with translation, sometimes heatedly— whether from an old man's weary exasperation or from frustration at the complexity of the problems involved—about the book of First Corinthians. Lars-Goren sat forgotten in a corner of the candlelit room, listening, with his hands on his knees. The text they were discussing was one he had never heard before and would have considered, at any other time, not worth haggling over, since it was a text never used in sermons. But today's context charged it with meaning in Lars-Goren's mind, though the meaning was nothing he had words for. The text read, roughly, "There are diversities of gifts, but the same Spirit; and there are differences of administrations, but the same Lord; and there are diversities of operations, but it is the same God which works in all." Like the priests, Lars-Goren sat forward, hanging on the specialists' words, his brandy glass on the table beside him, forgotten.

His hope that their arguments would resolve his unwordable question proved vain. They spent the whole time debating the meaning of the Greek word for which Brask supplied the translation "operations." The younger priest was urging such translations as "movements" or "events," possibly "changes and inner principles in things."

The bishop looked older and wearier by the minute. His left cheek trembled, and his mouth made a tight, thin line. "My young friend," he said, "it's not our business to *write* the Bible, just to translate."

"But it means the same thing," the young man insisted,

smiling falsely, eagerly, as if in hopes of deflecting the bishop's wrath. *"Operations—changes in things—*surely there's no real difference!"

"If that were true, you wouldn't be fighting me so heatedly," said the bishop.

The young man held out his hands, palms up. "It's a question of making ourselves clear to the people who read," he said. *"Changes in things* they'll understand—spring, summer . . ."

"You fool yourself," snapped the bishop, and let his eyes fall shut. "You want to make God say not what in fact he says but what the people will understand. What the people believe—what *you* believe—you want *him* to believe. The Greek is more vague than you like it—less, so to speak, sophisticated. You want him to compare the behavior of water in a river to the behavior of mayflies, or husbands and wives—make God some kind of universal alchemy. Perhaps up in heaven, listening to what you say, God is pulling at his beard nodding heartily in agreement. But at the time he, so to speak, spoke with Paul, he was talking about talents and governments, and somehow or another he forgot to say what, listening to you, he may be wishing now that he'd thought to bring to Paul's attention."

The young priest was checked in his opinion for only an instant. He drew his plump hand back to his mouth and said tentatively, not meeting the bishop's eyes, his whole body expressing his refusal to be beaten by the bishop's rhetoric, "It all depends what he meant, exactly, by 'administrations.' Perhaps he wasn't thinking exclusively of churches or political systems. Systems of philosophy, as Aquinas tells us, have their necessary logical 'government.' Trees, the arrangement of veins in mammals, the habits of badgers, as opposed to those of bees . . ."

"You know you're talking nonsense," the bishop said

crossly. "Human pride! Beware of it! What a pleasure it would be"—he smiled slightly, his eyes narrow slits—"to impose one's opinions on the world through the mouth of God himself!"

"If I've correctly followed the arguments of your books, they're as much your opinions as mine, my lord," said the priest, but feebly, looking at his knees, as if he knew the ploy would never work.

"True enough, they are my opinions," said the bishop. "Who knows, if the Lutherans win, they may someday be all men's opinions and taken for gospel. Give every man a Bible and let him read it as he likes, sooner or later what the Bible says will be what the news-crier says in the street. Truth will be whatever survives, generation on generation." He closed his eyes again, and for a moment it seemed to Lars-Goren that he'd fallen asleep. Then, without opening his eyes, he said, "It may all come to pass. No need to rush it."

With an effort, the old man raised his eyelids, then set down his glass. "I must sleep," he said. "Translate it any way you please. Whatever we do is presumably God's will." He pressed down on the chair-arms and rose.

The young man looked at him, distressed, his head full of arguments, but in the end, with the other priests gathering around him, he said nothing, but officiously rose to help the bishop to his room.

In the morning none of them referred to the midnight discussion. Perhaps, on reflection, the young priest had decided to take advantage of the old man's irritable concession and do exactly as Brask had ironically advised—translate any way he pleased. After matins and breakfast, as they were mounting their horses—the bishop stiffly, as if the pain he had still not mentioned were much greater now—the young priest asked, "Will you be passing through Dalarna?"

Glancing at the bishop, who showed nothing, Lars-

Goren answered, "No, that's out of our way. We'll be heading straight north."

"Ah," said the priest, and nodded.

Bishop Brask studied him with drawn lips. His old horse
stamped irritably, but the bishop held him in a moment
longer. He asked sternly, "Why?"

The priest shrugged. "There are always rumors of trouble in Dalarna," he said, and gave a laugh.

"What this time?" Lars-Goren asked.

With studied off-handedness, to show that he himself was
in no way involved, he told them of the Daljunker—the
young gentleman of the Dales—who claimed he was Nils
Sture, that young Nils was, after all, not dead but had escaped Gustav's wrath.

"That's absurd," Lars-Goren said, flashing anger. "What
wrath? Who ever said Nils Sture was dead?"

"He's not?" asked the priest.

Bishop Brask, heavy on his horse, flicked his reins
slightly, moving without a word of farewell down the path
toward the road. Lars-Goren looked after him, then nodded
to the priest and started out behind him, trotting to catch up.
The road was lightly speckled, like an eel's back, with light
and shadows. "More work of the Devil?" said Lars-Goren.

"Everything's the work of the Devil," said the bishop.

"Everything?" Lars-Goren asked, ironic.

"Nothing, then; whatever you like," said the bishop, and
said no more.

3 THEY RODE that day only as far as Lake Dalälven.
As on the previous day, the bishop sometimes rode for miles
without a word, at other times spoke freely. Once Lars-
Goren said, riding through a forest as dark as a cave except

for a few threads of sunlight—a forest so thick there was no underbrush, only a carpet of pine-needles—"It puzzles me, Bishop, that you decided to come north with me. Surely you had friends you could have turned to for protection. It hasn't escaped me that you ride like a man in some discomfort; back trouble, perhaps, or possibly something worse, though I hope not."

"Yes," Bishop Brask said, a sullen, disembodied voice in the darkness to Lars-Goren's right, "I'm old for a trip like this, that's true."

Lars-Goren waited, listening to the footfalls of the horses, and when the bishop said no more, he said, "Yet you've come. It does seem strange."

"Strange," the bishop agreed, and then, with a sigh, as if only to avoid further hounding on the question, "I hardly know myself why I decided to come. Perhaps just exhaustion. No doubt that sounds strange—to take a long, arduous trip out of exhaustion—but when a man reaches my age, or my mental state, call it what you like, it can sometimes seem easier to walk on foot to China than to wrestle over trivial decisions." He rode awhile in silence, then spoke again. "That was mere rhetoric, I'm sure you noticed. 'Walk on foot to China.' I live on rhetoric, like a spider on its threads. Perhaps I imagined I could outride the edge of my rhetoric. More rhetoric, you'll notice."

Lars-Goren said nothing.

"I remember when I imagined some connection existed between rhetoric and the world. I remember the feeling. Very pleasant, like the feeling of union between man and a woman when they couple. A *curious* illusion, when you stop to give it thought. I doubt that one would have quite that feeling if one did it with a sheep or, say, a unicorn. But one never stops to think about such things when one's young. 'I love thee, Kristina!' cries Sören; 'Sören, I love thee!' cries Kristina—and the world pops open like a flag. Oh yes, ah yes." He heaved a sigh. "I've watched it, *de temps à temps*. I remember young Gustav. How I envied him, there beside Lake Mora, full of faith in himself! Then Norby. Poor gudgeon, he had it too. That's one of the Devil's main tricks, of course. Fill a man with faith. What evils, what absolute horrors the noble sword of faith sends pouring into the world!"

"Strange words from a bishop."

"Yes, I admit it. I'm not at my best, I'm afraid. I might say this in my defense. . . . More rhetoric, you'll notice. '*I might say this in my defense.*' But never mind, never mind. I might say this, as I was saying: I haven't made the trip out of ignorant faith, like you, my dear knight. No offense! Merely an observation! You, Lars-Goren: with no place to turn, where do you turn? Back home! Not because your wife or your children can help you, or your peasants and villagers, most of whom have never seen a war. And even if they had, of course, even if every last one of them was a seasoned veteran, what could little Hälsingland do against all Sweden? Can your castle withstand a siege by Gustav? Will he forget you, abandon you to your family? Never! Then why have you come? Because you've come, that's all. Surely you're aware of it yourself, my friend. Home is, for no reason you can find words for, the seat of your power. If something will turn up, it will turn up—or so you imagine—there. You're wrong, that's my opinion, or at any rate my guess. It's a fool's faith. And yet you act on it! That's the beauty of faith. One acts on it."

"But not you, you claim."

"Not me. No."

"You've lost me again. Why is it you've come?"

Ahead of them, they could see light. We'll soon be out of

the woods, thought Bishop Brask. But only in the literal
sense, of course. That was one of the fundamental symptoms
of despair, it struck him now—the discovery that the literal
world was no adequate metaphor. He could write a book on
despair—who could do it better? But of course one couldn't
write in this condition. And what good would it do anyway, a
book on despair? Whom would it serve? On the other hand,
what difference if anyone was served? On the other hand, why
write at all?

Out of the dimness Lars-Goren was asking again: "Why
is it you've come?"

Strange to say, Bishop Brask thought, framing the words
he might say to Lars-Goren but did not have the energy to
say, I was once in love. Yes, me! Hans Brask, Bishop! It was
an illicit love—to say the least! A young man! and worse yet,
eunuchus ex nativitate. Nevertheless it was so. I was in love.

It was not a feeling one could explain to a man like Lars-
Goren, but it had been real, and powerful. He remembered
how his friend, a young prior, had changed the light and air
he walked in. Perhaps there were women who could have,
for some, the same effect; but it had seemed to Hans Brask,
and seemed to him yet, that nothing in the world could be
more beautiful than the gentleness of that man. When he
listened to someone arguing a position of some kind—
whether Brask or someone else—he had listened with a
strange openness of heart, his head slightly forward, encouraging, as if to say "Yes! Yes, good! That's an interesting
point!" He was like the Christ Hans Brask had in those days
imagined, divine in the invulnerability of his spirit. If someone attacked or insulted him, the young prior dismissed it
instantly as something he himself might have done if he had
misunderstood in exactly the way his attacker did, for no one
would hate anyone, he was persuaded, if understanding were

complete. He was a grinner and a nodder. You spoke, he nodded, pulling out your words as a fisherman pulls a fish. When he disagreed, he said so—but enough, enough!

Yet the thought of the young man would not leave him. He saw in his mind how his young friend had walked, head thrown forward, mouth sombre, as determined and prepared for disaster as a Jew, walking—almost running—as if rushing toward some encounter he feared but would not duck. Once, arguing some idiotic point of theology, Hans Brask had burst into tears and the young man had seized his trembling hands. It was the only time they'd touched, except, perhaps, for a casual pat on the shoulder, a collision—he remembered it distinctly—in the hallway. Yet the whisper of the priest's skirts at the door was slaughtering, his scent unearthly—but enough.

They came out into the light of an open field, a little village in the distance. Peasants were cutting hay, the last of the season. The scent of it was dizzying. Grasshoppers and honeybees were everywhere. It came to Bishop Brask that he had ridden for a long time in silence, not answering Lars-Goren's question. He said, "I'm sorry. You must forgive me. You asked me something—what was it?"

Lars-Goren rode with an easy comfort that made the bishop suddenly conscious again of the pain in his back and upper thighs. Lars-Goren cast back in his mind, trying to remember. Bishop Brask remembered first.

"Ah yes," he said, "why is it that I've come with you? that was your question." He thought about it, frowning hard. "I don't know," he said at last. He knew for an instant what the truth was—it leaped up in him like a shock of excitement, a remembered nightmare—but then his despair was back, and, wearily, he shook his head.

At Gästrikland, all one heard anywhere was excited talk

of the Daljunker. From the emotion he roused, he might have been the Messiah come back in glory. Lars-Goren and the bishop, after conferring together, veered toward the west, into Dalarna. It was evening when they arrived in Kopparberg. The city was in a furor. The Daljunker had arrived sometime this morning, they were told, and would speak to the assembly tonight. Lars-Goren and the bishop hurried to join the crowd.

Lars-Goren could not say what he'd expected, exactly—certainly a Dalesman, crude but impressive; otherwise why would the Dalesmen have rallied to his cause in such enthusiastic force? But whatever it was that Lars-Goren had expected, the Daljunker, when he appeared, was a surprise.

He was an elegant young man with golden hair and manners he could only have gotten from a life among aristocrats. If he'd been fostered in Denmark, his speech did not show it. Every slightest gesture was Swedish to the core. His attire was magnificent. King Gustav himself had no such fancy clothes, and even if he had, he could never have worn them with such a casual perfection. In face and figure, he was beautiful—authentically so: he was no womanish imitation, no painted doll, no fop. What he said was not true—Lars-Goren and Bishop Brask knew it. Was he simply a magnificent actor then? If so, he was the finest in the world. Was he mad? If so, he showed not the faintest hint of it.

His voice rang, though he did not seem to shout. The torchlight around him did not seem, tonight, like the torchlight of a stage but simply torchlight. Lars-Goren mused on it so deeply that he almost missed the Daljunker's words. Surely, Lars-Goren thought—and he had never thought more carefully, more critically than tonight—surely the Daljunker would have the same effect in the middle of the day. His confidence in what he was saying was hypnotic.

The Daljunker cried out, as if in authentic agony, that King Gustav, Sweden's great hope and the hope of the whole northern world, was dead. Listening, Lars-Goren for a moment believed it and was shocked to the bone. He glanced at Bishop Brask, who very slightly, glumly, shook his head. Lars-Goren stared in amazement at the Daljunker. "He was Sten Sture's kinsman!" the Daljunker cried. "He fought King Kristian and King Fredrik and Sören Norby and the bishops! He made us proud to be Swedes! It is said that he killed Nils Sture, but that is not true! So brilliantly and cunningly that even the international magnates were fooled, he slipped Nils Sture out of prison, so that here and now he can stand before you all and cry, *The king is dead—long live the king!*"

"*Le roi est mort,*" Bishop Brask whispered, not turning his head. "He must have studied in France."

Now the Daljunker spoke of Sten Sture. His voice betrayed him, cracking, though he struggled for control. Lars-Goren found himself mentally backing off in a way that obscurely frightened him. But however Lars-Goren backed off from it, there could be no doubt of the Daljunker's sincerity. His tears, his voice, were not an actor's effects. He meant and believed every word he said; his tears were no less honest, Lars-Goren would have sworn, than the tears of Gustav Vasa when the bodies burned on Södermalm hill. Yet the whole thing was a lie—absolutely a lie, though conceivably the handsome young man did not know it. The Daljunker, speaking of Sten Sture, who he claimed was his father, was now weeping openly, no longer struggling against the force of his emotion. The Dalesmen all around Lars-Goren and the bishop wept with him. "Madness!" Lars-Goren thought. But the word was not enough.

Lars-Goren caught himself up sternly. "Suppose I am mistaken," he said to himself. "Suppose Gustav Vasa is dead and has been dead for weeks"—so the Daljunker had claimed—"and I am mistaken. Suppose this is truly, this Daljunker, the king of the Swedes."

That instant Bishop Brask seized his elbow and said, "Enough. Let's go!" Lars-Goren studied the terrible weariness in the bishop's eyes and, almost unaware that he was doing it, hurled up a prayer.

Fool, thought Bishop Brask, *stupid moron fool!* His rage was beyond words as he forced Lars-Goren toward the back of the crowd, guiding him ferociously by the elbow. He might have laughed, if he could summon up the energy. Nevertheless, when they had escaped the outermost rim of the crowd, he for some reason did not let go of Lars-Goren's elbow but, instead, hung on as if Lars-Goren were dragging him back out of Dalarna, north toward Hälsingland, toward safety and hope, as in fact he was.

4 THE DEVIL took the form of a fly and sat on the mantel in the firelit hall. He felt the threat very strongly here, though it seemed to make no sense. "Perhaps," he said to himself, rubbing his front feet together in frantic agitation, "perhaps it's the form of the fly that makes me feel this way. A fly's a very vulnerable creature. Perhaps it's only that." As an experiment, he flew up into the darkest corner of the room and transformed himself to a spider. If anything, the feeling of foreboding grew stronger than before. He looked down, baffled, at Lars-Goren, his family, and their guest, sitting close to the fireplace, their outlines blurring against the white, swirling fire.

There was nothing he did not know concerning the mission King Gustav had assigned to Lars-Goren and the bishop; not a detail he did not know about their long trip north. He had been startled to laughter, hearing King Gustav charge them with his removal, and he was no less inclined to laugh now. Yet his sense of danger was as sharp as the smell of woodsmoke all around him.

He lowered himself on a strand of gossamer to listen more carefully to their talk. As he listened he began to feel not only foreboding but anger. Like all human talk, it was unimportant, senseless, and took forever to get said. Their talk was so trivial he could barely keep his mind on it from sentence to sentence; and as his impatience grew by bounds, so his curious sense of foreboding grew. It would be the death of him, he thought, this inability to concentrate on stupidity not worthy of his attention. Yet surely no one, not even God himself, could keep his mind fixed on this foolish, meandering conversation in which the words of a child had the selfsame importance as the words of Lars-Goren or his wife or Bishop Brask. Still in the form of a spider, he lowered himself to the flagstones and ran nearer, scampered to within half a foot of Lars-Goren's wife's shoe.

Now Bishop Brask, to the Devil's disgust, was spouting poetry. He recited in a high, thin goat-voice, rocking a little in rhythm with the words, his shadow rising and falling on the wall behind him. Lars-Goren and his wife stared into the fire, listening or dreaming. The smaller children watched the bishop with their mouths open. It was an old Swedish tale of love and war, funerals and marriages. Soon, though he fought with all his might against it, the Devil was fast asleep.

5 THEY STAYED three weeks at the castle of Lars-Goren, sometimes riding out to watch the peasants at work or to pass an evening in one of the village inns, sometimes sitting with Lars-Goren's family, the dog nearby, under trees

or in front of the fireplace. Bishop Brask was increasingly impressed by the native intelligence of his friend—for indeed, he was beginning to think of Lars-Goren as just that, a friend, though their beliefs were far apart. Once, returning from a long ride to watch timber being marked to be cut for the coming winter's fires, the bishop said, "You have a good life here in Hälsingland, Lars-Goren. I see how your peasants look up to you, how your wife and children love you, and I'm filled with amazement, exactly as a man might be if he visited Eden."

They had stopped their horses side by side on a high ridge looking down over fields and the castle. The sun was low on the horizon, the sky deep red above the jagged pines. The dog, Lady, looked up inquiringly.

"Yes, it's good here," said Lars-Goren. He sat with his hands on the pommel of the saddle, his face solemn, waiting for the qualification he knew must come.

"But unreal," said the bishop, with a glance at Lars-Goren. Then he looked down into the valley again.

"Unreal?" Lars-Goren echoed.

"Like Eden," said the bishop. "It's a depressing thought, I admit, but inescapable."

"I don't follow," said Lars-Goren.

The bishop nodded at the valley with its long shadows, the castle set on its hill like a ruby full of light. "It's one of those dreams of innocence, this place. It's easy enough to live justly here. What's to prevent it? But who can live in Stockholm as you live here in Hälsingland? Or think of Paris—Vienna—Rome! The future's with the cities; you know that yourself." He gave an apologetic little shrug. "Cities are where the wealth is, and the power that makes your little hideaway safe or not safe. And what are the cities but hotbeds of rivalry and cunning, fear and exploitation? It's the old story

—Abraham and Lot: Abraham up there with his sheep in the mountains, Lot struggling to stay honest down in Sodom and Gomorrah. That's where the Devil keeps house, we like to say: down in the cities where merchants show their wares by uncertain light and pine sells for fruitwood, where sly politicians thread their lies through truths and half-truths till not even they themselves know which is which. Who can help growing greedy and corrupt, in places like that? Cheat or be cheated, that's the rule—and the rewards of shrewd cheating are visible on every hand: fine togs in every window, fine leather carriages under every lamp, fine stone houses filled with light. Lords steal in one way, beggars and cut-throats in another, but in the end it's all the same, rob and be robbed; it's the norm, down there." The bishop tipped his head, sadly smiling, his eyes queerly merry.

"Ah yes," the bishop continued a moment later, as if answering something Lars-Goren had said, "complexity's a terrible thing. That's what our retreats to the country make us see. How monstrously dull it is, every time we go back to Gustav's court and catch up on the latest plots and counter-plots, learn which new schemer has stuck his head up to tempt the axe! How rich life is here in the wilderness where people can be above-board and open with one another! How clear things become! as they were for Achilles, John the Baptist, St. Francis! No wonder your great religions come from inhospitable regions, and no wonder they tend to sicken when the wilderness gives way to the vast golden cities of Solomon! It's the same with the arts, or so it seems to me. How fine the old viking carvings are, or the primitive statues of Africa, or the square-cut tomb of King Edward the First of England—I suppose you haven't seen it. But then great cities rise, artists grow wealthy, their vision grows confused and complex. What a pity! Irony comes in. Paradox. Soon the only powerful emotion artists feel is nihilism. 'If I can't have my Eden, I'll destroy you all'—the same words the man of religion says when the world grows confusing and complex. 'The axe shall be laid to the root of the tree!' Ah yes, poor humanity! Poor Sweden!"

"I don't know," Lars-Goren said, surprised by the bishop's sudden shift, "as kingdoms go—"

"Yes, I should have guessed," the bishop said. "You have great hopes for our dear little Sweden. Why not? Why should we ever lose our innocence, like the French, the Italians, the English? We're a race of commoners. We always were, but now especially, thanks to Kristian's bloodbath. We're farmers, peasant villagers, priests in frayed cuffs. We have the miners, of course; an unruly crowd. But even they have a certain love of order, as we see in their meetings, if there's nothing out there frightening them. Perhaps little Sweden will become a model for all the world, you think. The basis of a universal ethic."

"You have reason enough to speak ironically," Lars-Goren said, just a trifle stern. He crossed his hands on the pommel and looked down in the direction of the dog. "Your own life has not turned out exactly as you might have wished, or so I gather, and you've witnessed many other failures of vision. King Gustav, perhaps. He was once the kind of innocent you describe, yet now—" He sucked in his lips and mused for a moment, then nodded as if to himself. "No, on second thought, even now a part of him believes in openheartedness and reason, I think. Why else this rage to see the Devil gotten rid of?"

Bishop Brask laughed, youthful for an instant. "He does even now believe in reason, that's true! You've heard, I take it, that he's ordered that public debates be held between the Lutherans and the Church? *There's* faith in reason for you!"

"You think the dice are loaded?"

"Not at all—at least not by Gustav! The fittest will survive—naturally." He smiled, wry and indifferent.

"The Lutherans, you think?"

"The Lutherans, yes. And after the Lutherans—" He shrugged. "A man could build a great many huts with the stones and leaded glass of Chartres Cathedral. Now that we have the printing press, and paper, and tawdry bindings, how vast the potential for, so to speak, 'literature'!"

"Nevertheless," Lars-Goren said, "if the Devil were out of it, and people could quietly argue things out, apply the Golden Rule with an appropriate measure of self-love, if you follow me—"

"Oh, I follow you all right," said the bishop, and tipped his head back, looking up at the darkness above them, an empty sky made darker by the blood red glow on the horizon. "Your views are very clear, and even if they weren't, any sensible child could construct them. It's easy to see what you think of as good, here in the country, surrounded by your family, your faithful dog, your well-cared-for peasants: openness of heart, the willingness to tell a man frankly what you think. A man could build a whole ethic of that, as indeed the Old Testament Jews did: evil as the closing of the heart, refusal to communicate. What was Adam's fall but a turning toward secrecy, self-interest?"

"I've heard worse definitions of good," Lars-Goren said.

"Of course you have!" said the bishop warmly, leaning forward in his saddle as if trying to see into his vision more clearly. "It's an excellent theory, or so it seems at first glance. I could argue it myself! Say a mother is beating a child before my eyes. What should I do? That is, what would be good and reasonable? Should I use force against the mother? But what is the evil in the beating I am witnessing? That the child feels pain, or that the mother feels the torments of malice instead of the joy of love? Surely it's in both, by the theory we've just advanced. A man on his own can do no evil; evil is lack of communication between people. If I want to act, then, I should act to restore communication between the mother and the child. If I use force on the mother, do I get rid of the lack of communication? No, I introduce a new lack of communication, between the mother and myself. I must reason with her, then. But suppose that, in her fury, the mother is screaming as she beats her child, and the child is also screaming. How do I get their attention?" Quickly, to prevent Lars-Goren's interrupting, he raised his hand. "I know, I anticipate your answer: I use force, but only such force as is needed to stop the ruckus and make the two pay attention. I use measured response. *Then* we sit and reason."

"It may be inconsistent," Lars-Goren said, "but it's reasonable enough. One must be sure of one's motives, needless to say. But it seems to me a man knows when he's acting for justice, not out of personal fury—that is, when he's acting by the Golden Rule and when he's not." His tone had an edge, as if he suspected the bishop of hair-splitting.

Bishop Brask stretched his arm out, conciliatory. "Say that's true," he said, "though of course I'm not as sure as you are that we always know our motives. But say it's true! You must surely see the problem it raises for me, a city man. Say there are four mothers, all beating their children at the same time, each for a different reason. Say there is also a small group of cannibals, over on a streetcorner off Ostengräd, not far away, preparing to put a priest in their boiling pot, and just beyond them there's an Arab who, misunderstanding the language, believes he has just purchased some fisherman's wife. What am I to do in this case? whip the various offenders to submission and tie them to cartwheels till I can get to them, one by one, and argue them to reason? Suppose I do this and then *you* come along just as I'm tying up the last of the offenders—you come along, that is, and see me tyrannizing these innocent strangers, as it seems to you. Do you knock me unconscious to get my attention and run around untying the people I meant to reason with? My example annoys you; I'm making things more complex than they are, you think. I admit the examples are a little facetious, but life in the city may be even more complex than I've suggested. What is one to do to get open communication where Swedes, Germans, Frenchmen, Poles, Russians, Finns, and even an occasional Lapp are mixed together like left-over herring sauces, each with his own way of thinking, his own old codes?

"That's why I said earlier that it's unreal, this Eden you live in, this Platonic Form of right behavior. It's refreshing, I don't deny it! It fills a man with hope and good sense, rejuvenates his spirit. But what if it's all snare and illusion? I don't mean to offend you, I hope you understand! No one could be more grateful than I am for the numerous kindnesses you've shown me, this glimpse you've given me of the pastoral life. No one could be more worthy of love than your wife is—I'm honored to have met her! But you see my reservation. We like to say gloomy, grim cities are the haunt of the Devil, but tradition is against us: it places his home in the unpopulated North—perhaps some such pastoral scene as that valley there below us, shining like a garden."

Lars-Goren smiled oddly, an expression Bishop Brask could not penetrate—perhaps annoyance, perhaps rueful acknowledgement that it might be as he claimed. With anyone else, Bishop Brask knew, he would at this point have fallen silent, withdrawing to his familiar hopelessness, for clearly he had won; but Lars-Goren had, and had had for some time, a queer effect on him, a way of forcing him—or inspiring him—to say more than he'd intended, as if arguments that only made him weary at other times took on interest when advanced against Lars-Goren. However certain

Lars-Goren might be about the motives of his actions, for the
bishop there was always some doubt, and never more than
now. Whether he continued in the desperate hope of corrupt-
ing Lars-Goren, smashing his ill-considered optimism, or in the
hope that Lars-Goren might somehow, by his stubborn innocence, "save Brask's soul"—a distasteful phrase, to the
bishop—he had no idea. It was perhaps both at once. Whatever
the case, he found himself arguing on, urgently, gesturing
like a man selling relics to a man with no faith in them. The
dog looked up at him in alarm, and he lowered his voice.

"Who can say ideals aren't the Devil's chief trick?" he
asked. "Isn't it possible that in the country, secure in the love
of his family, a man learns faith and serenity that outside the
country can only produce madness or tyranny or both?
Think about it, that openness of heart or willingness to
communicate that we've defined as the root of all good. Let
us consider what we mean by it, exactly. Where do we put
ignorance in our ethical scheme? The ignorance of the miners of Dalarna, for instance, or the pirate Sören Norby. What
good is the willingness to communicate in a man who's got
his facts all wrong? There may be no evil in the hearts of
such people, but surely they put evil into the world. Never
mind, you say; ignorance can be overcome by education—
another form of communication, in this case communication
between the culture and the individual. Yes, perhaps. Perhaps! But perhaps it's precisely this education which makes
the soul fold its wings. Perhaps education leads *inevitably* to
weariness and despair. As we civilize a child by beating or
cajoling or shaming him, do we not perhaps beat, cajole, and
shame what breeds hope in a man—individual will, every
man's innate sense that he's descended from the angels—to a
dreary acceptance of what's taken for necessity, the tiresome,
dispiriting laws of the docile herd?

"I will not pursue the point; I leave it to your judgment. I ask, instead, where does madness fit our scheme? the Dal-junker, for instance, convinced to the soles of his boots that he's Sten Sture's son? How does the culture communicate with a madman? Not only does he have his facts wrong. In defense of his sacred, individual will, he denies dull reality with all his might, claiming he's King Nero or Jesus, insisting that the infirmary or dungeon where we converse is not what it is but a castle in Spain. Or this, my friend: what of the well-meaning and canny political manipulator, a man like Gustav Vasa in his early days—the man who communicates truth, or so he'd claim, by simplification: complicated truth reduced to slogans? How in heaven's name do we communicate with him, or with those he has taught to use his methods? There's the future, I think. Power bloc against power bloc, lie against lie, until finally no one knows anymore that he's lying; fact and that-which-seems-desirable-in-the-long-run become hope-lessly confused, and the man who tells the truth, that is, sticks to the plain facts, is dismissed as a lunatic, or troublemaker, an enemy of the good. You think it's *reason* the Lutherans have introduced into human affairs? It's a new and terrifying tyranny—I think so. In the old days we knew who the tyrants were: King so-and-so. Bishop so-and-so. Queen X. Judge Y. The tyranny was official, however covert. We knew whom to watch. In the future every dog will have his plot and his secret arsenal."

He broke off abruptly, watching Lars-Goren's face, wait-ing for some answer. Instead of speaking, Lars-Goren, with a look of faint distress, raised his long arm and pointed into the valley. When he turned to look, Bishop Brask saw, below them, a horseman approaching, galloping as if the Devil were at his tail. They urged their horses forward, cantering down the slope to meet the man—the dog leaped up to follow—

and when they were fifty yards away Bishop Brask recognized the rider as Lars-Goren's fat groundsman.

"My lord," the man shouted when he was near enough to make himself heard, "you must flee at once! King Gustav has sent men—" He gasped for breath, and Lars-Goren, drawing close, reached out to touch the man's arm and calm him.

"Take your time," Lars-Goren said.

When he was able to speak, the groundsman said, "There's been a massacre in Dalarna. King Gustav's gone mad; it's the only explanation. And now he's sent men in armor after you and the bishop. They're in Hälsingland already. Nobody knows what the charge is, but I think you'd better run."

Lars-Goren nodded. "Very well," he said. "Don't worry yourself, old friend. We have everything ready." He glanced at Bishop Brask, then up at the darkening sky. "Very well," he said again, and together they started at a canter down toward the castle.

6 It was the saddest of partings. Lars-Goren's wife and four children stood at the arch, silent, Bishop Brask crooked on his horse, favoring his back, smiling wanly, as if casting in his mind for a suitable parting line or gesture and finding nothing that would do.

"God be with you," said Lars-Goren's wife, her hand on the metal armor on Lars-Goren's knee. Her nose was red and swollen like a peasant's. As she'd helped him into his underdress and armor, then the heavy fur that made his final layer, she'd been weeping. The groundsman stood anxiously shifting from one leg to the other, again and again casting a look down the road toward the trees.

"Will it be cold in Lappland?" little Andrea asked.

"Hush," her mother said, rather fiercely, as if the thought of the cold alarmed her.

"Don't worry," Lars-Goren said, smiling down at the child but speaking to put his wife at ease. "They'll meet us at the border. They'll know we're coming."

"I wish I could come with you, Father," Erik said. "I'd be a help. You'd see!"

"Next time," said Lars-Goren, and instantly shifted his eyes away.

"My lord, you must hurry," said the groundsman, wringing his hands.

Lars-Goren looked sadly at his beautiful older daughter, then at Andrea, then at his sons. "Take care of things while I'm gone," he said to Erik. "And you—" He glanced at Gunnar. "Keep your big brother out of trouble."

Gunnar grinned, his dimple flashing into view among the freckles. "I will," both boys said at once. "Don't worry."

"Bring me a reindeer-horn ring," said Andrea. "Promise!"

"I will if I can," Lars-Goren said and smiled. Then he bent down over the saddle and kissed his children, first Pia, then the others, finally his wife. Now all of them were weeping.

"God bless you, Bishop Brask," said Lars-Goren's wife to the bishop. "Take care of yourself."

"I'll be fine," said the bishop with a smile. "Remember me in your prayers."

Abruptly, Lars-Goren spurred his horse. The bishop followed. Gunnar tugged at the leash, keeping Lady from following.

7 IN NINE DAYS, moving first through frost, then snow, they reached the border of Angermanland and Lappland. There, surrounded by blinding white, an old woman stood barring their way, her bare hands lifted in a peasant salute. Lars-Goren made a sign to Bishop Brask, who stared in amazement, and they stopped their horses, got down from them, and approached the old woman on foot. Though there was wind, a steady, thin whine in their ears, her black shawl and dress, too thin for the weather, did not move. Her bare face and hands seemed indifferent to the cold, though it was fierce enough to freeze the nostrils.

Lars-Goren bowed formally and waited for her to speak. When she said nothing, he spoke himself. "I see that you have come from another world," he said. "I am sure that you have some urgent business with us or you would never have made such a troublesome journey. My name, as perhaps you already know, is Lars-Goren Bergquist. This man beside me is Bishop Brask. If you have anything to say to us or ask of us, I hope you will say it or ask it."

Snowdust whirled and snarled around the dead woman's feet. The dead eyes stared as if with indifference at Lars-Goren, but seeing that she did not step aside or turn her eyes, Lars-Goren knew it was no ordinary human indifference. Perhaps, he thought, it was the indifference of a judge, or perhaps the indifference of a divine messenger, one who had no stake in this at all.

"If it seems to you proper," he said cautiously, bowing like a servant, "may I ask your name?"

As if a feeble spark of life had come into her, the dead woman smiled. The lips moved stiffly, like old leather. After a moment, in a voice hoarse with disuse, she spoke.

"You would not remember my name, Lars-Goren, though you heard it once or twice. I was a peasant on your estate. You who should have been my protector were my murderer."

Lars-Goren stared, a blush of anger rising into his cheeks. Even from the dead he was not a man to tolerate a slander. Yet something made him hesitate, and the dead woman spoke again.

"I was an excellent servant in my younger days," she said. "I worked hard, in my hut and in the fields, and I raised twelve children, nine strong boys and three girls. But evil times came. With your lordship's blessing six of my sons moved south to join Sten Sture and his war, and there they lost their lives. Then the six that remained to me died one by one, four by the plague, two by accidents. My husband sickened with grief and hanged himself; you yourself signed the paper that refused him Christian burial. Suddenly I was alone in the world, avoided by all my former friends because they thought me bad luck or possessed. Children tormented me, men and women avoided me; soon they would not let me into their fields. It was said I was a witch, and though at first it was not true, in time it became so: by curses and charms I kept myself safe from my Christian tormenters. I kept them afraid of me, and by my power to make them tremble— worse yet, by my power to do evil to and for them—I kept myself in clothing and food. No one was ever less evil at heart than I was, at least in the beginning; but I grew bitter, as one does. I learned to enjoy my malevolence, for it gave me revenge on those who tormented me, stronger than myself. But of course it could not last. They were many; I was alone. The strength was in the end all on their side. They spoke with your lordship. You ordered me burned—burned alive, the most painful and shameful of all deaths. An old woman, a faithful servant for years and years, and a miserable victim to whom a just man would have shown mercy! Did you ask me why it was that I behaved as I did? Did you think of my humanness and misery at all? No, you listened to my enemies and condemned me as you would some old dog that has turned to killing sheep. But a dog you would have killed with a gun—one flash of pain, then peace. A dog, you would have buried. Such is the justice of Lars-Goren, advisor to King Gustav, a lord with whom neither those above nor those below find fault, except for me. Lars-Goren, whose power comes from God himself, so we're told. Vicegerent of angels! Then God damn the angels in heaven, says the witch!

"Now in rage and misery I roam the world's edges, restless and unappeasable, for I refuse to go to the place appointed to the wicked, because I hate the injustice of my damnation, and refuse too to go to the place appointed for the just, though nothing but my anger prevents it. I have deigned to offer only one small prayer to heaven, that you and I might meet somewhere on common ground, at the edge of our two worlds, that I might strike at your devilish complacence with my tongue; and today that prayer is answered. Though it may not bring me to rest, I have been given the chance to say what I have to say to you: that if I am damned, then you are ten thousand times damned, Lars-Goren. You are called a great fighter and a wise counsellor, and you are praised as a man who is afraid of nothing in the world except the Devil. But I have come to tell you you are a coward and a fool, for you shiver at a Nothing—mere stench and black air, for that is what he is, your wide-winged Devil—and in the presence of the greatest evil ever dreamt of, the fact that we exist in the world at all, helpless as babes against both evil and seeming good, you do not have the wit to blanch at all."

All this, in spite of the rage in her heart, she spoke calmly.

Lars-Goren, on his side, though he now understood that the ghost was incapable of doing him harm, was like a man with the wind knocked out of him; try as he might, he could not draw breath or speak. Whether it was rage or horror he felt, it had nothing directly to do with the old woman. "So this is the Devil!" he thought. "So this is existence!"

But Bishop Brask, the great cynic and disbeliever, felt nothing of the kind. He had known for many years that the world is full of sickness and evil. He was thinking of how Lars-Goren had left his family and home, riding to his almost certain death, or at any rate a bitter life of exile. If he was guilty, and he was, he was guilty in the same way the angry old witch had been: a victim of chance and unreason. He acted, or at any rate so he believed, by the commandments of a god who had not spoken to anyone sane for fifteen centuries.

Bishop Brask cried out, "Old woman, what right have you to chide like this?" His voice was sharp with indignation, his face twisted by both anger and the pain shooting up in him, almost past bearing; and, not like a ghost impervious to his power but like a fearful peasant, the old woman turned her eyes to him and clasped her bony hands. He raised his arm as if to strike her. "Wretched creature," said the bishop, his face wildly trembling, "even in death you're an animal, not human! Here you are, free as a bird in the realm of the eternal, free to learn the secrets of everything—free by your own admission to roam heaven and hell if you please—and all you can think of is petty human spite! Have you sought out the children and husband who died before you? No! Not even that! And you ask divine wisdom and love of Lars-Goren? Admit it, walking dung-heap! You were a witch from the day you were born!"

"Stop!" Lars-Goren whispered, his face dark red. His

right arm moved, wobbly, toward the bishop's elbow. Now a frail thread of his breathing came back. He straightened a little, making both of them wait. Even for a man whose condition was normal there was little enough air, in the sharp, icy wind, to breathe. After a full minute, when he'd filled his lungs, insofar as was possible, Lars-Goren spoke again. "She's right, and you're right. We all are," he said. "It's right to cry out for justice beyond anything else. If *we* can dream of justice, surely God can too, if he's still conscious. No harm that she blames me for her misfortunes. We taught her the system, we aristocrats. 'Look to us,' we said. 'We'll take care of you.' If we too were victims of a stupid idea, that's not her fault."

Bishop Brask stared at him with distaste, as he'd have stared at an insect, bit his lips together and kept silent.

"Old woman," Lars-Goren said, "I accept the ten thousand damnations you put on me. I take it all in your place. Now go where you belong. I absolve you of all guilt. Go at once!"

The old woman's eyes narrowed. They seemed to have come to life. "Are you God then?" she asked bitterly. "Are you a priest now?"

"Accept it," Lars-Goren said. He thought of saying more. He thought of reasoning with her, showing her that all human beings make mistakes, that knowledge is progressive, if it exists at all, that the justice he offered her came in fact from her own thought or dream. But he was sick with reflection and not immortal, like her; he had no time, no strength. "Go where you belong," he said, speaking very sternly. "Go to the place appointed." He raised his fist as if to strike her. "Go now, this instant, or I warn you—"

Suddenly, where the woman had stood, there was only clean snow. Lars-Goren and Bishop Brask stood staring, their blue lips parted. Then, without speaking, they turned back to their horses. When they were mounted again, and moving northward into the blinding light, Bishop Brask said: "Very well, we've learned this much. The Devil is mere stench and black air, and the evil is life itself."

Lars-Goren said nothing, staring straight ahead into the whiteness. "Yes," he thought, "my wife was right as usual. It was rage that made me tremble; fear that the chaos is in myself, as in everything around me."

Abruptly, he stopped his horse and stared blankly into the light. Bishop Brask stopped a step or two later and waited. Lars-Goren said, "I ordered her to judgment—ordered her there with my iron-clad fist raised, prepared to strike."

The bishop nodded.

"The strange thing is," Lars-Goren said, "that she vanished. Where did she go?"

"No doubt we'll find out when we're dead," said Bishop Brask.

"No doubt?" Lars-Goren echoed. "No *doubt*, Bishop?"

"Don't make too much of it," said the bishop, "it was merely an expression."

Lars-Goren said nothing, but started up again, bending his head against the wind.

"It was merely one of those things people say," Bishop Brask insisted, "mere habitual language. That's the chief source of our illusions, surely. Habitual language. What we have words for, we imagine exists. We walk all our lives through a mad dream constructed of language. We invent the word *love*, and from then on we moan and sigh over love. Who knows if it exists or has the slightest significance in nature?" He winced, a pain worse than most shooting up in him. "We invent the word *pain*," he said, smiling grimly. Lars-Goren rode lost in thought. The bishop grew more testy.

He shook his head, riding cocked sidewards against the pain shooting through him like needles of ice. "Ah yes," said the bishop, as if speaking to himself or some invisible observer, "his lordship does not choose to speak with us. And why should he, of course? He knows better than his peasants and commands them, even when they're dead, as he would order little children around—only for their good. Why not the same with a bishop? There's no authority in the world but the wisdom of a man's own heart—that's the ultimate wisdom, these days. 'I make you your own priest,' as Virgil tells that foul, cranky Lutheran Dante. Have no fear, Hans Brask! Lars-Goren will take care of you! It's the great modern Christian mystery: each man is the ultimate judge of the world, and it's the duty of all other men to bow humbly and accept each man's judgment or pay through the nose! Confusing? When were the holy mysteries not confusing?"

Abruptly, severely compressing his lips, Bishop Brask reined up his horse and stopped. Lars-Goren stopped too and looked at him, grimly waiting. "As you see," Bishop Brask said crossly, bowing to Lars-Goren, "I've stopped. I go no further. This is the place I choose for turning myself to an equestrian statue made of ice." Mockingly, angrily, he struck a noble pose.

"Don't be a fool," Lars-Goren said. "Keep me company. We'll ride on a ways and freeze together."

"No," said Bishop Brask. He knew well enough that he was behaving like a petulant child. For a man accustomed to respect it was a queer situation, and if he could have thought of a way to seize the mastery he would have done so. Then he'd have ridden on. But he could think of no way, and he was willing to put up with the indignity, since he seemed to have no choice. As a matter of fact, it was pleasant, in a way, to play a role more or less new to him. "Old peasant women, dead or alive, you rule by force," he said. "Me you try to rule by charm." He mimicked Lars-Goren's tone: " 'We'll freeze together.' Well, *no*, that's my answer. I'll freeze when and where I choose."

"Ah, Brask, what a difficult man you are," Lars-Goren said, softly yet bitterly. "Shall I *reason* with you, now that I have your attention? Is that what you want?"

In spite of himself, Hans Brask opened his mouth in mock dismay and put the spurs to his horse. Grimly, Lars-Goren laughed.

In the whiteness all around them there were now vague shapes. At first they seemed swirls of dark snow, perhaps trees. As they circled nearer, he made out that they were Lapps and reindeer.

8 In his tent of skins, the magician sat tapping on the drum with the tips of his fingers. There was no one else in the tent except the child, kneeling beside the drum, black-eyed and beaver-faced, like the magician, watching intently as the three stones danced on the drumhead. One stone was black, the second stone was white, the third was gray. All three had been formed in a reindeer's stomach. *Lokk, lokk, lokk,* sang the magician. His voice made hardly any sound. On the drumhead there were lines, most noticeably one running from east to west, painted in reindeer blood. Two stones, the black and the gray, were on the west side; the white was on the east. In the silence of Lappland, far north of Jokkmokk, the gentle tapping of the magician's fingers was like thunder.

In Stockholm, King Gustav sat writing at his desk. He was ordering the execution of his enemies, real and imagined. He wrote with his tongue between his teeth, his eyes full of light. *Whereas I, King Gustav, took this throne to make peace and bring harmony to my people . . .*

Lars-Goren and Hans Brask lay asleep in a house made of reindeer skin and bone. There were shelves, chairs, tables, all of reindeer parts. Sometimes one of the Lapps came in, moving in perfect silence, with black, wide eyes. Sometimes a reindeer paused outside the door, listening with lifted ears, dark eyes empty. Lars-Goren, sleeping, dreamed that the Devil came and seized his shoulder, shaking him awake.

"Lars-Goren," the Devil said, "I know what your mission is, and I've come to reason with you." The Devil's eyes were wide with alarm.

"Very well," Lars-Goren said, holding his breath.

The Devil opened his hands like a man pleading innocence. "You want to kill me," he said. "I ask you, what justice is there in that? What harm do I do? Do I exist at all, in fact? The old woman you killed: was that *my* doing? She was a witch, people say, and so she herself admits. Did *I* make her a witch? Did *I* make the people turn against her? Perhaps you will say, 'Ah ha! Not directly! But you murdered her children!' Come, come, I answer. Is the Devil *bad luck* then? Is that what you think? Have you come to destroy *bad luck*? What makes people strong? What makes horses strong, or trees? Destroy bad luck and you'll turn the whole world to fat! Oh, it's true, it's true, we'd all like bad luck in gentle measure—just enough bad luck to make children brave and strong, never enough to kill them. But what nonsense, my lord! Imagine a world without death in it, without serious pain. A world of mild toothaches. Who'd need a castle in a world like that? Or a church or a museum—even a family? What's good, with no evil to judge it against? What's order without chaos? What's the beauty of a rose in a field of bright red? Bad luck and good, that's the principle of life

itself! I exist insofar as life itself exists. Rid the world of me
and the world will be a barren stone rumbling without purpose through space. It's the mission of an idiot, this mission
you're on. Not that I blame you. It was Gustav's idea. He's a
madman, as surely you understand. He began with the best
of intentions, of course; but bad luck has overwhelmed him.
It's the usual situation: he failed to get his way—as we all do,
we all do! So now he turns on the dearest of his friends like a
maniac. Kill him, that's my advice. You could do it, you
know. You could be king yourself. Dalarna will support you.
I don't say it to tempt you—nothing of the kind. I'm slan-
dered on every side: it's life itself that does the tempting—
life and reason. What good is Sweden in the hands of a
maniac? I don't say kill him to advance yourself. Kill him for
the sake of justice, and pray for the best—for yourself, I
mean: pray that you prove luckier than he was. It's only a
suggestion, you understand. To me it's a matter of complete
indifference, I assure you. The fit will survive; that's the
world's only law. The fit—" He broke off, his eyes grown
suddenly vague, as if he'd lost his train of thought. Lars-
Goren raised his head from the pillow of skins, struggling to
see deeper into the Devil's mind, and by moving wakened
himself. The Devil disappeared. The house was cold and silent.

"Is *that* it?" Lars-Goren thought. But the thought was
half sleeping, half waking, and now when he tried to think
what it was that had dawned on him, the thought would not
come clear. "I must make the world safe for Erik," he
thought. He grimaced. "Now there's an illusion for you," he
thought bitterly. "How can anyone make the world safe for
his son?" Nevertheless, he was seeing his family in his mind's
eye, and rational or not, he was thinking he must make the
world safe for them.

In his house, the magician closed his eyes, stopped drumming, and smiled. On the drumhead, the white stone had moved nearer to the line and was in danger of falling over. With one finger, the child moved the white stone back where it belonged. Now, though the sun was no higher than before, it was morning.

Bishop Brask said: "I had the strangest dream. I dreamed the Devil came to me and said, 'Why should you kill me? Think, my dear Bishop! What am I but love, poetry, religion? Call them evil if you like—I don't deny that they lead in the end to disappointment. But of what earthly value is this mortal life without them? You, you pride yourself on reason. As a child, you loved books, but you came to understand that they were tricks and illusions. They told you love stories, but you looked at the world and you saw no such love—on the contrary, you saw people struggling to find the kind of love they'd seen in books, and you saw the illusion destroying marriages. Very well, you said to yourself, I'll be fooled no longer! And what was the result? Despair! The inability to act! Books, religions, the idea of love—they're all lies, I admit it, though I'm the father of such lies. But they give goals, shape quests: they give point to your brutal mortal striving. No doubt you'd disbelieve me if I told you God himself is a Devil's lie. You'd suspect me of interest. Very well then, I won't say it. But this much you'll agree with, I'm sure: God is Truth. And what is the truth about this paltry existence and its ending?' So he spoke, in my dream, and a great deal more in the same vein. But what's interesting is this: at some point he made a mistake, and I knew I had him. I felt a shock as if lightning had struck me, but that instant I woke up, and whatever the insight was, it was gone."

"I too had a dream," Lars-Goren said. He slowly rubbed his hands against the cold and told the bishop his dream.

In Stockholm, King Gustav signed his name with a flour-ish and folded the parchment, then sealed it with wax. He struck the bell to call his messenger, then rose and paced. "When I was young," he thought, but then the thought es-caped him. He stopped, lips clamped tight, staring out his window at the snow.

In her house, Liv Bergquist stopped suddenly, alarmed by a voice. What it said she could not make out, though she knew. "Erik!" she called. When her son came to her, she said, "See who's at the gate."

The headman of the Lapps said, "Very well, we will take you to the Devil." He shrugged, as if the mission seemed foolish to him. He had a small, wrinkled face and, on his hood, reindeer horns. All around him, the Lapps stood rhythmically nodding. In the endless snowfall, one could not tell which of them were men, which of them were women, which of them reindeer. The Lapps called their reindeer "the people of six eyes." It was a reference to their queer alert-ness, their attunement with the wind and snow. The Lapps did not really think the reindeer were people, for only in a limited way could the reindeer think. Between them, the Lapps and the reindeer divided all knowledge; so the Lapps believed. Lars-Goren and the bishop took their seats in the sledge, their horses tied behind. Gently, carefully, the Lapps covered the two men with skins. An old woman kissed Lars-Goren on the forehead, making a warm place that remained with him. When the reindeer started up—no one gave a sig-nal, or so it seemed to Lars-Goren—it was as if they'd been running all along.

The Devil sat enclosed in his wings, baffled. Even with his hands over his eyes he was blinded by the brightness. "This is a very foolish thing you're doing," he said to himself. He spoke in a child's voice, exactly like a child playing house.

"Foolish, is it?" he said. "Yes, foolish." He shuddered, but he could not seem to stop himself. "Why foolish?" he asked. "I'll tell you why foolish." "Yes, tell me." "Very well." "No, don't tell me!" "No, I'd like to." "You're a fool! Go away!" "A fool, you think?" "A fool! A fool!" He felt forms around him. With a part of his mind he struggled to awaken, but the voices were still running, childish, idiotic, blocking out the world. "Pay attention!" cried one. "I *am* paying attention!" "No, fooling around! That's all you ever do—fooling around." He shuddered again. The line was not right. "That's all you ever do—fool around." But the rhythm was wrong. Now the forms were closer, minuscule disturbances around his hooves. He struggled to wake himself. "Despair, then? You, the inventor of despair, you're caught in it?" "Nonsense!" His cheeks were freezing cold. It dawned on him that he was weeping, the tears turning to ice. "Suicide?" cried one of his voices. "Has it come to that?" With a violent effort, he opened his terrible eyes.

The magician's fingertips drummed softly, but the sound was like thunder. The child watched in silence. The three stones moved toward the line, mighty forces in near balance.

"We call them 'six-eyes,'" a young, smiling Lapp said, his hand on the reindeer's flank. He did not know or care that they'd been told already. He smiled as if that were enough, simply saying it; no more need be said. He too, Lars-Goren thought, was a creature of six eyes: in tune with the wind and snow, the heartbeat of the reindeer, the mind of God. It was true of course, as his son had said, it was not possible to be like the Lapps. Yet also it was true that it was good to know that Lapps existed, not dreams or illusions, real people, living at the extreme.

They had come to the foot of a great, dark mountain. The horses shook with cold as Lars-Goren and the bishop

mounted. All the Lapps stood looking up. They seemed to look at nothing and everything at once, at the mountain, the blinding white sky, the reindeer, each other. It was a look he had seen before somewhere—but he had no time to think where. In the windy silence he seemed to hear his wife's voice, distinct, right beside him: *Erik, see who's at the gate.* The mountain had two foothills. Lars-Goren's blood froze. The foothills were enormous cloven hooves.

He spurred his horse and started up. Bishop Brask was beside him, wincing with pain. "Why does he put up with it?" Lars-Goren wondered. The instant he asked it, he seemed to see deep into the bishop's mind, as if he'd remembered the secret of the Lapps. But the insight had no words. "Very well," he thought, "there are truths that have no words." In his belt Lars-Goren carried a knife made of reindeer bone. Here steel was of no use. Ice would dull it, the cold make it snap on impact. He wore, today, no iron gloves, only skins; nor was he dressed in his armor. He looked like a man from the world's first age, indistinguishable from a furry beast. In the terrible cold he found it difficult to think. He kept his mouth closed tight, lest the cold shatter his teeth. When it had begun he could not tell, but now the wind was howling. The bishop had to shout to make Lars-Goren hear. "Suppose we succeed," he yelled, "what will be changed?"

Lars-Goren could think of no answer and so rode on in silence, his head tucked down against the wind and flying ice. They were now on the flat of the Devil's thighs, moving toward his hands, the fingers extended, huge drifts, each one higher than a horse.

"And *how* do we succeed?" Bishop Brask called, his voice just a whisper above the wail of the wind. "What's our plan? What's our strategy?" He laughed, a kind of wail of despair.

Lars-Goren had no idea. He rode on, breathing shallowly. The air was like acid in his throat. When he reached the Devil's splayed fingers he dismounted. Only when they bumped one another did he realize that Bishop Brask was right beside him.

"We'll never make it," Bishop Brask yelled. "The whole thing's nonsense!"

Mother, his son's voice called, *it's some old woman.*

Without ropes, digging deep to clutch the hair of the Devil's robe, they scaled the Devil's silent upper arm. Hours passed. They hardly noticed, struggling for every breath. On the ice-crusted shoulder they rested.

"Lie here too long," Lars-Goren called, "and we'll freeze." At once he shut his mouth again.

"You think such laws apply here?" Bishop Brask wailed back. Lars-Goren could not even see him in the swirling snow and ice, though he was six feet away.

Even to Hans Brask it was a strange business, a kind of miracle. He had meant to cry out from despair, as usual, and he had reason enough: he was beyond pain, numb to the heart; yet what he felt was the wild excitement of a child or an animal. He would not be fooled by it. He was a sick old man, and he knew there was no chance of getting back from here alive. Bishop, man-of-God, whatever, he had no faith in God. As surely as he knew he was alive he knew God was dead or had never existed. What was this euphoria but an animal pleasure in existence at the margin—the joy of the antelope when the tiger leaps? Yet the joy was real enough. Absurdly, for all his philosophy, he was glad to be alive and dying. It was this that his books had prepared him for: the candleflame's guttering. He knew well enough that he wasn't thinking clearly, that at home in his study he would scorn this emotion, but now, this instant, that was irrelevant, unspeakably trivial. "This is poetry, this is love and religion!"

he thought. He crawled closer to Lars-Goren, filled with excitement, almost laughing, though no sound came out and his cheeks were all ice from his tears. With his mouth only inches from Lars-Goren's ear, he cried, "What a stupid fool you are, Lars-Goren! You know as well as I do that all this means nothing!" The words were thrilling to him, whatever their effect on Lars-Goren. "We've reasoned it all out: God and the Devil mean nothing whatsoever. We exist and we die—that's the glory of our existence. All the rest is mere language!" He could feel, below him, the Lapps looking up with their animal stupidity, their thoughts indistinguishable from reindeer thoughts, one with the universe—meaninglessly, idiotically one—whereas he, Hans Brask, was a bursting star of intellectual energy, magnificently separate from everything, everyone. "Pride?" he yelled, "tell me about pride, pretty Jesus!" He laughed, clenching his half-frozen fists in his joy. Lars-Goren, he realized now, was not beside him. He had a vague memory, light as the movement of a hair on his forehead, of Lars-Goren's having spoken, telling him, no doubt, that it was time to move on. That stood to reason. Everything stood to reason! Stood and fell! He laughed. Bishop Brask rose to his knees, then sank down again, laughing at his clumsiness, filled with numb joy. Now the three stones on the stretched skin of the drumhead were perfectly balanced, the black on one side, the white on the other, the gray stone balanced on the line. The magician grinned, lost in his trance, mindless. Abruptly, impishly, the child reached out and struck the drum. The gray stone leaped eastward, as if by will. In Dalarna, three men looked up suddenly in the darkness of the mine where they worked. It seemed to them that something had groaned, sinking toward the center of the earth. Lars-Goren, clinging to the ice that sheathed the Devil's neck, seized his knife of bone.

Suddenly the Devil was filled with terror. He shaded his

eyes with both hands, bending his head forward, trying to make out what it was that was wheeling around him. *The Lapps!* he thought. *It was the Lapps from the beginning!* But he could make out neither the Lapps nor their reindeer in the blinding whiteness. It was as if, for an instant, all existence had become one same thing, at the center of it a will, a blind force more selfish than the Devil himself, indomitable, too primitive for language, a creature of awesome stupidity, wild with ambition. And now all at once came a smell of Sweden into his nostrils. *The Swedes!* he thought, and the truth of it almost made him laugh. *Of course, of course!* he thought, raging. He had always known, he knew now, that it had to be the crafty Swedes.

What a fool, what a poor, stupid fool, thought the Devil, smiling in his despair. *First Sweden, then the world!* For it was now all perfectly clear to him: after the bloodbath of Stockholm, there were only the people—no kings, no lords, only fools like Gustav Vasa and a few threadbare bishops. There he lost his train of thought. *That's my problem*, he thought. *I lose my train of thought. What wonder, though*, he thought, *in this utterly senseless . . .* Again he could not remember what he'd been thinking.

Something tickled his neck, a colder place on the coldness of his skin, and he raised his hand to swat at the annoyance, but then a voice came to his ears, and he hesitated. It was the voice of Bishop Brask. "Dreams, illusions," the bishop was shouting. "It's for yourself you do this, my dear Lars-Goren! No one but yourself! What's your love for your children and wife but greed? What's your love of justice, your love for all so-called humanity, but a maniac's greed? Do you think they've elected you God, Lars-Goren? You're a tyrant! Mad as Tiberius! You'd kill them all as readily as you'd save them, you know it! And if killing proves fittest, then it's killing that will survive! How can you act, then, confronted by such knowledge? Maniac! Animal!" The voice was full of joy and rage, a kind of cackling, crackling glee. It was as if the man's mind had gone as blank as the face of Bernt Notke's carved statue, decadent art in all its curls and swirls—ten thousand careful knife-cuts and a face more empty of emotion than the face of the world's first carved-stone god. *I repent me that I ever made man,* thought the Devil. His ice-crusted eyebrows jittered upward.

Slowly, thoughtfully, he felt along his shoulder until he came to the bishop's little body, perched like a cockroach at the end of his collarbone. Almost gently, respectfully, he crushed it. Then he frowned. Had the bishop's loud crying, right there in his ear, been a trick of some kind? When he shook his head and tried to speak to himself, he understood that his throat had been cut.

"Whatever it may mean," said the old woman at the gate, "the Devil has been killed."

"And my husband?" said Lars-Goren's wife.

"In fourteen days he'll be home," said the old woman. "Tell him I came." She spoke proudly, as if what she had done was a wonderful thing, a feat no one, living or dead, could conceivably rival. No one's eyes, even the Devil's, ever shone with more pride. Liv Bergquist winced at the sight of such terrible arrogance. Then the old woman vanished.

"So Lars-Goren has destroyed the Devil!" Liv Bergquist thought. She smiled, raising her head. She'd known when she married him that Lars-Goren was no ordinary mortal. Otherwise, she'd never have consented to be his wife. She could have had any man she pleased.

She smiled at her son, who stood with his arms folded, beaming as if he himself had killed the Devil—and he could have, she thought; he *would* have.

In Stockholm, King Gustav was seized by a sudden thought. "No," he said, "stupidity!" He had a vision which he scarcely understood and, in the heat of it, tore the parchment to shreds. "Let the Riksdag decide," he thought. "'What concerns all should have the approval of all.'" He smiled, pleased with himself. With his printing press, he'd write a letter to his people, and he would make the press available to his people for response. They'd be reasonable, he knew. They would not dare behave otherwise.

The sky outside his window was as red as blood, whether the blood of God or the Devil Gustav Vasa did not think to wonder.

"Who'll tell the story?" said the child to the magician. "People should be told."

"Never mind," said the old man, smiling like a beaver. "For centuries and centuries no one will believe it, and then all at once it will be so obvious that only a fool would take the trouble to write it down."

Now the red of the sky was fading. In Russia, the tsar, with ice on his eyelashes, was declaring war on Poland. "Little do they dream," he said, "what horrors they've unleashed on themselves, daring to think lightly of the tsar!" All around him, his courtiers bowed humbly, their palms and fingertips touching as if for prayer.

And now, like wings spreading, darkness fell. There was no light anywhere, except for the yellow light of cities.

A NOTE ON THE TYPE

The text of this book was set on the Linotype in Fairfield, the first type face from the hand of the distinguished American artist and engraver Rudolph Ruzicka. In its structure Fairfield displays the sober and sane qualities of a master craftsman whose talent was long dedicated to clarity. It is this trait that accounts for the trim grace and virility, the spirited design and sensitive balance of this original type face.

Rudolph Ruzicka was born in Bohemia in 1883 and came to America in 1894. He designed and illustrated many books and created a considerable list of individual prints— wood engravings, line engravings on copper, and aquatints.

Composed by Maryland Linotype Composition Company, Baltimore, Maryland, and printed and bound by American Book–Stratford Press, Saddle Brook, New Jersey

Typography by Camilla Filancia